THE ANOMALY

A DELPHI GROUP THRILLER

JOHN SNEEDEN

Want a FREE novella by John Sneeden?

Sign up for John's newsletter and get the novella *Betrayal* for free. You'll also be the first to learn about John's future releases and special discounts. You can sign up here:

www.johnsneeden.com/newsletter/

The process is quick and simple, and your email address will not be sold to anyone else.

PROLOGUE

Deep Beneath the Ellsworth Mountains, Antarctica

His lungs burning, Dimitri Pudovkin knelt on the cavern floor and took in deep gulps of breath. The toll on his body was real, but that would soon go away. It was the mental damage he was worried about. The images he had seen would likely remain with him for the rest of his life.

As an officer of Spetznas, the Russian Special Operations Forces, Dimitri had encountered almost every horror imaginable —death, torture, and abuse on a level most people had only read about in books. And yet none of that compared to what he had just witnessed.

Still, he had to press on. The Terror—the name he had given the thing that had taken the lives of his men—could still be out there. And if it was, it might eventually pick up his trail.

After letting his body rest for several more minutes, Dimitri stood and used his flashlight to examine the area ahead. At the outer edges of the light, he saw the nearside of the ice bridge they had crossed earlier. A sense of relief washed over him. The bridge would take him across the chasm and into the tunnels that led back to the surface. If he moved quickly, he might make it back to base camp within the hour.

While the thought was comforting, Dimitri remembered how treacherous the ice bridge's surface was. Eight hours earlier, two of his men had almost slipped off of it—a fall that would have meant certain death. This time, there would be no one to save him if he found himself sliding toward the edge.

In the end, it was an easy choice. He had to cross the bridge or risk being overtaken by the Terror.

As Dimitri continued on, he thought back on all that had happened. They had come to Antarctica to find the ultimate prize, the discovery every government in the world wanted to get their hands on. The Americans certainly wanted what was buried there, and they had already dispatched a team to find it. Dimitri hoped to finish the job long before they arrived.

After establishing a base camp in a mountain cave, Dimitri had sent his men out to explore the network of tunnels underneath the Ellsworth Mountains. On the second day, two of the men had reported finding a massive cavern, which seemed like the kind of place that might hold the treasure they were looking for.

Excited by the news, Dimitri had set out with his team that morning. The two men who had made the discovery led them through the tunnels and across the ice bridge. Once on the other side, Dimitri marveled at the stunning sights—towering stalagmites and a cavernous ceiling that was higher than most indoor sports arenas. It was a place of great beauty, but they hadn't come there as tourists. They were in a race to claim a prize.

After hours of searching the cavern, they hit pay dirt. One of Dimitri's soldiers stumbled across a fissure in one of the cavern's walls. That break had led to the Holy Grail of human discovery—the exterior of an extraterrestrial spaceship.

As soon as the image of the ship formed in his mind, Dimitri quickly pushed the memory aside. He didn't want to think about what had happened once they'd boarded it or what had become of his team.

But it wasn't just the horrifying images he wanted to suppress. He also wanted to forget the painful truth that he had deserted his own men. When given the chance to fight or flee, he had chosen the latter.

The decision to run reminded Dimitri of something he had heard as a young man. He and a friend were going camping on the Kamchatka Peninsula of Russia, and the two teenagers were afraid they might run into one of the massive brown bears that roamed the forests there. When he had shared those concerns with the family, Dimitri's grandfather had comforted him with some humorous words of wisdom.

"As they say, you don't have to be faster than the bear," the old man had said with a twinkle in his eye. "You just have to be faster than your friend."

Although his grandfather's words were meant to be funny, they were emblematic of what had just taken place. When given the opportunity to escape, he had taken it. And while some might find what he had done repulsive, he knew it had been the right thing to do. Staying would have only resulted in one more death.

A distant *thump* pulled Dimitri out of his thoughts. It sounded like something heavy hitting the ice floor of the cavern. He turned around, directing the beam of his flashlight behind him. *Nothing.*

Perhaps he had imagined the noise. As he thought it over, another sound reached his ears. It was subtle, as if something was moving stealthily along the ice. It also seemed to have come from the left side of the cavern.

The left side of the cavern.

That's where the ship was located. *And if the sound was coming from there...*

His heart pounding, Dimitri stepped onto the bridge and

moved quickly toward the other side. After reaching the midway point, he slowed his pace. Even though he would've preferred to keep running, he knew he was about to pass through the area where his men had almost fallen off. Fortunately, they had learned something from that near disaster that would help him now. They had discovered that the center of the path was relatively flat and textured. In other words, if he kept to the middle of the bridge, he would probably be fine.

As Dimitri continued, he became certain something was approaching from behind. He resisted the urge to look back. He already knew what it was, and stopping to look would only slow him down. He also decided to keep his flashlight on. While the beam gave away his location, he wouldn't be able to make it the rest of the way across without it.

To his relief, Dimitri was able to make it past the treacherous section of the bridge without any trouble. He hoped the Terror wouldn't fare as well. While it likely possessed a high level of intelligence, it wouldn't be familiar with the nuances of the bridge's surface. If it veered slightly to the left or right, then it would plunge to a certain death.

After reaching the other side, Dimitri exhaled. He wasn't out of the proverbial woods yet, but he was getting close. All he needed to do was make his way back to camp. Once there, he would use his satellite phone to call a Russian research station a few hours away.

Fueled by adrenaline and thoughts of an impending rescue, Dimitri sprinted into the tunnel. Then disaster struck.

He'd been focused on getting to the surface as quickly as possible and hadn't noticed the deep indentation in the tunnel floor. The toe of his boot went into the crevice, twisting his ankle and splintering the bone. The Russian flew through the air and landed hard, his body tumbling across the ice. After coming to a stop, he felt hot spears of pain shooting up his leg. He grabbed his ankle and cried out. Having experienced a number of fractures over his career, he knew this break was bad.

Clenching his teeth, Dimitri managed to rise on one elbow. His flashlight had rolled a few feet away, its beam trained on the nearby wall. Grunting, he used his arms to drag himself in that direction. As he did, he heard the sound of something skittering along the ice.

He stopped moving and looked back toward the bridge, wondering if the thing behind him had somehow managed to make it across.

No. Please, no.

He tried to explain the noise away, but there was no denying that *something* was out there. Fleeing was no longer an option. At that point, the only option was to defend himself. At least he had the means to do so.

Reaching into his coat pocket, he quickly pulled out his MP-443 Grach pistol. He thought about retrieving the flashlight then thought better of it. It might allow him to illuminate his attacker, but it would give away his position.

Silence fell over the tunnel.

His arms trembling, Dimitri rose into a sitting position and lifted his pistol with both hands. *Where is it? Did it go back across the bridge?*

A low hiss sounded about twenty yards away. Claws skittered across the ice.

Death was moving in Dimitri's direction at a frightening speed. The only thing between it and him was the pistol shaking in his hands. The Russian officer directed the muzzle back down the tunnel and opened fire.

1

Delphi Headquarters
Arlington, Virginia

AFTER EMERGING onto the office building's roof, Zane Watson went straight to the little arrangement of patio furniture and slid into his favorite chair. Like others in the Delphi organization, he went there at least once a day when he was in town. It was a place where one could sit and enjoy the stunning views of downtown Arlington, but it was also a place to think through the difficult issues that arose on the job. There was something about the open air and isolation that seemed to stimulate his mind.

But on this occasion, he wasn't there to figure out some work-related mystery or to strategize a plan for an upcoming operation. No, his visit was much more simple than that—he had come to suffer in silence.

To say he had endured a difficult day was an understatement. He had just broken up with Katiya Mills, his girlfriend of the last couple of years. As someone who didn't have much family, she had been everything to him.

In his mind, the two had been the perfect match. Both were driven in their jobs, had an intellectual curiosity about the world around them, and were loyal to a fault. They also enjoyed many of the same leisurely pursuits. They often dined in fine restaurants, curled up on the couch to watch a good detective series, and hiked through some of America's most beautiful locales together.

Despite everything they had in common, Zane had known for some time that this day would come. He and Katiya loved their jobs, and both were good at what they did. But while their commitment to work was a positive thing, it also meant that their time together was limited to the occasional weekend. Most relationships couldn't handle such long periods apart, even a relationship as strong as theirs.

In light of their sporadic time together, the two had long known their relationship might not last a lifetime. Still, that hadn't made the breakup any easier. When they had parted ways, Katiya said their story was like a Shakespearean tragedy—two souls bound together in a love story that was moving toward an inevitable and painful conclusion.

As Zane saw it, the only positive was that the breakup had been mutual. Earlier that afternoon, they had spent three hours walking along the National Mall, sticking to the tree-lined trails that ran between the Lincoln and Jefferson Memorials. They ended their time together in a tight hug. Neither one said anything during the long embrace.

The two had actually broken up one time before, but Zane knew there was a stronger sense of permanence to this one. Katiya had told him that she felt it as well. Even so, the two knew that one of them might be tempted to resurrect the relationship in a weak moment. That was why they had agreed not to contact the other unless there was important news to pass along, such as the death of a family member or a serious illness. Zane wondered if they would be able to stick to their own rules.

As he sat in silence, Zane's thoughts transitioned to what had taken place over the last hour. After taking Katiya to the airport, he had received a text from his boss, Dr. Alexander Ross. Although he knew Zane was on vacation, Delphi's CEO had asked him to come in for an important meeting that would take place that evening. Knowing it would be an inconvenience to his senior operative, Ross had lured him in with the promise of an extra day off somewhere down the line.

Already in a dark mood, Zane had been irritated by the request. Ross could have asked one of the other operatives to handle whatever came up. Carmen Petrosino was out on assignment, but Amanda Higgs and two other operatives were available. Even if Ross wanted Zane to eventually take the reins of the operation, the others were fully capable of gathering all the necessary information.

Zane also found it frustrating that his boss had been coy about the meeting's agenda. After being pressed, he would only say that a Danish intelligence officer wanted to pass along some important information, which in turn made Zane wonder just how important it could be. After all, he had worked in espionage for years and couldn't remember anything of critical importance happening in Denmark. The small country wasn't exactly a hotbed of clandestine activity.

A honking car on the street below pulled Zane out of his thoughts. He looked at his phone. The meeting was still an hour off, which meant there was time to do the one thing that might take the edge off of his day. Reaching into his shirt pocket, he pulled out a Cohiba cigar. After lighting it, he took several quick puffs then sat back in the chair.

His gaze ran to the north. Night had fallen, and a full September moon hung over the Potomac. Zane had read reports that the US was in the process of establishing the first lunar colony in history. According to several unnamed sources, the project would be a joint initiative between NASA, the military's Space Force, and several private companies, including one that was owned by a famous British billionaire. It was said the first buildings of the settlement would be in place in approximately two years, although Zane found that hard to believe.

He took a long pull on the cigar. As the smoke slowly escaped from his mouth, his thoughts went back to the meeting that was about to take place. He found it odd that Ross had been so evasive about what the Danish intelligence officer was going to share. *Why the secrecy? Is it because Ross doesn't know much himself?* Zane doubted it. The Delphi CEO never agreed to take on work unless he had a very good idea of what it would entail.

Maybe he had withheld the information out of respect for what Zane was going through after the breakup with Katiya. Maybe he didn't want to burden the operative with too much information in light of all that had happened that day. While Zane appreciated such a gesture, it still irritated him that Ross hadn't asked someone else to sit in on the initial meeting.

Zane had just taken another draw on his cigar when his phone flared with an incoming call. He looked at the screen. *Ross.*

He shook his head. *Can't I even finish my cigar?*

Exhaling, he answered the call. "Yes."

"Boy, someone's in a good mood," Ross said. "Where are you?"

"Right above you."

"I hate to do this, because I'm guessing you're enjoying a smoke, but I need you to come down in ten minutes."

Frowning, Zane ran a hand through his long hair. "I thought we were starting at eight."

"Our Danish colleague is a few minutes out. Apparently, she decided to come straight here before checking into the hotel."

"Do I need to bring anything?"

"Just that incredibly perceptive brain of yours."

Ross's lame attempt at flattery only served to irritate Zane even more.

"Brett's going to take notes, so you won't even need to do that," Ross explained.

"If Brett's going to be there to take notes, then what do you need me for?"

After a short pause, Ross cleared his throat and said, "Look, I know this wasn't convenient—"

"No, it wasn't. It's also an insult to our other people, who are fully capable of handling whatever is on the agenda."

"Watson, I need *all* of you on board tonight." Ross paused for a moment. "You know I wouldn't have called you in unless it was absolutely necessary."

"You're telling me some piece of intelligence from Denmark is of critical importance?"

"This goes beyond Denmark. Trust me on this. Once you hear what this agent has to say, you'll be glad I called you in."

I doubt it. After disconnecting the call, Zane mashed the tip of his cigar into the ashtray and stood. It was time to see what secrets were about to be revealed.

2

As Zane went down the stairs, his thoughts turned back to the comment Ross had made at the end of their call. He claimed Zane would be thankful for being called in. *What could Danish intelligence have uncovered that would be so intriguing?* Zane wondered if Ross had exaggerated the whole thing in order to get him on board with a mundane task.

No. The man could be frustrating at times, but he wouldn't do that. Alexander Ross was many things, but he certainly wasn't a liar. If it was a routine operation, then he would have said so.

Given that, Zane had no idea what the woman was going to reveal or why she was bringing it to *them*. Delphi was a private organization that was hired by the US government to look into the dark and mysterious corners of intelligence. Their investigations involved such things as foreign adversaries developing futuristic technology and the suspicious deaths of Americans overseas. In short, they investigated matters the CIA and other agencies were unwilling or unable to.

More recently, that narrow focus had started to expand. The intelligence community was burdened with a greater workload than before, and that was primarily due to the rise of cyber threats against the United States. Small-time players could suddenly hack into government servers, retrieving everything from military secrets to breakthroughs in technology. Given the wider spectrum of threats, US intelligence agencies were asking private organizations to take on more of their work. That meant Delphi was being tasked with conducting routine espionage activities such as surveillance and tracking.

Normally, Zane would have assumed that anything being passed along by the Danes would relate to the latter type of work. But that wouldn't square with Ross's cryptic comment. If nothing else, Zane had to admit his curiosity had been piqued.

A half minute later, Zane entered Ross's office. Four people stood in a circle a short distance away, talking among themselves. Brett Foster was one of them. The dark-haired computer whiz was Delphi's chief technology officer. A master of all things digital, Foster had never encountered a system he couldn't hack into.

Also in attendance was Amanda Higgs, another senior operative at Delphi. The athletic blonde had joined the organization through a strange set of circumstances. While investigating the mysterious death of Amanda's father, Zane and fellow operative Carmen Petrosino had noticed Amanda's acute investigative skills. That, coupled with her background in archaeology, made her the perfect fit for an organization that often looked into the bizarre.

Zane assumed the fourth person in the room was the Danish intelligence officer. She had shoulder-length brown hair that matched a pair of big brown eyes. Adding to the woman's brown tone was a small mole that was situated above the left side of her mouth. She was attractive, but she also had a simple style that probably enabled her to work a room without being noticed.

"There he is," Ross said as the operative came toward them. "Watson, I'd like you to meet Freja Larsen."

He stepped forward and shook her hand. "Nice to meet you."

"The pleasure is mine," she said in flawless but accented English.

"As you probably guessed, Freja works for PET," Ross said.

Politiets Efterretningstjeneste was the Danish intelligence agency responsible for counterintelligence and national security. PET agents typically worked on Danish soil, while Forsvarets Efterretningstjeneste, also known as FE, worked in the area of foreign intelligence. Despite racking his brain, Zane couldn't recall working with either of the two agencies in the past.

Ross gestured toward the sitting area in one corner of his office. "Since time is of the essence, let's get started."

So there *was* an urgency to whatever the Danish agent had come to discuss. *The plot thickens.*

Freja slid onto one of the couches, and Zane selected the cushioned chair directly across from her. When someone was sharing critical information, he liked to study their expressions. He had found that the subtle movements of the speaker's face often conveyed as much as the words themselves.

After everyone had settled into their seats, Ross said, "Freja, please tell them what you do and why you came to see us."

"Thank you." She sat up straight, her eyes moving from one person to the next. "As Dr. Ross said, I work for PET. More specifically, I work in the area of Russian counterintelligence. I speak the language fluently, and I'm well versed in all things related to the country, its people, and its intelligence tactics."

"A Russian specialist in Denmark?" Zane asked. "You must not be very busy."

Ross shot him a look.

Despite the jab, Freja forced a smile. "Keep listening, and you might be surprised." After pausing to gather her thoughts, she continued, "About three months ago, we received reports of suspicious activity at a farmhouse in a suburb of Aalborg, a city in northern Denmark. As you may know, we don't have a large population of immigrants, and we certainly don't have many people from Russia or any of the former Soviet bloc countries.

"Since we didn't know what was going on, our director asked us to take things slowly in the beginning. After all, we do have some Russian immigrants, and to the best of our knowledge, most if not all of them are law-abiding citizens.

"We started with video surveillance. We placed several cameras on the hill overlooking the site, and we also put a few drones in the air. While we weren't able to determine exactly what was going on, we did confirm there were a lot of people coming and going. Too many for this to be an ordinary residence.

"Then, about a month later, something totally unexpected took place. The Russian ambassador to Denmark made a visit to the farm, and he did so in the middle of the night."

"I assume he wasn't there to buy fresh produce," Amanda remarked.

Freja smiled. "No, he wasn't. But we grew more concerned once we were able to analyze some of the images more closely. In one of them, we learned that he was accompanied by a Russian man we believe to be an officer with the FSB."

"A high-ranking federal security officer was at the farm?" Brett asked.

"Yes, but what makes it even more interesting is that he's based out of the Russian embassy in Helsinki, Finland. Officially, he's a pleasant diplomat who attends social events and makes platitudes about good relations with the West. In reality, he's a spy."

Zane considered what she had just shared with them. Finland bordered Russia, which meant it was a country of great strategic importance to the FSB. It was common knowledge that the Russian intelligence agency had stationed some of their best people in the Scandinavian country.

The more he found out, the more he had to admit Ross had been right. Freja Larsen had his attention. The FSB wouldn't show up at a farm under the cover of darkness unless something nefarious was going on. *But what? And why Denmark?* He assumed he was about to find out.

"At that point, we knew we had a lead. In addition to camera surveillance, we decided to place two agents in the area to monitor the site. We also monitored all incoming and outgoing calls. To make a long story short, we eventually realized the farm was being used to train spies who were going to assimilate into Western society."

"Like Anna Chapman?" Brett asked.

Chapman was a Russian spy who had operated in both the UK and the United States.

"Yes, with one slight difference. To the best of my knowledge, Anna Chapman never concealed her Russian background. We believe at least some of the spies being trained at the Aalborg farm were going to pose as people born or raised in the West."

"So did you take action, or did you just continue to watch?" Amanda asked.

"The decision was made for us," Freja replied. "About a month after we began to monitor things more closely, all activity at the farm ceased almost overnight."

Zane frowned. "Was that because the training was complete?"

Freja shook her head. "No. We think they knew they were being watched, and we have no idea what tipped them off. Even though we operated our drones at very high altitudes, it's possible they spotted one of them. It's also possible they saw one of our human assets. To be honest, I doubt we'll ever know for sure what spooked them."

"So I take it you searched the farm for evidence?" Amanda asked.

"On the day we were supposed to go in, a lone individual arrived in a van. He was undoubtedly a cleaner."

Zane leaned forward in his seat and smirked. "I'm betting you don't mean the kind who scrubs toilets and mops floors."

Freja nodded. "He was about to remove all traces of activity, including fingerprints and any small items that might have been left behind. Once we realized his purpose, we decided to make our move." She sighed. "Apparently, this particular asset had been told not to be taken alive. When we approached, he pulled out a semi-automatic rifle and opened fire on our agents. It was a fight he had to have known he wouldn't win, and yet he engaged us anyway."

"And the evidence?" Zane asked.

"Looking back, there probably wasn't much for him to clean up. The Russians had done a very good job of doing that when they left. In fact, they had probably been taking things out for weeks, a little bit at a time."

"Well, you're here talking to us right now, so I assume you must have found something," Zane said.

"We did. The cleaner was using a burner phone, and he had done a pretty good job of erasing every text that was sent or received. But we got lucky because one had come in about the time we made the raid. There was a short cryptic message in Russian, which I was able to translate. Once the Aalborg job was complete, he was to make contact with their Operation Whiteout contact to see what was needed. Just so you know, the words Operation Whiteout were typed in English."

"Operation Whiteout?" Amanda asked. "What does that mean?"

Ross cleared his throat. "I can answer that. Operation Whiteout is an American operation. The US government is sending a team down to Antarctica to investigate a discovery that was recently made there."

Zane's brow furrowed. "Something in Antarctica is so important it requires a secret operation?"

"I think it will make more sense once I explain what was found," Ross said. "There are nine people at Ellsworth Station, including seven astronomers. As the name suggests, the station is located at the base of the Ellsworth Mountains. A while back, the team noticed that a small building at Ellsworth had begun to sink. Fearing that the ice underneath the station was unstable, a technician was sent in with a ground-penetrating radar system. As he surveyed the substratum, a large metallic anomaly was detected. We're talking very large." He paused for a moment to let that sink in. "I wasn't given the precise measurements, but they told me it was at least the size of a football field."

Zane wondered what object of that size could be buried under the ice.

"As you can imagine, the US government is anxious to learn more about this object," Ross continued. "So anxious that they've put together a team of experts to investigate."

"Operation Whiteout," Zane said.

Ross nodded.

"I get that they want to know what's down there, but why all the secrecy?" Amanda asked.

"Our scientists have examined all available data on the anomaly," Ross replied. "After ruling out a number of possibilities, they've come to the conclusion that we could be sitting on top of an extraterrestrial spaceship."

3

SILENCE FELL over the room as each person digested what they had just heard. While Brett didn't seem surprised, it was clear that Amanda and Freja were hearing the news for the first time. Ross had done a good job keeping things under wraps.

Zane was no stranger to extraterrestrial activity. Several years ago, he had encountered an alien spaceship during an operation in the Amazon basin, although he had recently begun to question some of his memories of the event. Despite that experience, he would need more information before concluding that the radar had picked up an alien craft underneath the ice.

Freja removed her phone and began tapping the screen. "Have they considered the possibility that this is a large sea vessel? I don't know the word in English, but there are some that are used to cut through ice."

"Icebreakers," Zane said.

Freja stared at her screen. "It looks like the Ellsworth Mountains are located along the Ronne Ice Shelf. If my memory serves me correctly, that shelf is a thin layer of ice that sits on top of the ocean." She looked at Ross. "It's the perfect place for a shipwreck."

"The Ronne Ice Shelf is on the north side of the Ellsworth

mountain range, and our station is south of it," Ross explained. "The buildings are sitting on fifty to seventy-five feet of ice, and below that is terra firma."

"You said they brought in the GPR because one of the buildings had sunk into the ice," Amanda said. "Did they ever find out what caused that?"

"They don't believe it was this object if that's what you're asking," Ross replied. "There are a series of natural tunnels along the edge of that mountain range, so it's thought one or more of the tunnels may have collapsed."

"Let's go back to Freja's theory that this might be a lost sea vessel," Zane said. "I don't know anything about that part of the world, but I'm guessing the topography has changed quite a bit over the centuries. Can they really rule that out?"

"Yes, they can," Ross said. "Think about it. The only vessels that might fit from a size perspective are aircraft carriers and destroyers, and we know the topography hasn't changed since those ships came into existence. No ancient vessels would fit in terms of size or material."

Zane nodded.

"Unless those ground-penetrating radars aren't accurate," Amanda noted.

"That's a fair point," Ross said. "We certainly can't rule out equipment malfunction. That's why, at some point, we need to get down into those tunnels to confirm what's there."

"Have they considered anything else?" Freja asked. "It just seems odd to jump to the conclusion that this is some sort of spaceship."

"Yes, they have considered a few other options," Ross answered. "One of those is that the anomaly is an underground building of some kind."

Amanda frowned. "An underground building?"

Ross nodded. "One CIA analyst told me she believes it could be an outpost of some kind, perhaps one being used to spy on our operations at Ellsworth. In any event, the shape doesn't seem to fit, and we feel pretty certain that no country would've done something so bold. Even our Russian and Chinese friends."

"Speaking of the Russians, why are they so interested in Operation Whiteout?" Zane asked.

"I was just about to get to that," Ross said. "As you probably know, the Russians and the Chinese monitor everything we do. Over the last decade, they've been hacking into the servers of US businesses and research facilities in order to steal trade secrets and technology. The Chinese are probably the worst offenders, but the Russians are major players as well.

"To make a long story short, the CIA believes the Russians were probably monitoring all communications going in and out of the Ellsworth Station. If so, that means they probably know about the anomaly."

"Let's assume that what you just said is correct," Zane said. "It would explain that text Freja and her team found on the cleaner's phone."

"Exactly. It's clear the Russians found out about Operation Whiteout. And since this cleaner in Denmark worked with spies who are going to be assimilated into the West, we believe that might indicate the operation has already been compromised."

"A mole?" Zane asked.

Ross nodded. "Something else has come up that I need to make you aware of. About twenty-four hours ago, the CIA lost all communication with the team of astronomers I mentioned before. We think it may be due to a series of bad storms moving across that part of Antarctica. From what I've been told, they're some of the worst storms the continent has seen in over a decade. We're talking blizzards that make the ones here look like a spring picnic. So while it's certainly bad for the Ellsworth team, it might explain why communications were knocked down."

Zane considered what Ross had just said. Yes, strong atmospheric activity could certainly cut off radio and satellite signals, but there was still something about the whole thing that didn't seem right.

Freja leaned forward, her eyes lit with concern. "What if the Russians sent in a group of commandos to take the station over? The blizzard would provide the perfect cover for that sort of thing."

"I suppose we can't completely rule it out, but I seriously doubt they would do something so brazen," Ross said. "If they're caught, that could set off the next world war. Not only that, but they would also have no reason to insert a mole on our team if they had already taken over the station."

Freja nodded. "That makes sense."

"So why are we here?" Amanda asked. "What does Delphi have to do with any of this?"

It was a question Zane had been about to ask.

"You're here because I want you and Watson to be on the team that's going down to Ellsworth. Your primary goal will be to detect the mole, assuming that one exists. You're also going to provide security at the site while the experts look into this anomaly.

"Even though we think they're fine, it's also possible the team of astronomers will need to be safely evacuated. If this storm is bad enough to knock down communications, then it's possible they've experienced other problems as well. Depending on wind speed, the buildings they're in could have experienced some damage."

Zane nodded. "Assuming that's correct, then why not send an extraction team from one of the other stations? I don't know much about Antarctica, but I do seem to remember there are quite a few stations on the northwest peninsula."

"Under normal circumstances, we'd send a team from Parks Station, which is the largest in the area," Ross replied. "It's where most of the planes fly in, including the one you'll be on. But Parks is about three hundred miles away from Ellsworth, and the weather is just too bad to make an attempt. The astronomers just got a large delivery of food and other supplies, so they could survive for another month if they had to. As long as the buildings hold up, they should be fine."

"If the weather is that bad, then how are we supposed to get there?" Amanda asked.

"Although Antarctic forecasts are notoriously unreliable, we've been told there is supposed to be a pause about the time you arrive. We have no way of knowing that with any certainty, so it's possible you'll have to wait at Parks until conditions improve."

"That sounds like a barrel of fun," Zane said.

"It's why we pay you the big bucks," Ross said.

"And that's why my government pays me as well." Freja fixed her gaze on Ross. "I want to be on your team."

Ross hesitated, clearly taken off guard by the request. "As you probably know, we're a private organization, and I'm not in a position to authorize that. My people are leaving tomorrow, so I'm afraid it would take too long—"

"With all due respect, you and I both know it would just take one phone call," Freja said.

Zane smiled to himself. She was feisty. He liked her already.

"Remember what I do for a living," Freja continued. "If there is a mole on this team, then I'm the one best able to see through their cover. I've spent my life studying Russian assets. I know how they think, and I know the little idiosyncrasies that set them apart from other spies."

"We don't even know if your people would approve of your participation." Ross threw up his hands.

"Fine. We'll make two phone calls," Freja said.

Ross looked at Zane as though trying to gauge the operative's thoughts on the matter, and Zane gave his boss a subtle nod. There was no reason not to bring along someone with her background. From the sounds of the mission objective, they would need an expert on all things Russia to succeed.

But it wasn't just the Danish agent's knowledge that would make her a valuable asset. After watching her butt heads with Ross, Zane could tell the woman was a bulldog, the kind of person who would pursue something until it got resolved. Given the nature of this operation and the conditions under which they would work, she was exactly the sort of teammate he wanted.

"Fine, I'll make a call," Ross finally said. "But if they tell me no, then I'm not going to pursue the matter any further. Time is of the essence, so I need to be focused on getting my people down there."

"Fair enough," Freja said.

Ross turned to Brett. "Now let's give them a brief overview of the team they'll be going down with."

4
―――

Three Days Later
Parks Station, Antarctica

PARKS STATION WAS the largest research operation in the northwest quadrant of Antarctica. Owned by the United States, the United Kingdom, and Australia, the facility consisted of a dozen buildings, several garages, an aircraft landing strip, and a network of ice tunnels that were used for storage. The research conducted at Parks encompassed the full spectrum of scientific disciplines. At one point or another, geologists, earth scientists, marine biologists, and oceanographers had called it their home.

But Parks wasn't just a research site. Due to its large size and proximity to South America, it also served as a regional airport and supply depot for the smaller stations that were scattered across the peninsula. As a service operation, it housed a number of mechanics, cooks, pilots, and supply managers.

Zane Watson entered the Parks Station mess hall about a quarter to eight in the evening. Tables were spread across the large space, which he guessed could seat fifty or more people. The room was devoid of human activity, but he could hear the clanking of pots and pans in the kitchen.

Still suffering from exhaustion, he sank into one of the chairs to wait for the others to arrive. The last two days of travel had been brutal. First, there had been the overnight flight from DC to Santiago, the picturesque capital of Chile. Once the CIA-owned Gulfstream G550 had been refueled and restocked, they were in the air again for the four-hour flight to Punta Arenas. Located at the southern tip of the South American country, Punta Arenas was one of the most popular bases for travel to Antarctica. Many commercial cruises originated there, as did all direct flights to the various research stations in the Antarctic continent's northwest peninsula.

Zane, Amanda, and Freja had spent the previous night at a hotel in Punta Arenas. Shortly after noon, they had boarded a new plane for the final leg of the journey, a six-hour flight south to Parks Station. They had touched down around half past six that evening. Their host, British helicopter pilot Niles Hawke, told them to take an hour and a half to unpack and rest before their meeting at eight. Zane had thought about taking a quick nap but eventually opted for a long shower instead.

In the mess hall, he glanced at the time on his phone. *7:47.* The others would be arriving soon.

"How are you, mate?"

Zane looked up at the sound of the distinct Australian accent. A man with dark hair and a thick beard stood behind one of the long serving tables. He was holding a tray stacked with brown paper bags.

"Good evening," Zane said.

The Aussie set the tray down on the table. "Are you with the Ellsworth group that just flew in?"

"I am."

"You probably had dinner on the plane, but we threw together a few sandwiches in case you're still hungry."

"We did eat, but only if you use the word 'dinner' in the loosest sense. Anyway, I appreciate you putting that together."

"Don't expect anything fancy." The Aussie pointed at a large metal tub at the end of the table. "We have drinks as well. Help yourself, mate."

As the man went back into the kitchen, Zane stood then walked over to the tub. He wasn't hungry, but he felt a little parched from all the flying. Buried in a large mound of ice were a variety of bottled drinks—water, orange juice, and a wide array of soda. There were even a few beers mixed in.

He settled on bottled water.

"Well, hello there."

Zane turned to see a middle-aged woman coming toward him. She had short blond hair that was styled into a bob. The professional look was completed with a pair of dark-framed glasses.

Morgan Martini.

She was one of the two experts assigned to Operation Whiteout. Zane knew from her dossier that she worked for the Office of Naval Intelligence. More specifically, she was the head of the now-famous Unidentified Aerial Phenomena Task Force. Established a year ago, the group's strategic objective was to "standardize collection and reporting" on unidentified aerial phenomena. UAP had slowly begun to replace UFO as the acronym of choice among academics, researchers, and military experts.

She approached and extended her hand. "I'm Morgan."

"Zane Watson," he replied.

"It's good to finally meet you."

The two had talked by phone once in order to discuss logistics, as well as the role of the Delphi team. Due to time constraints, their conversation had been brief.

Martini nodded at the bottle in his hand. "Water? I was told we'd have some booze available."

Zane nodded at the tub. "They do have beer."

"And you're not partaking? It might be the last chance to get our hands on alcohol for a while."

"I'm getting older. I rarely miss an opportunity to hydrate my skin."

She smiled at his lame attempt at humor. "I suspect I'm quite a bit older than you, but hydration is taking a back seat tonight." She plucked a bottle of Michelob Ultra from the tub then twisted the cap off. "So when did you guys get in?"

"About six thirty. You?"

"Yesterday morning." She took a swig of beer. "How was your trip?"

"Let's just say I'm happy to be on solid ground. It was a pretty nasty ride."

"Turbulence?"

He nodded. "Those last two hours were pure hell."

"I'm sorry to hear that," Martini said.

"How was your flight?" he asked.

"It was fine, but my sleep here last night was a different story."

Zane smiled. "I take it this place isn't exactly the Hyatt."

"Actually, the mattress was fine. I just can't get used to all the winter darkness. Thirty-six hours in, and my body clock is already screwed up."

Antarctica only had two seasons, summer and winter. Given a choice, no one would ever voluntarily come there in winter. In addition to the frigid temperatures, the entire six months were spent in complete darkness, a phenomenon known as polar night, which was the result of the earth tilting on its axis. During the winter, the region was tilted away from the sun, keeping it below the horizon.

It was early September, which meant that summer was still

three or four weeks away. Unfortunately, that also meant Operation Whiteout would have to be carried out in darkness.

"Is that a beer I see in your hand?" a deep male voice called out.

Two men had entered the room and were coming toward them. In terms of appearance, the two couldn't have been more different. One of them had dark hair that fell to his shoulders and an unruly black beard that looked like it had the texture of a Brillo pad. The other man was clean-shaven with short blond hair. Both wore V-neck T-shirts that were stretched across muscled frames.

US Navy SEALs.

"You must be Captain Watson," the dark-haired SEAL said.

"I'm certainly no captain, but that's me." Zane took the man's hand.

"Rod Cignetti."

"Otherwise known as the Rodfather," the blond-haired SEAL said.

"Rodfather?" Zane asked. "That sounds a little intimidating."

"He's got a nasty temper if he doesn't get his beauty sleep. Most of the time, he's all bark and no bite—unless you're a sexy lady," the second SEAL quipped. "I'm Colton O'Connor, by the way."

Zane shook his hand.

Cignetti nodded at Morgan's beer. "Where did you get that?"

She pointed at the tub. "Help yourself."

"I think I will."

"And there are sandwiches over on the table," Zane said.

Cignetti smiled. "Nice. A little grub is just what the doctor ordered."

Zane waited until the two walked off then turned to Morgan. "Since you're the official head of the UAP taskforce, I have to ask you a question."

"Shoot."

"What do you think we're going to find down in that ice?"

"You get right to the point, don't you?"

Zane smiled. "You may want to get used to that."

She took a pull on her beer. "As you might guess, I don't have enough information to give you a definitive answer. After all, that's why we're down here."

"What does your gut tell you?"

Her gaze went briefly to the SEALs, who had taken their beer and sandwiches over to one of the tables. Satisfied they were out of earshot, she turned back toward Zane. "My honest opinion? I agree that it is an extraterrestrial craft, and I'm someone who's normally pretty cynical about these kinds of things."

"So what makes you so sure?"

"For one, the shape is much too geometrically symmetrical to be some large deposit of metallic ore, which to me is the only other possible explanation."

"What about a seafaring vessel of some kind?" He knew others had pretty much ruled that out, but he wanted to hear what she had to say.

She shook her head. "Impossible. The shape isn't right, and it's much too large."

Zane was about to ask a follow-up question when he heard the din of voices across the room. He turned toward the sound. Amanda and Freja had just entered along with a woman and three men. Zane recognized them as the four remaining members of Operation Whiteout.

The woman was the team's nurse—an attractive twenty-seven-year-old Korean American. Sunny Lee had porcelain skin, brown eyes, and dark hair that was colored with red highlights.

On the far left was a tall, slender man who appeared to be in his mid-thirties. He had a thin face with a mop of blond hair that hung down over his eyes. *Brady Arnott.* The man who would be cooking their meals for the next few days. A food lover, Zane hoped the man could live up to his reputation.

Unfortunately, he wouldn't have much to work with given the climate.

Next to Arnott was Vince Stone, a bald Black man with a medium complexion. According to his dossier, Stone was one of the most experienced mechanics in the employ of US intelligence agencies. It was said he could fix everything in their fleet, from airplanes to tanks to motorcycles. Keeping transportation running was vital on any trip to Antarctica.

The third man was short, probably five-six or five-seven. He had neatly trimmed dark hair, a unibrow, and beady eyes that never seemed to stop moving. Zane immediately recognized him as Lucas Reimer, DARPA technology specialist. He was the other expert on UAPs.

Zane watched as Reimer scanned the room. He was looking for something or someone. When his eyes finally fell on Morgan Martini, he peeled away from the group and walked briskly in their direction.

"You didn't tell me you had already come down," Reimer said to Martini by way of greeting.

"Sorry, I didn't realize I needed to check in."

The man shrugged. "I thought we had talked about me coming by your room to get you on my way down."

Martini gestured at Zane. "Lucas, this is Zane Watson, our new head of security."

As the two shook hands, Reimer fixed his gaze on Zane. "No offense, but it seems like a bit of a waste to bring you down here."

"What makes you say that?" Zane asked.

"This is a research expedition, not a covert intelligence operation," Reimer said.

Due to the possible presence of a Russian asset, Delphi's strategic objective hadn't been revealed to any of the participants. And that was because no one, including Martini and Reimer, had been ruled out as the mole. The team members had simply been told that Zane, Amanda, and Freja were employed by a private security organization that specialized in overseas operations of a sensitive nature.

Zane had expected that their role might raise a few questions, but he hadn't expected to be confronted so early on. Lucas Reimer seemed almost irritated by their presence.

"It's a research expedition that's of vital interest to the United States, and there are concerns about the conditions under which it's going to be carried out," Zane said.

"What sorts of concerns?" Reimer asked. "Killer penguins? Too much snow on some of the buildings?"

Already in a foul mood, Zane resisted the urge to lash out at the little weasel. The last thing he needed was to get caught up in a tense verbal exchange the night before they set out. Instead, he decided to strike a calmer tone. "Antarctica is the harshest environment on the planet, and it just happens to be going through some of the worst storms to pass through the region in over a decade. As I'm sure you know, communications with Ellsworth Station have been cut off. I think it was reasonable and prudent for the government to have concerns about the safety of the team."

"Having an additional level of security certainly can't hurt, Lucas," Martini said.

Reimer nodded at the SEALs, who were seated close by. "That's what they're here for. I think they can handle anything that might come up."

Zane was about to make a retort when a knocking sound carried across the room. Someone was banging their knuckles on one of the tables.

"Okay, everybody! Can I have your attention?" a voice shouted above the din.

All heads turned toward the man standing at one end of a long table in the middle of the room. He had wavy red hair and razor stubble. Zane hadn't seen him come in.

"That's Niles Hawke," Martini whispered to Zane.

Zane nodded. "Yes, I met him and the other pilot earlier."

Niles Hawke and Patrick Rider were both former helicopter pilots with the British Army Air Corps. No longer in the military, they were now the chief transportation specialists for Parks Station. As such, they had been hired by the US government to fly the team down to Ellsworth Station. Because their participation was limited, the two men hadn't been given the full nature of the operation either. They had simply been told that one research team would be taken down to replace another.

"Can everyone please gather around?" Hawke called out. "That will keep me from having to shout."

As Zane and the others moved in that direction, he saw a laptop on the table in front of Hawke. He also noticed the British pilot's face was etched with concern. Zane wondered if they were about to hear that the storm had worsened.

Once everyone was near, Hawke began. "Cheers to you all. Sorry to skip the small talk, but there is something I need to tell you. As you probably know, we were scheduled to depart tomorrow morning at zero seven hundred hours. We planned it that way because there was supposed to be a break in the storm around that time." His eyes scanned the faces around him. "As some of you know, meteorological forecasts are pretty spotty down here, and unfortunately, that was the case with the information we previously received.

"The pause in the weather that we thought would begin tomorrow morning actually started this evening. A large front just passed through, and winds are down to about nineteen knots. The next front is about nine or ten hours away, which gives us that window we've been looking for."

"So what are you saying?" Cignetti asked.

"I'm saying that everyone needs to get packed up. We leave for Ellsworth Station in forty-five minutes."

5

In the Air Over the Antarctic Peninsula

The sleek Agusta Westland 139 helicopter cut through the frigid polar air like a white falcon soaring over the frozen tundra. The bird's powerful engine hummed with surprisingly quiet efficiency as it followed the southeastern curve of the Ellsworth Mountains.

Still awake despite the late hour, Zane stared out the window to his right. Even though darkness still ruled over the continent, he was able to make out the white terrain below. The topography was even more rolling than the last time he'd looked, a sign they were probably drawing close to the station.

As he continued to watch, Zane noticed a few snowflakes swirling underneath the big bird. Interestingly, snowfall was a rarity in Antarctica. In fact, the entire continent was technically considered a desert. The precipitation produced by the current system of storms was quite unusual. Still, much of what they would see over the next few days was likely existing snow being blown off the mountains or stirred up from the ground.

"How close are we?" someone whispered.

The soft voice pulled Zane out of his thoughts. He turned to see Sunny Lee staring at him, noise-canceling headphones still clamped over each of her ears.

Earlier, the two had spent some time getting to know one another. He had asked her about the basics—her background, her job, and what she did and didn't like about living in DC. Although she was kind and personable, she also seemed like the kind of woman who wasn't easily fazed. That kind of inner strength probably came in handy for someone who worked in stressful conditions.

"The last time I spoke to Hawke, he said we were about an hour and a half out," Zane replied. "I guess that means we have another thirty to forty-five minutes."

Sunny pulled down her headphones. "I'll bet the other team will be happy to see us."

"You would think so. Can't be too pleasant to be trapped out here."

Sunny rubbed her eyes in what seemed like an attempt to wipe away the fatigue. "So, what's going to happen when we touch down? We were told the astronomers would be taken back to Parks right away, but that was before the change in plans."

"If the conditions are still reasonably calm, that's still the plan."

"If you don't mind, I'd like to take a look at them before they depart. They've been through a lot, mentally and physically."

He nodded. "Just remember we're operating on a tight schedule. The important thing is to get them back to Parks as quickly as possible."

"It won't take long. I really just want to ask them a few questions about their health. If any concerns are raised, then I'll look into it."

Zane was about to add something else when Niles Hawke

caught his eye. The pilot had turned around to look at them then motioned Zane up to the cockpit with his hand.

"Excuse me, but I think I'm needed," Zane said.

"Is something wrong?"

"I don't think so. I think Hawke probably wants us to prepare for landing."

After slipping past her, Zane made his way up to the front. Despite telling Sunny that nothing was wrong, he had to admit there had been a bit of urgency in Hawke's movements. Perhaps the weather had worsened. The chopper felt steady, so he didn't think that was it. Nor did it sound like the engine was having any problems. Whatever it was, he didn't want to think about the possibility of having to land and walk the rest of the way.

"We haven't been able to make contact with our mates at Ellsworth," Hawke said as Zane came up. "Which is odd because we're well within radio range."

"Have you tried multiple channels?"

"I have, although they're supposed to monitor one specific channel in case of an emergency."

"How far out are we?" Zane asked.

"Nineteen minutes. It may be nothing to worry about, but I wanted you to be aware."

Zane nodded. "Thanks for the update. I'll get everyone ready for arrival."

6
―――

ELLSWORTH STATION, Antarctica

CLOUDS OF SNOW and ice billowed through the frigid air as the chopper descended through the darkness. From his seat behind the cockpit, Zane watched as the vague outline of a two-story structure came slowly into view. Having familiarized himself with the station's layout, he knew he was looking at the main building, which contained the living quarters, the dining room, and the communications center.

As the snowy haze dissipated, Zane noticed dim light spilling out of several windows on the second floor. He hoped it was a sure sign of life. Then again, Hawke still hadn't been able to reach any of the astronomers yet. *Why aren't they responding?* The station abutted a mountain, but there were no signs of an avalanche or any other calamity that might have brought on an emergency.

Zane felt a pinch of concern growing inside him. There was something about the whole situation that didn't feel right.

Seconds later, the chopper's skids settled onto the helipad.

The wind had picked up substantially over the last half hour, but Hawke and Rider had maneuvered through it with skilled precision. A pilot himself, Zane was impressed at how the two men had performed under the worsening conditions.

Hawke flicked a control that powered down the rotor.

"No welcoming committee," Rider said as he stared through the glass.

"Maybe they're asleep," Hawke said.

"With all the noise we made coming in?" Rider asked.

"Do they typically keep normal hours during the polar night?" Zane asked.

"It differs from one station to another depending on what they do," Rider replied. "Most researchers try to keep their body clocks in the same place it was when they arrived."

Zane looked at Hawke. "So you've been out here before?"

"Yes, many times. We're their taxi service, and we also bring supplies when they place orders."

"I want to take a small team in to check things out first," Zane said. "Since you know the layout, I'd like at least one of you to go in with us."

Hawke nodded.

"I want to make sure everything is safe before we bring the others in," Zane said.

While the two pilots shut the helicopter's engine down, Zane went to the back and brought the team up to date. He selected a few of them to go with him to scout the station and make sure everything was suitable for entry. Joining him would be the two SEALs, Freja Larsen, and Niles Hawke. Amanda asked to go, but Zane wanted her and Rider to remain behind with the others in case anything happened to their counterparts.

"So the rest of us have to sit out here freezing to death while you go in and look around?" Reimer asked, his words more a statement than a question.

"The main building is one hundred yards away," Zane said. "We'll be in touch via comms. If all is clear, then—"

"How long is this going to take?" Reimer snapped.

Zane did the best he could to quell the anger rising inside of him. He needed to put a lid on the situation before things got out of hand. He could tell already that Reimer was the kind of person who always needed to be in control. His comments to Morgan Martini back at Parks Station were another example of that.

"It will take as long as it needs to," Zane said emphatically.

Reimer's face turned red.

"I think he's right," Sunny said before he could respond. "It's a bit surprising that no one is coming out. I think it's smart to send in a few people to see what's going on."

Reimer shook his head but said nothing.

Zane looked at the others. "Like I said, we don't know how long this is going to take. Hopefully, not too long."

"While we're gone, please get your things together and be ready to disembark," Freja said.

As Zane moved toward the side door, he stopped next to Reimer and whispered, "If you get too cold, I'm sure one of the ladies could lend you their coat."

* * *

THE ADVANCE TEAM had just gotten off the chopper and were making a final check of their headsets. Zane and the two SEALs had established code names to use when communicating by radio. Rod Cignetti was the Rodfather, the nickname he always used when operating in the field. O'Connor was Ghost, an apparent reference to his ability to operate in the shadows. Zane had a call name he normally used with Delphi, but Cignetti had insisted he go by Samson, a humorous allusion to the operative's long hair and fit physique.

"Testing one, two, three," Zane said into the tiny microphone that wrapped around the front of his face.

Cignetti's voice crackled through Zane's earpiece. "I read you loud and clear, Samson."

In quick succession, the others indicated they could hear as well.

Even short walks in Antarctica could be dangerous if participants weren't dressed appropriately, so Zane did a quick assessment of everyone's attire. The SEALs wore pants and parkas colored with white-and-gray camouflage, the standard military garb for operating on the frozen tundra. Hawke and Freja were also covered in several layers, including heavy coats, knit caps, gloves, and fleece balaclavas. The extra layer of balaclavas was an absolute necessity in that part of the world because large patches of exposed skin could freeze in seconds.

Satisfied his team was ready, Zane turned to Hawke. "Take us in."

Hawke turned on his flashlight and led them toward the cluster of buildings. Cignetti and O'Connor split apart to cover each flank. Both of the SEALs carried M4 rifles, the weapon of choice for US Special Forces. Although they weren't expecting trouble, both men's heads were on swivels as they checked for potential threats.

Thick clouds of snowflakes swirled around them, stirred up by the stiff winds sweeping across the landscape. While the gusts weren't yet a concern, Zane wondered if they were a sign that the next storm front was arriving sooner than expected.

For now, he was just happy to be moving again. The Delphi operative had worked all over the world, but the cold there was unlike any he had ever experienced before. The only exposed part of his body was the small area around his eyes, and the skin there was already starting to burn.

The group was now at the line of smaller buildings at the periphery of the station. On the left were a small water tower and an above-ground fuel tank. On the right were three structures—a garage and two large storage facilities.

"The main operating facility is directly ahead," Hawke said.

"A few lights are on, but I don't see any movement inside," O'Connor added.

"At least we know their generators are working," Freja said.

"What concerns me is that no one seems to have noticed our arrival," Hawke said. "Our bird makes a lot of noise."

Zane felt another pinch of concern, this one a little stronger than before. Hawke was right. It was strange that no one had come out.

"Maybe they're asleep," Freja said.

Hawke shook his head. "I doubt all of them would be."

"Do they have weapons?" Freja asked.

"They shouldn't," Hawke replied. "Why?"

"Just don't want to go in and wake up a bunch of trigger-happy astronomers."

"We're fine."

A half minute later, they arrived at the main building, which was situated at the base of a mountain. A set of black metal stairs ran up to the front door. Hawke stopped at the bottom of the steps and looked back at Zane for guidance.

"Try knocking first," Zane said. "Even though they probably aren't armed, I don't want to go storming in unless we have to."

Hawke nodded then climbed the steps. He used a gloved hand to knock heavily on the door.

"That ought to wake them up," Cignetti said.

While they waited for someone to answer, Zane lifted his gaze to the two lighted windows on the second floor. As best he could tell, there was no movement in either room. No one was peeking out to see who was there, nor were there any shadows moving against the wall.

Seeing no further signs of life inside, he turned and looked behind them. The inability to make out anything over the wind concerned him. As bundled up as they were, it would be virtually impossible to hear anyone approach. He wasn't expecting any hostiles at the isolated station, but he had learned to trust his gut, and his gut was telling him that something wasn't right there. First, the communications had gone down, then no one was responding to their knocks.

"Try again," Zane said.

Hawke banged on the door a second time, even louder than before.

"Hear anything inside?" Zane asked.

"Negative," Hawke replied. "Although I'm not sure I could with my ears all covered up."

At that point, they had done everything they could. Zane hoped they would be pleasantly surprised to find some cold-but-healthy astronomers inside, but it would be prudent to go in expecting the worst.

He started up the steps. "Let's go in."

When they reached the top of the stairs, Hawke was already holding the door open.

"It wasn't locked?" Zane asked.

Hawke shook his head. "No, but that's not unusual at these remote stations. Other than a few nosy penguins, you don't expect to have any visitors out here."

The interior was mostly dark, with a small amount of ambient light coming from other parts of the building. While still cold, the temperature inside was significantly higher than it was outside. It was a clear indicator the heat was working, which also meant the team hadn't frozen to death.

Zane looked around the space. They were standing in a nondescript foyer. Directly ahead, a set of stairs ran up to the second floor. On either side of the stairs were corridors that ran toward the back.

Zane lowered the part of the balaclava that covered his mouth and called out in a loud voice. "Is anyone here?"

There was no response.

The others pulled their balaclavas down as well.

"Nobody's home," Cignetti said.

"Not good," Hawke said.

"I just thought about something," Freja said. "Don't they keep some of those special trucks here at the station? I forget the word in English. Terrain trucks or something like that?"

"All-terrain vehicles," Hawke replied. "Yes, there are supposed to be two Hagglunds in the garage."

Having done a little reading on the way down, Zane was familiar with Hagglunds. The over-snow carriers were commonly used in Antarctica to transport people from one station to another.

"If that's the case, then maybe they tried to take one of them back to Parks," Freja said.

"I suppose anything is possible," Hawke said. "But why would they leave? They should have plenty of supplies, and we know the generator is working."

"Communications are down, so they may have been concerned about making it through the storm," Freja said.

"It's possible they're here," Zane said. "I studied an architectural sketch of this building, and it's massive. They could be on the other end."

"Could be," Freja said. "But I'm willing to bet they aren't."

"There is only one way to find out." Zane looked at Hawke. "Where are the living quarters? Let's start there."

"If my memory serves me correctly, I believe they're on the second floor."

Zane pointed to Hawke and the two SEALs. "Why don't the three of you check those rooms out? Freja and I can start down here."

"Roger that," Cignetti said.

"Let us know the minute any of you makes contact with one of the residents," Zane said. "Remember to keep things calm. If we find someone, they're liable to be surprised by our presence."

It was sound advice, but Zane didn't believe they were going to find anyone. For whatever reason, the astronomers appeared to have deserted the station. Maybe Freja was right. Maybe they were on their way to Parks Station in one of the Hagglunds.

After Hawke and the SEALs departed up the stairs, Zane turned to Freja. "There are two hallways. We can work them together, or we can split up."

"We can cover more ground alone." She patted the pocket of her coat, indicating the pistol that was hidden there. "I'll be fine."

Zane nodded. "I assume the two halls connect at the back of the building. If not, I'll come find you when I'm done."

"Copy that."

As Freja moved off, Zane entered the corridor on the right. It was even darker than the foyer, so he pulled out his flashlight and thumbed it on. About ten yards down, he stepped into the first room on the right. Feeling around on the wall, he found a panel and flicked the switch up. Light filled the space, revealing what appeared to be an office area of some kind. Several desks were lined up along the near end. Each was covered with mounds of papers, folders, and a few large sheets that looked like maps or charts.

Zane scanned the opposite end of the room where a few cubicles were clustered. There was no movement. In fact, it didn't look like the place had been used in quite some time.

Seeing no evidence of recent activity, Zane turned the lights off and exited into the hall. He had just started walking toward the next room when Cignetti's voice crackled through his headset. "This is Rodfather, do you read?"

"Go ahead, Rodfather," Zane said.

"We need you to come take a look at something. Second floor, third room on left."

Zane wondered why Cignetti hadn't told him what they had

found. Either he wasn't sure what it was, or there was bad news that was difficult to share. Although Zane hoped it was the former, his gut told him it was the latter. "Roger that."

When Zane returned to the front vestibule, he found Freja waiting for him.

"That was quick," Freja said. "I hope it's good news."

Zane nodded but said nothing. If it was good news, then Cignetti would likely have given some indication of that.

The two took the stairs up to the second floor. Just down the hall, light spilled from an open doorway on the left. As they moved toward it, Zane's nostrils began to fill with a faint but pungent odor. It was a natural smell that seemed to have been suppressed by the cold temperatures. Suddenly, he realized what it was, and dread crept over him.

Hawke arrived from the opposite direction, then the three of them entered together.

Despite the distinctive smell, Zane still held out hope that they might find the two SEALs talking to a drowsy astronomer who had just been woken up. Instead, the two men were standing in the middle of the room, their flashlights trained on something against the far wall.

Hearing the others shuffle inside, the SEALs stepped apart so the rest could see what they were looking at. Zane noticed the stains before he saw the body. Dark stringy lines, smudges, and spots. It was as though someone had flung a small pail of paint across the floor.

Then, when the body came into view, Freja let out a gasp.

7

It was hard to set aside the feeling of shock one had after seeing the ravaged body of the victim, but Zane knew he had to do exactly that. There would be time to process the scene later. Right then, he needed to protect the members of his team from a killer that might still be close by.

His adrenaline pumping, Zane told Freja and Hawke to watch over the astronomer's body while he and the two SEALs went out to escort the others into the building. He had no way of knowing where the killer was, but it was clear everyone would be better off inside. Exposed out in the storm as it was, the helicopter was a sitting duck.

After bringing everyone in, he tried to get them to assemble in the office he had found earlier. Unfortunately, the team could sense something was wrong and demanded that he bring them up to speed at once. Zane had wanted to keep the news under wraps until they had more information but soon realized that it wasn't the kind of thing that could be kept a secret. He had to give them the truth of what they were facing.

Without going into a lot of detail, Zane told the group that a man—who they assumed was one of the astronomers—had suffered a horrific death. Despite their initial shock, each member of the team expressed a desire to visit the scene to see what had happened for themselves. While it wasn't ideal in terms of morale, Zane knew he was dealing with people who worked in the world of military and intelligence. In other words, death was something they were familiar with.

After giving them a final warning about the gruesome scene, Zane led the group up to the second floor. Before letting them into the room, he told Cignetti and O'Connor to clear the remainder of the building. He then asked Hawke and Rider to place a call to the Parks Station using their satellite phone. They needed backup, and they needed it fast.

As the four left to carry out his instructions, Zane finally let the others come in. There were a few initial gasps, followed by stunned silence.

To Zane, the scene looked like something out of a horror film. The brown-haired man lay on his back under the window, his face mauled beyond recognition. Unfortunately for him, the gruesome wounds didn't end there. One of the astronomer's arms was bent at an impossible angle, and one of his legs had been nearly ripped off. His navy sweater was riddled with tears and stains, indicating that he may have been stabbed many times as well.

Despite the carnage, nurse Sunny Lee stepped forward and crouched near the body. She moved her head back and forth, her eyes taking in every detail. It was almost like she was trying to make sense of it all, something Zane didn't believe possible.

"Who or what could possibly have done something like this?" Martini whispered, breaking the silence in the room.

Sunny said nothing. Either she was too stunned to answer, or she was so caught up in her analysis that she hadn't heard the question.

"It had to be an animal," Reimer said.

"There are no large predators on Antarctica," Amanda said. "At least not any that live on land."

Reimer shook his head. "All I can say is, no man would kill like that."

"They might if they were trying to torture information out of him," Vince Stone said.

Although he understood why the mechanic might think that, Zane doubted the astronomer had been tortured to death. It seemed too over the top. Most torture involved smaller, more precise wounds. Missing fingernails. Broken fingers. Small burns in delicate places.

Sunny stood then took a few steps back.

"Any thoughts?" Zane asked.

She shook her head. "Amanda's right about there not being any predators down here, but I still can't help but think an animal did this."

"And a predator would have consumed what it killed," Zane said.

"What about dogs?" Stone asked. "Maybe the team kept dogs here."

"There was no mention of any pets in the information we received." Amanda nodded at the astronomer's severely dislocated arm. "Besides, no dog could do that."

Sunny nodded. "Whoever or whatever did this was powerful. Extremely powerful."

"What about a powerful man?" Martini asked.

"A strong man with a weapon could have," Sunny said.

"Or several men," Reimer noted.

Zane was having a hard time envisioning a human being responsible for such carnage, and yet he knew it was certainly within the realm of possibility. *But why?* Maybe Stone was right. Maybe the astronomer had been tortured by someone who didn't know how to do it. But if so, he wasn't sure what information the killer had been after. *Were they trying to find the location of the anomaly?*

"Can you tell how long he's been here?" Brady Arnott asked the nurse.

"That's a good question," Sunny said. "There are no obvious signs of bloating, which I believe begins three to five days after death." She crouched near one of the man's legs. She then pulled up one pants leg and placed her hand on the calf muscle. "His muscles are still fairly stiff."

"What does that suggest?" Freja asked.

"Well, rigor mortis begins within a few hours and can last from one to three days. After that, the body goes limp again."

"So he could've just died?" Amanda asked.

Sunny stood. "As I said, the calf muscle felt pretty stiff. I'm guessing he's been here for one to three days. Then again, I'm not an expert on human decomposition. My job is to keep people healthy and alive."

Zane was about to add something when a voice crackled through his earpiece. "This is the Rodfather. Samson, do you read?"

"Go ahead, Rodfather," Zane said.

"I think we found something you need to look at."

Zane frowned. "What's your location?"

"First floor. Head straight to the back until you enter a large atrium."

"Roger that. Be right there." Zane looked at the others. "That was Cignetti. I need all of you to wait here."

Zane asked Amanda to remain with the others then signaled Freja to follow him out. Once in the hall, he removed the Glock pistol that had been tucked in his coat pocket. Although the SEAL hadn't mentioned a specific threat, he wasn't taking any chances.

"Let's hope it's not another body," Freja said as they went down the stairs.

"I was just thinking the same thing."

After arriving on the first floor, they turned down the hall Zane had started to explore earlier. The dark corridor seemed to stretch on forever. Zane had known the building was large, but he was just now getting a true sense of just how massive it was. It was going to take them a long time to clear it.

A minute later, they emerged into an expansive atrium that stood at the intersection of several hallways. Zane's gaze was immediately drawn to a glassed-in area on the far side. It looked like the soundproof room of a recording studio. The interior was lit up, and Zane could see Cignetti and O'Connor standing inside.

As they moved toward it, Zane saw a half dozen computers, as well as what appeared to be radio equipment. The room must've served as some sort of communications center.

"It's completely destroyed," Cignetti said as they entered.

There was no need to ask what he was referring to. Pieces of crushed electronic hardware were strewn across the floor.

"I guess it wasn't the storm that prevented them from radioing in," Freja said.

O'Connor nodded. "Someone didn't want them communicating with the outside world."

"Any signs of the other astronomers?" Zane asked.

Cignetti shook his head. "No, but we still have a lot of ground to cover. This is a large building, and we're just getting started."

Suddenly, a voice came through Zane's earpiece. "This is Niles. Do you read?"

"Yes, go ahead, Niles," Zane said.

"We can't call out," Hawke said.

"Why not?"

"Because we don't have a signal. That front is moving in quicker than we thought. The wind has picked up quite a bit in the last few minutes."

Zane swore under his breath. He had counted on satellite communication to bring in help.

"Did you find the radio?" Hawke asked.

Zane looked at the electronic debris at his feet. "We did, but it can't be used."

"Why not?"

"I'll explain later."

"I think we may have a workaround," Hawke said. "Patrick wants to take the chopper about ten or fifteen miles out and try to place a call from there. The storm has just arrived, which means there is a lot of atmospheric activity overhead. If he can get far enough out, there might be a signal."

"Can it be done safely?" Zane asked.

"At this point, nothing we do is going to be safe. This is Antarctica, and there is a nasty storm coming in. But Patrick is going to fly low, and if he's unable to keep going, then he's promised to set the bird down and hike back."

"That sounds like a suicide mission," Zane said.

"He and I know this region better than anyone, and we know how to survive under the worst of conditions. As long as he's able to land it without any problems, he'll make it back. That I guarantee."

"There is a fuel reservoir here," Zane said. "Can he fill up and take some of our team back to Parks?"

"Unfortunately, there isn't enough time. Not only that, but if he has to set the bird down, you don't want inexperienced people trying to hike back through this mess."

He was right. At that point, the plan for Rider to fly out in search of a signal was probably their only hope of making contact with the outside world.

"Okay," Zane finally said. "Just tell him not to do anything stupid."

8

In the Air North of Ellsworth Station

Patrick Rider glanced at the satellite phone for the third time since leaving Ellsworth Station. There was still no signal. He was beginning to wonder if he would ever get one. He was flying along the leading edge of the storm, and he was already experiencing some of the worst conditions he had ever seen in all his years working on the continent. The winds were blowing at approximately thirty knots, with the occasional gust that he figured was well over forty.

For the moment, he kept the chopper about two hundred feet above the surface. Such a low altitude wouldn't normally be a problem when operating over the flat terrain, but the darkness and the mountainous curves made the path extremely treacherous. Even so, he didn't have a choice. With powerful gusts becoming more and more frequent, he needed to stay near the ground in case a quick landing became necessary.

A few minutes later, the chopper came around a sharp ridge. Hoping the signal might be better, he decided to check the phone

one more time. If there wasn't a signal, he would attempt to set the bird down and hike back to Ellsworth as planned.

As he reached for his phone, a tiny point of light flared on the far side of a nearby ravine. It stood out against the dark landscape. Rider frowned. There were no other stations in the area, nor were there any temporary outposts or camps. That being the case, then where had the light come from?

Suddenly, an image flashed in his thoughts. It was a memory from his deployment to Iraq. During one particularly vicious battle with ISIS insurgents, he remembered seeing flashes of light coming from the terrorist encampments. Those flashes were similar to the one he had just seen.

"Stinger," he whispered, remembering the handheld surface-to-air missiles. His blood ran cold. Someone had been hidden along the base of the mountain, ready to fire at any aircraft coming in or going out of Ellsworth.

Another point of light flared in the same location. A second missile had been fired.

At most, Rider had maybe ten or twenty seconds to get out of harm's way. Looking through the cockpit glass, he noticed there was a rocky ravine at the base of the mountain to his right. That gave him an idea. It seemed impossible, but at this point, it was his only chance of survival.

Knuckles white, he slammed the collective throttle down, angling the helicopter into a sharp descent.

9

Ellsworth Station

With one astronomer dead and the others missing, Zane, Hawke, and the two SEALs began the process of clearing every square foot of the station. They needed to make sure the perpetrator wasn't hiding somewhere, ready to go on another killing spree. Due to its mammoth size, the main building took a full four hours to search. Once that was complete, they ventured outside to check the three exterior structures.

Zane told the SEALs to check the two storage buildings, while he and Hawke went to the garage. The Hagglund vehicles as well as other various pieces of equipment, from backup generators to snow blowers, were housed there. After a thorough search of the interior, they found no signs of anyone hiding inside. Nor did they find anything that seemed out of the ordinary. If the killer was still at Ellsworth, he wasn't in the garage.

Once he and Hawke were done, Zane radioed the SEALs. "The garage is all clear, Rodfather. Can you give me an update?"

Several seconds later, Cignetti's voice came through the head-

THE ANOMALY

set. "We cleared the first storage building and are in the process of clearing the second. So far, we've found nothing of concern."

"Do you want us to come over and help you finish up?"

"Negative. We're almost done. We'll meet you back inside."

"Copy that."

"So far, so good," Hawke said after Zane signed off.

"I agree, but I still get this feeling there is more to this place than we know."

"What do you mean?"

"This station was built out over several decades. In some cases, it looks like some prefab structures were put on top of existing structures. That means you could have some gaps in the construction that would make a nice hiding spot. I also want to start looking for the tunnels."

"But how would an attacker know about that? They would know even less about this place than we do."

The file Zane had been given on Operation Whiteout indicated that the astronomers were going to try to enter a series of tunnels in an attempt to reach the anomaly. Hawke wasn't supposed to know about the discovery, so Zane answered without disclosing everything he knew. "We were told that the building had experienced some structural problems, and according to the report, those problems might have been caused by a network of underground ice tunnels."

"It's the first I've heard of it, and I've been working down here a while," Hawke said.

"Who knows? It may not even be true. But we need to rule that out."

After switching off the garage lights, the two exited into the storm, which was getting worse by the minute. The temperature had dropped precipitously, the gusts blowing the snowflakes sideways. Although he wasn't a meteorologist, Zane was reasonably certain the wind speed was at least thirty knots.

Since they hadn't yet heard from Ryder, they assumed the

pilot had been forced to make an emergency landing and walk back. The thought of someone traveling across that terrain on foot was more than a little concerning. Even someone dressed for the trek might have a hard time surviving for more than a few hours. Still, Hawke remained certain that the pilot would find a way to get back. Zane wasn't so sure.

Heads down, the two men marched briskly toward the main building. Zane hated being exposed outdoors even for a few seconds, but it would be useless to try to scan the area for hostiles. The only positive was that any attacker would have to deal with the same lack of visibility they had.

When they reached the front entrance, Zane unlocked the door using one of several keys they had found in a utility room. Once inside, he spoke through his mic. "Rodfather, I'm locking the front door. We'll see you in the dining room."

"Copy that, Samson. We'll be there soon."

Zane locked the door then tucked the key into his coat pocket.

As the two men crossed the building's foyer, Hawke turned toward Zane. "Okay, you want to tell me what's really going on here, mate?"

"What do you mean?"

"We've got a dead man upstairs, and you didn't even seem fazed by it. If I'm not mistaken, it almost seemed like you *expected* to find a body."

"When I'm in work mode, I don't display much emotion," Zane said.

"Okay, so you keep your game face on in difficult situations." He paused for a moment. "Then can you tell me why you brought along two soldiers who seem suspiciously like US Special Forces? I'm former military myself, so I can spot those guys from a mile away."

Zane considered how he should respond. Hawke and Rider hadn't been in on the Operation Whiteout findings, nor had they been told about the possibility that a Russian mole might be hidden among the Ellsworth operatives. The original plan had been uncomplicated where the British pilots were involved. They'd been supposed to take Zane's group down to Ellsworth then return the other team to Parks in a quick swap.

Unfortunately, the dead body and the missing astronomers had changed matters. Not only that, but Hawke was smart enough to know that the US government wouldn't send armed soldiers down unnecessarily. He'd likely realized that the Ellsworth team was facing some form of danger that would require the use of weapons. Keeping secrets from the man wasn't going to be so simple.

By that point, Zane knew he had to give Hawke something. The hit squad that had killed the astronomer was still probably close by, which meant the possibility of another assault was likely. Given the dire situation, Zane was going to have to rely on Hawke to watch his back. Besides, the British pilot deserved to know what was going on.

As the two entered the dark corridor, Zane said, "The astronomers found something under the ice. Something the US government is very interested in. And before you ask, I can't tell you what it is. It's classified, and none of us is sure what's down there."

"Bloody hell," Hawke whispered.

"And there is something else I need to tell you. We believe the news of that discovery may have leaked out."

"Which explains the dead body."

Zane nodded.

"Why didn't you tell me about what we might be up against?"

"First of all, none of us believed you and your co-pilot would be in any danger. The plan was to send you back right away. Second, I honestly had no idea what we'd find here. I knew that word had likely gotten out, but I didn't think that those in possession of that information would have been able to mobilize so quickly. If I had known that, I would've brought an entire squad down here."

Hawke nodded but said nothing.

"At some point, I knew I was going to have to share what intel we had," Zane said. "You just beat me to it."

"Okay, tell me this. Who do you think is out there? Who killed that man?"

"We're not sure."

It wasn't a truthful statement, but Zane wasn't about to get into his speculations on the attack. Nor was he going to tell Hawke about the possible presence of a mole. That detail would have to remain locked down.

"I'll just assume it's one of the usual suspects like China or Russia."

"That's probably a safe assumption."

"So what now?"

"We lock this place down as much as we can, then we wait to hear from Rider. Speaking of which, has he contacted you?"

Hawke shook his head. "Not yet."

"Let's just hope he landed the bird all right and is trying to make it back here on foot."

"No sense in worrying," Hawke said in a solemn tone.

They both knew that Rider wasn't going to fly back. Not even a large helicopter like an Agusta Westland could operate safely in these conditions. Zane was troubled by the thought that the pilot might be out there on his own, but at that point, there was nothing they could do. Rider had known about the danger he was facing, and to his credit, he had been willing to do whatever was necessary to get help. Even though it hadn't been the plan, Zane hoped the man had had the sense to continue on to Parks.

A minute later, Zane and Hawke entered the dining hall. The other team members were seated around several tables at the far end, talking in muted tones. Brady Arnott, the group's chef, was bringing out plates of food.

Zane went to the table where Amanda and Freja were sitting.

"Everything check out?" Amanda asked by way of greeting.

Zane nodded. "Cignetti and O'Connor are finishing up and should be here shortly."

Zane noticed the two were eating off of paper plates. Arnott had put together an interesting mix of canned tuna, rice, and bananas.

Amanda saw him looking at her plate. "Want some?"

Zane shook his head. "I'll grab something when we're done."

"How did the Hagglunds look?" Freja asked. "We might need them to get out of here."

"They looked fine, but honestly, I wasn't paying close attention to their condition. I just made sure no one was hiding inside. At some point, I'll send Vince out to take a closer look at them. We also need to make sure the fuel tank is working."

"I can go with him," Freja said. "I worked on a farm when I was a teenager, so I've had some experience with trucks and heavy machinery."

"A jack-of-all-trades." Zane looked at Amanda. "Did you put together our sleeping arrangements?"

"Yes, we were just putting the finishing touches on it when you came in. We're going to put everyone in rooms that are nearby. The good news is that there were quite a few that weren't being used by the astronomers, so we won't need to move a lot of stuff out."

"Thanks for doing that." Zane looked out across the tables and raised his voice. "Everybody, listen up."

As they turned in his direction, Zane could see expressions ranging from extreme fatigue to deep concern. He understood their anxiety. Until help arrived, they would have a difficult road ahead. In addition to the possibility of an attack, they were going to be living under conditions that could sap the life out of anyone. The lack of sunlight and extreme cold were enough to send even the most hardened individuals into a state of depression.

Zane decided to be as positive as he could. "First, I have some good news. We've completed our sweep of the station, and it seems to be clear."

"Do we know where the other astronomers are?" Martini asked.

"No, we don't."

"Why not?" Reimer asked from his seat next to Morgan. "You were brought along as our security expert, and now you're telling us you don't have any idea what happened to these people?"

Once again, Zane managed to tamp down his anger. "Our first priority is keeping everyone safe. We'll start the search once we're confident the building is locked down. We also need a little rest."

Reimer shook his head. "There are people who might be injured or in danger, but we haven't even started looking for them."

Reimer's protest reminded Zane of a certain Bible story. In it, Judas complained that the expensive perfume had been wasted on wiping the feet of Jesus when it could have been sold and the money given to the poor. The Bible made it clear that Judas cared nothing about the poor but instead was a thief who had been stealing from the moneybag. In a similar way, Reimer was trying to take the moral high ground in their situation. If Zane had emphasized the search for the missing researchers above everything else, Reimer would have certainly complained that he didn't feel safe.

Zane fixed his gaze on the DARPA scientist. "In case you didn't realize it, the search of the station also allowed us to look for the missing astronomers. Now that we've secured the building, we'll be able to conduct a proper search without having to look over our shoulders."

"I think you're doing a fine job," Stone said. "I'm glad you're in charge instead of these other yahoos."

Reimer glared at Stone.

"Let's talk about sleeping arrangements," Zane said before Reimer could say anything else. "Amanda and Freja have put together room assignments."

"Room assignments?" Martini asked.

"We're trying to put everyone as close together as possible," Zane said. "More specifically, we want everyone to be close to someone armed."

"We should *all* be given a gun," Reimer said.

"I think Lucas is right," Martini said. "In light of what we found, it would be nice if each person was at least given a pistol. I suspect most of us have handled one at some point in our lives. I certainly know how to use one."

"Unfortunately, there aren't enough weapons to go around," Zane said. "There are five of us providing security, and it's imperative that we have the weapons we need to do our jobs."

What he'd said was true enough, but even if there were enough weapons to go around, Zane wouldn't have allowed it. With the possibility of a mole operating in their midst, it would be foolish to arm everyone.

"If there are no further questions, please come see Amanda and me for your room assignments," Freja said. "I'd also encourage each of you to get as much sleep as possible."

Martini stood, but instead of following the others toward Amanda's table, she walked over to Zane. As she came toward him, he braced for what was probably going to be a complaint about not having a gun.

"I want to apologize for Lucas," she said in a soft voice.

Zane blinked, more than a little surprised by the sudden apology. But he was relieved that he wouldn't have to argue with her.

"I've known him for a while now," she continued. "He's not a bad guy. But he's a perfectionist, and when things are chaotic, he can get a little frustrated and angry."

Zane nodded. "We're all in the middle of a very stressful situation, which means people are going to react in very different ways. I'm used to dealing with that."

"I appreciate your understanding. We're all going to have to pull together."

"Indeed, we are. By the way, don't worry about not having a weapon. You'll always have protection close by."

She nodded, although it was still clear she didn't agree with him. "Thank you."

As she walked off, Zane considered her words. While it was nice of her to play the role of peacemaker, he found her comment about Reimer troubling. *She's only worked on a couple of projects with the guy and is already familiar with his temper?* No matter what kind of spin she'd tried to put on it, that wasn't a good look for Reimer.

10

Arlington, Virginia

Carmen Petrosino removed her Washington Nationals coffee mug from the top shelf then closed the cabinet door. It was a little after eight in the evening, which was well beyond her normal cutoff time for caffeine. But tonight was different. She needed to get started on her new Delphi assignment, and to do that, she was going to require a lot more energy.

Her extreme fatigue was in no small part related to the three weeks she had just spent on a job in Taiwan. The work itself had been grueling, and the long flight home had only added to her physical and mental exhaustion. She had traveled for well over twenty-four hours, and she was starting to realize that it might take weeks for her internal clock to get back to normal.

After landing at Dulles that afternoon, Carmen had taken an Uber back to her apartment in Arlington. Her initial plan was to go home and get in bed without checking her messages. Her colleagues were fully capable of fighting any fires that might be out there. Besides, she wouldn't be much help in her exhausted state.

But curiosity soon got the better of her. While riding in the backseat of the Uber, she used her phone to access the secure Delphi portal, and that was when she found the new assignment file waiting in her inbox.

Her work in Taiwan had kept her off the grid, which meant that all the information Ross had placed in the file was new to her. She had never heard about Operation Whiteout before, and she certainly hadn't heard about the discovery of an anomaly below a US research facility in Antarctica.

From the moment Carmen started reading, she was hooked. It was a case that was both fascinating and important to American interests. She even felt a little stab of jealousy that she wasn't down there with Zane and Amanda.

Despite her disappointment, she knew she still had an important role to play. Ross had asked her to take a deep dive into the lives of everyone participating in Operation Whiteout. He was convinced that someone on the team was working with FSB, the Federal Security Service of the Russian Federation. It would be Carmen's job to identify the likely suspects, and she would do that by probing into their backgrounds.

Carmen grabbed the pot and filled her mug to the rim with Lavazza Classico coffee. An Italian by birth, she had mostly made the conversion to American culture while still managing to keep a touch of Italy in her life. She still clung to many of the products she had grown up with, including Lavazza.

After taking a few sips of the hot brew, she went to her living room, took a seat on the couch, then opened her laptop. On the screen were the images of every person participating in Operation Whiteout. A visual person, Carmen preferred to study photographs of the people she was looking into. She wanted to immerse herself completely in their lives, and she couldn't do that unless she studied their appearances.

She examined each photograph again, associating a few words with each suspect. Morgan Martini, the UFO expert. Lucas Reimer, the DARPA guy. Rod Cignetti, a US Navy SEAL. Colton O'Connor, the other SEAL. Sunny Lee, the nurse. Vince Stone, the mechanic. Brady Arnott, the chef.

"Which one of you is the bad apple?" she whispered to herself.

After going through the photographs several more times, Carmen toggled over to a Word document where she'd noted the basic information on each member of Operation Whiteout. The first name at the top was Vincent Stone, the mechanic.

She had listed Stone first because he looked familiar to her. She remembered his handsome features from when she had rented an apartment in Alexandria the year before. She was certain she had seen him in her building on several occasions. The two always seemed to arrive at home around the same time each evening. But after looking at his straightforward background, that was probably just a coincidence.

Stone had been one of the US Army's top mechanics for the better part of a decade. In fact, he was so good that the CIA had scooped him up shortly after he'd left the armed services. US intelligence agencies owned massive transportation fleets, from the sedans used by Langley staff to the corporate jets that were flown around the world. A fleet of that size required a full contingent of mechanics, and Stone was second-in-command of that group.

Seeing nothing out of the ordinary, Carmen opened her web browser and made a quick sweep of the social media sites. While she doubted that someone paid by Russia would leave a trail of clues strewn across the Internet, she still needed to check the box.

After a half hour of searching, she came up empty, which was odd. Vincent Stone had no online footprint whatsoever. No social media accounts. No record on the White Pages website. Nothing.

She found the discovery bizarre. Yes, he was an employee of the world's largest intelligence agency, but he wasn't working in a position that required secrecy. Carmen knew a few people who held administrative positions at both the CIA and NSA, and all of them had a fairly significant online presence.

Carmen toggled back to the Word document and made an entry under Vincent Stone. *No online presence. Strange.*

11

Ten Miles North of Ellsworth Station

A loud *bang* echoed across the frozen terrain.

Patrick Rider looked over his shoulder just in time to see a pillar of flames, smoke, and debris burst into the night sky. It was just what he had hoped for. The blaze had finally reached the helicopter's fuel tank, triggering a mammoth explosion. Anyone who came to examine the downed chopper would assume that all the passengers were dead.

Realizing he was exposed by the light of the flames, Rider turned and hobbled away from the wreckage. His knee throbbed, making it difficult to move faster than a brisk walk. At that point, he was just thankful he could put weight on his leg.

After seeing the missiles coming toward him, Rider had made the tough call to place the chopper on a course that would crash it directly into the wall of the ravine. Once the autopilot was set, he had used the few seconds he had to grab his backpack, open the side door, and jump.

Some might have called it a clever and brave decision. In reality, it was the only viable option he'd had left. Trying to avoid the incoming missile already targeting him would have been an exercise in futility. The Agusta wasn't equipped with decoy flares, nor did it have enough maneuverability to take evasive action. Attempting a normal landing would have taken far too long.

The fall was approximately twenty feet, and Rider had had no idea what the terrain was like below him. Had there been boulders or jagged ice, he probably would have died on impact. Fortunately, the center of the ravine was filled with more snow than usual due to the recent storms. As a result, his only injury had been a twisted knee. He could live with that.

A loud *pop* brought Rider back to the present. Another piece of the engine had just exploded behind him. He was about fifty yards from the crash site, but it wasn't enough. The people who had fired the missile would arrive soon to check for survivors, which meant he needed to be as far away as possible when that happened.

A gust of wind howled through the ravine, blowing the snow sideways. Rider's body shivered in response. Not only did he need to get away from the flames, but he also needed to find a place to escape the chilling wind. A cave. A fissure. Anything.

He had glanced up at the lip of the ravine. His initial plan had been to climb it, but that wouldn't be possible with the injured knee. He turned and looked toward the bottom of the mountain. While flat ground would be better on his knee, that direction wasn't an option either, because whoever had fired on him would likely be coming from that way.

As if on cue, a tiny beam of light suddenly appeared at the base of the ravine. Seconds later, another beam appeared. Then a third. Before long, there were seven beams in all.

They're here.

Rider's chest tightened as he watched the lights move in his direction. He guessed the enemy would go straight to the burning wreckage. With their attention on the chopper, he wondered if he might be able to slip past them. While tempting, he quickly dismissed the idea. His knee was barely functional. If the enemy didn't take long to examine the downed bird, they would probably catch up to him on their way back down.

At that point, his only option was to take cover. Turning, he let his gaze run over the terrain behind him. Almost immediately, his eyes settled on a snowdrift that was piled up against a rocky ridge. It was perfect for what he had in mind.

Sidling over to it, Rider dropped to his good knee and began scooping away the snow. The flakes were soft and fluffy, making the job easier than he had expected. Still, he hurried on. Every second was critical.

After carving out a large recess, he opened his backpack and pulled out the pistol Zane Watson had given him. At the time, it hadn't seemed all that important. But at any moment, it might save his life.

Rider chambered a round, grabbed the backpack, then maneuvered into the recess. Once he was positioned horizontally, he began to wiggle his left arm and leg, shifting so that the snow above him fell over his body in piles. Within seconds, he was mostly covered. It wasn't a perfect hiding place, but at least it gave him some measure of cover.

Situated, Rider looked toward the downed chopper. The seven attackers had just arrived and were circling the wreckage, looking for any signs that someone might still be alive. Each of the men had on a coat, a pair of pants, and boots that were all camouflaged with splashes of white and gray.

Commandos, he thought. The elite soldiers must've been carrying out some mission. *Who sent them?* Rider examined the rifles slung over each man's shoulder. Each one had a light mounted on the barrel, which Rider momentarily mistook for a flashlight. He also noted the long box magazines extended from underneath each weapon. *Kalashnikovas.* Probably AK-74s. They were the rifles of choice for armies across the world, mostly in

Eastern Europe, the Middle East, and Africa. But Rider happened to know that only one of those countries had a large presence in Antarctica—Russia.

He frowned. *What are Russian commandos doing here?* Perhaps they'd been sent to kill the astronomers at Ellsworth. If so, why? For that matter, he wasn't sure what the Americans were up to either. Rider had suspected there was more to Zane Watson's mission than he had been told, but he had decided not to ask any questions. After all, he was only being paid for a simple transport job.

But the situation had changed drastically—a group of Russian commandos had just tried to kill him. Like it or not, that meant Rider was involved in a battle. *But a battle over what?* It was a question he would have to answer later.

Movement near the chopper pulled Rider out of his thoughts. Three of the commandos were fanning out in different directions, and one of them was moving directly toward the snowdrift where he was hiding.

Rider's pulse quickened. He tried to remember if he'd left footprints behind him. He had purposefully walked on his toes, and the small indentations should have been covered by the snow still being whipped across the ravine. But the man seemed to be following something.

To Rider's surprise, the commando halted about twenty yards away. He leaned over as if looking at something in the snow. Then his gun light ran up the incline toward Rider.

The British pilot's hand tensed around the pistol. He hoped he wouldn't have to use the weapon. Any gunfire, even a single shot to eliminate the immediate threat, would bring in the other six commandos. The cover of darkness might give him some measure of protection, but it wouldn't be enough to save him. A man with one pistol and a sore knee had no chance against a half dozen elite soldiers with automatic weapons.

There was movement again. The light from the commando's

gun swept back and forth as he moved up the slope. If it illuminated the drift, then the enemy would undoubtedly see that the snow had been disturbed. That couldn't happen.

His body tense, Rider began a slow count to three.

One.

He moved his finger over the pistol's trigger. If he could somehow take the commando down quickly, he could at least grab the man's rifle and use it against the others.

Two.

Rider readied himself to act, but before he could, a shout sounded from across the ravine.

Confused, the commando straightened up and looked back over his shoulder. The soldiers who had remained with the wreckage had kicked something out of the flames. Rider squinted as he tried to figure out what it was. Then it hit him. It was his pilot's helmet. He remembered flinging it off just before jumping out.

Cursing under his breath, the commando turned and strode back down the slope.

12

Ellsworth Station

Amanda opened the door and flicked on the overhead light. Like all the bedrooms at Ellsworth, that one had a distinct dormitory vibe, with plain white walls and a simple desk topped with shelves. The accommodations were certainly Spartan, but that didn't bother her. As long as she had a mattress, a pillow, and some warm blankets, she would be fine.

Sunny Lee came in behind her. For the time being, the two would be roommates. They had gotten to know each other a little on the way down, and since the bedrooms available were limited, they had decided to share.

"I haven't slept on one of those since I was twelve," Sunny said.

Amanda turned to see the nurse staring at the metal-framed bunk bed that stood against the right wall. "Nice."

"Have you ever slept on one?" Sunny asked.

"I was an only child, so I never had a bunk bed. I did sleep on them a couple of times at friends' houses though."

"Most kids think they're the coolest thing, but the novelty wears off pretty quickly. After a few months, it's just a place to sleep."

"That's the same thing people have told me about swimming pools." Amanda set her duffel bag on top of the desk. "I really wanted a bunk bed, but it was kind of hard to convince my dad since it was just me."

"If you want to live on the wild side, I'll let you get on top."

Amanda chuckled. "I may take you up on that. As a kid, did it scare you to sleep up there?"

"Early on, I had some dreams of falling off. But after a few weeks, those went away." Sunny put her bag at the foot of the bed. "What made ours really cool is we had one of those slides that ran from the top bunk down to the floor."

"Uber cool. I remember seeing those advertised on TV."

Sunny laughed. "I can assure you, all the neighborhood kids were jealous."

Amanda unzipped her bag and removed a Sig Sauer P226 pistol, three magazines, and several boxes of ammo. After setting the items on the desk, she examined the magazines to make sure they were full and ready to go.

Sunny stared at the gun. "You work in security, so I'm thinking you must be pretty good with that thing."

"We're at the range three times a week." Amanda snapped one of the magazines into the Sig and chambered a round. "I'm not quite as good as a few of my coworkers, but I can hold my own."

"I'm not really a gun person, although I must say it's comforting to have a trained user around in light of all that's happened."

"So you've never shot a pistol before?"

Sunny shook her head. "No, but I've always wanted to learn how."

"If you'd like, I can show you a few of the basics while we're here. The parts of a gun, how to load it, and how to grip it properly."

Sunny removed a book from her bag then sat down on the bed. "I'd actually like that."

Amanda nodded at the book. "It looks like all this talk of weapons has bored you already."

"No, this is my Bible. I just wanted to have it ready for later. I like to read it before I go to sleep."

Amanda's eyes widened. "You're a believer?"

"Yes, you?"

"I am."

Sunny beamed. "It's interesting that we ended up in the same room." She set the Bible aside and crossed one leg over the other. "I'll have to share my testimony with you sometime. I received Christ when I was a teenager, then I had one of those journeys into the desert of worldly living for a while before finally recommitting myself to the Lord several years ago."

"Our walk of faith can be a roller coaster sometimes, but God is always faithful. My testimony is a little like yours. I've certainly had my ups and downs, I can tell you that."

Sunny frowned.

Amanda looked at her. "Something wrong?"

"Did you just hear something?"

"Hear what?"

"That tapping sound."

Amanda shook her head. "Nope, not a thing."

"Come over here."

Amanda set the pistol down and went to the other side of the room.

"Hear it now?" Sunny asked.

After remaining perfectly still for several seconds, Amanda heard a distant tapping. Although it was hard to tell with any certainty, it sounded like metal on metal. *The ductwork?* She searched the walls and the ceiling. "I think it's coming through a vent."

Sunny got up and moved toward the foot of the bed. "Here's one."

The two crouched next to it. Amanda placed her palms on the floor then lowered her ear to the louvered vent cover. She had been right. The tapping was clearly coming from somewhere inside.

"What do you think it is?" Sunny asked.

"I'm not sure. The heating system is probably old, so it may just be the way it always sounds."

"I didn't notice it when I first came in."

As Amanda continued to listen, she realized the taps weren't regular, which was what she would have expected if it was just the furnace knocking. She looked at Sunny. "I think you're right. Let's see if we can find the source."

"How?"

"We'll start at the room next door. If it's louder there, then we'll know we're getting closer."

The two stood then moved toward the door. Their room was at the end of the hall, which meant there was only one adjoining room. Having made the sleeping assignments, Amanda knew that Freja Larsen was that room's sole occupant.

Amanda knocked three times. Seconds later, the Danish operative opened the door. She had on headphones and reading glasses. She seemed surprised to see them.

"Can we come in?" Amanda asked.

Freja hesitated for a moment then stepped back and waved them in. "Of course."

"I hope we didn't wake you up," Amanda said.

"No, I was just listening to some classical music while I looked over a few things. It's hard for me to sleep with so much going on." Freja lowered the headphones onto her shoulders. "Is there a problem?"

"We heard a noise coming from inside the air ducts." Amanda nodded at the headphones. "I assume you haven't heard it."

"No, I haven't. In fact, I just barely heard your knock."

Amanda noticed the vent in Freja's room was in the same corner. She went over and crouched beside it.

Freja stood over her, waiting. "What kind of noise is it?"

"A tapping sound," Sunny said. "We thought you might be closer to the source."

"Do you think there is something wrong with the heating system?" Freja asked.

"We're not sure what's going on," Sunny replied. "It's probably nothing."

Amanda couldn't hear anything, so she put her ear flush against the grille. Once she did, she was able to make out the tapping, but it was fainter here. "I think this room is farther from the source than ours."

"We're at the end of the hall, so where should we look next?" Sunny asked.

Amanda stood. "The furnace is on the first floor, so the duct line may come up to our room then run down this side of the hall. Let's go have a look downstairs." She turned to Freja. "Want to join us?"

Freja smiled. "Since I can't sleep, I might as well."

After Freja put on a pair of shoes, the three exited into the hall. As they hurried toward the stairs, Amanda wondered what might be causing the noise. The more logical side of her brain believed it was something mundane like a noisy old furnace. But her experience as an operative told her it could be something more sinister. Perhaps someone was trying to break into the building. She considered going back for her pistol then pushed the idea aside. There was no reason to jump to conclusions.

"Where are you ladies going?"

Startled out of her thoughts, Amanda looked up to see Zane coming toward them, accompanied by Vince Stone.

"We're going to check out a noise," Amanda said.

Zane stiffened. "A noise?"

Amanda quickly described what they had heard.

"When air flows through shoddy ductwork, it can knock against things," Zane said. "But you're right. It's probably worth checking out. We'll join you."

The group of five took the stairs down to the first floor then entered the hall, which ran parallel to the one above. That floor was much larger than the second, which suggested that their level had been added to the structure later to provide additional sleeping quarters. Amanda scanned the hall, trying to guess which of the first-floor rooms was directly below the one she and Sunny were sleeping in.

After a moment, Amanda picked a door that seemed to be in the approximate location. It appeared to be unoccupied, so she entered, felt around on the wall, then flicked on the light. Along all four walls were metal shelves filled with cleaning supplies. Brooms, mops, and buckets were clustered in one corner.

As the others trailed in, Amanda held up her hand, indicating they should all remain perfectly still. She couldn't hear anything yet, which meant either she had chosen the wrong room or the noise had stopped. If someone was trying to break into the building, then perhaps they had heard them approach and ceased their activity.

"I was in here earlier when we cleared the building, and I didn't hear anything then," Zane said.

In response to his voice, a loud knock sounded from inside one of the walls. Amanda scanned the room for a vent. She didn't see one, which meant it was probably hidden under the stacks of supplies. "Help me find the vent."

"I think I found it," Sunny called out.

Amanda turned but didn't see her.

Stone was already moving toward the door. "She's in the hall."

They followed him out and found Sunny standing in front of

a massive grille set into the wall on the opposite side of the corridor.

"It's the return air duct," Stone said. The vent looked big enough for a person to fit inside.

"Did the sound come from in there?" Zane asked.

"I thought so," Sunny said. "Then when I came out, it stopped."

"Then let's take a look inside," Stone said.

Zane unholstered his pistol as Stone reached down and pulled out the two latches that held the cover in place. As he lowered the grille, Amanda heard something moving around behind it. Her body tensed. The noise hadn't been made by an old furnace or wobbly ductwork—something was alive in the ductwork.

Stone released the grille, which banged against the floor. Zane directed his flashlight beam inside while the rest of them crowded behind him. A writhing mass of tangled red appeared in the cone of light. It quivered like the fur of some startled creature ready to launch itself out of the vent.

Sunny put her hand to her mouth and stepped back.

As the fur shifted, Zane lifted his gun.

"Wait." Amanda's eyes narrowed. It wasn't fur they were looking at. It was a messy shock of hair.

The head slowly turned toward them, and the frightened face of a woman appeared underneath the matted strands. Her eyes were weak slits, and her cheeks were covered with cuts and dark smudges.

"Help me," the woman managed to say.

Zane tucked the pistol into his holster and looked at Stone. "Give me a hand."

"I'll take the flashlight," Amanda said, and Zane handed it over.

The woman was crammed into the space, so the two men carefully maneuvered to get their arms around her before lifting her out. Once she was clear of the vent, they lowered her to the floor, resting her back against the wall. Unlike the unfortunate astronomer who'd been killed, she had on a pair of old jeans and a thick black coat with a fur hood.

"They're here," the woman said with a slurred voice.

Zane got down on one knee. "Who's here?"

Her eyes slowly focused on him. "They came out of the tunnels."

"Who did?" Zane asked.

She seemed to not hear his question. "We... we never should have gone down there."

Amanda frowned. The woman was clearly delirious.

"Who are you talking about?" Zane asked. "Did more people come here to the station?"

Sunny put a hand on Zane's shoulder. "She'd dehydrated. We need to take her to—"

"You don't understand, do you?" The woman's eyes widened with fear. "These weren't people."

Zane furrowed his brow. "Then what were they? Animals?"

"Zane," Amanda said. "Sunny's right—"

"We need to leave before they return," the woman said, her voice trembling.

Crouching, Sunny grasped the woman's hand. "Everything's going to be fine."

The woman's eyes turned to Sunny. "You really don't understand."

Zane gently held her wrists. "You're safe now. Who is coming?"

Sunny stood. "I can't allow this to continue. We have to take her to the infirmary."

Drained of energy, the woman's head collapsed onto her chest.

Zane nodded. "Sorry. You're right. I'll carry her."

Stone stepped forward. "Let me help you."

"No. I can give her better support if I do it myself."

Zane looped one arm around the woman's shoulders and the

other underneath her legs. As he lifted her, Amanda noticed something sticking out of the woman's pants pocket. It looked like a white card.

She put a hand on Zane's arm. "Hang on for a second. She's about to lose something." Amanda withdrew the paper. "Okay, go ahead."

As everyone moved off toward the infirmary, Amanda looked at the item in her hand. It wasn't a card after all but a small stack of papers held together by a money clip. First, she slid a small photo out from the clip and turned it over. It was a picture of a couple sitting on a beach towel. Even though the woman wore sunglasses and had pulled her hair up in a ponytail, Amanda knew it was the same person they had just rescued from the vent.

Amanda slipped the photograph into her pocket then turned her attention back to the clip. In it, she found some US currency, a credit card, and a laminated ID. Amanda read the lines of information printed on the ID:

CHRISTINE PAGEAU
ELLSWORTH STATION
AUTHORIZED RESEARCHER #10274
DOB 02/15/1987

CHRISTINE PAGEAU. Amanda remembered the name from the list of astronomers she had reviewed on the trip down. She hoped the survivor could provide them with some useful information about what had taken place at Ellsworth.

As Amanda put the clip away, the woman's haunting words echoed in her thoughts. "They came out of the tunnels. We never should have gone down there."

13

AFTER ASTRONOMER CHRISTINE PAGEAU was transported to the infirmary, Sunny covered her with a thermal blanket and turned on a space heater as the others looked on. While the patient warmed, Sunny started an IV then conducted a thorough examination of the woman's body. Apparently satisfied that there were no significant injuries, she cleaned up some of the cuts on the woman's face and gave her a mild sedative to encourage rest.

Once Pageau succumbed to the drug, Freja Larsen and Vince Stone returned to their rooms. With a long day ahead, both wanted to get a few hours of sleep. Zane and Amanda wanted to stay with Pageau, but Sunny wouldn't allow it. Having been traumatized, the patient needed undisturbed rest.

Having been dismissed, Zane and Amanda decided to go to the dining hall in order to wait things out. They had planned on discussing the latest developments, but instead, both ended up nodding off in their chairs.

Zane was the first to wake up and seek out caffeine. Fortunately, the station's kitchen had been well stocked with coffee. It was cheap, but at that point, he would take what he could get.

As he started a pot, Amanda stirred and asked for a cup as well.

Ten minutes later, Zane came out of the kitchen with two mugs. He set one in front of Amanda. "I think you like yours with sugar and no cream?"

"Thanks." She took a sip then set her mug back on the table. "How long did we sleep?"

"Two hours."

"Did you hear from Sunny?"

He shook his head. "I've only been up for fifteen minutes or so."

Amanda pulled out the ID she had found in the clip and slid it across the table. "This is the identification card I was telling you about earlier."

"Christine Pageau." Zane stared at it for a moment then gave it back. "Did you find anything else in that clip?"

"Nothing important." Amanda took another sip of coffee then paused for a moment. "So, do you believe what she said about these attackers coming out of the tunnels?"

"I do. We already have a victim, so it fits with our knowledge of the situation."

"She said they came out of the tunnels. Doesn't that strike you as odd?"

"Not necessarily. We were told there were natural ice tunnels and cavities under this station. Maybe that's how the killer or killers slipped in."

"She also said the attackers weren't human."

"That part of it I don't buy," Zane said. "She's been through a lot over the last few days. Sunny said she's severely dehydrated, which means she's probably a bit delirious."

"But you believed the part about the tunnels."

"That's what happens when someone's been through a great deal of trauma." Zane took a sip of coffee before continuing. "They get some of the story right, and other parts are embellished or fabricated. You and I have both seen it before. Hell, it's happened to me."

"So you think it's the Russians?"

He nodded. "That would make the most sense. They know about Operation Whiteout, and they could have sent a team in quickly. There are a number of Russian stations down here too."

"I thought their stations were on the other side of Antarctica."

"They are, but they could still get here quickly."

Amanda leaned forward and put her elbows on the table. "Let's assume it was the Russians. You saw that man's body upstairs. Why kill him that way? Why not just put a bullet in his head?"

"The attacker had to have been human. There are no large predators in Antarctica. No wolves. No polar bears." He thought for a moment. "There are killer whales, but the last time I checked, they don't sneak into buildings."

"But why would they carve that man up like a Thanksgiving turkey?"

"The more I think about it, the more I believe they *were* torturing him for information and just did a sloppy job."

"Torturing him? About the anomaly?"

He nodded.

"If that's true, then where are they now?" Amanda asked.

"They probably got word we were on the way and retreated to a nearby camp."

"Elite commandos run off because a tiny American extraction team is on the way?"

"You're assuming they know our size and capability. They may not have had detailed information."

Amanda nodded but said nothing.

"Well, what do you think happened, then?"

"At this point, I'm not ready to rule out anything. Except for orcas." She smiled at him. "If you read between the lines, Pageau seemed to suggest this attack had something to do with the anomaly itself."

"As I said, she's been traumatized by what took place here. That probably explains why she mentioned something coming out of the tunnels. At some point, her mind started conflating the attack with the discovery of the anomaly."

"So you don't think there is an alien craft down there?"

He shrugged. "Even if there is, then how would it relate to what happened up here? You really think that the beings who crash-landed here are going to stick around?"

"Who knows? Maybe they didn't have any choice. Maybe they're stuck here. That craft may have been down there for decades or centuries."

"Then how have they survived for this long?"

Amanda paused for a moment before answering. "All I know is that I saw fear in that woman's eyes. She experienced something that was burned deeply into her psyche. Although I can't rule it out completely, I'm just not so sure a bunch of men storming the station with guns would do that."

"I disagree. Imagine what took place. You're riding out a storm a week or two before your assignment ends, then these men dressed in white camo come out of the tunnels. Some are killed by the initial gunfire, and the others are tortured for information while you cower in a vent."

Amanda nodded. "Maybe you're right. I guess we'll have to see what she says after getting enough rest."

The two sipped their coffee, each lost in their own thoughts.

"We should never have gone down there." Pageau's cryptic words echoed in Zane's thoughts. He wondered if it was true that some of the woman's colleagues had gone down to look for the anomaly. If so, they might have encountered the Russian team in the tunnels beneath the station. That would explain why they had only found one body in the station so far. Although it was a macabre thought, he realized more bodies might soon be found.

A voice came through Zane's radio, breaking the silence in the room. "You two still awake?"

Sunny.

Zane picked up the device. "Define awake. I suppose we both meet the minimum threshold of sentience."

"I was afraid of that." Sunny paused on the other end. "She wants to talk to you."

"Christine wants to talk to me?"

"Well, she asked to see the man with long hair, and against my better judgment, I agreed to radio you."

Zane rose from his chair. "I'm headed your way."

"Hang on. I need you to understand something. I'm giving you five minutes. She's been under a lot of stress. You hit the wrong button, and you may worsen her mental state, and I'm not going to allow that to happen."

"I understand," Zane said before slipping the radio into his pocket.

"Pageau's awake?" Amanda got up to follow him.

Zane nodded. "Sunny is giving me five minutes."

At that point, Zane was just grateful for the opportunity to talk to the astronomer. He agreed that she should be handled with kid gloves, but he also knew that her information could lead to other survivors out there. And if there were any left, time was of the essence. It would also help if he could learn more about the attackers, whether they were men with guns or something else.

After they arrived at the infirmary, Zane entered the dimly lit room while Sunny and Amanda waited outside the door. Christine Pageau was lying on the bed, her shock of wavy red hair splayed out across the white pillows.

Zane pulled a chair next to the bed and sat down. He gently placed a hand on her arm. "How are you?" he asked in a soft tone.

She turned toward him, a look of surprise on her face. It was as if she had just realized he was there. "Where is Paul?"

Her voice was slurred, which was probably a side effect of the sedative she had been given. Zane realized it was going to be like talking to someone in a drunken state.

"Paul?" Zane asked.

"Do you know where he is?"

Zane vaguely remembered seeing that name on the list of researchers stationed at Ellsworth. "Did you work with him here at the station?"

She nodded. "He's a wonderful man. He told you where to find me, didn't he?" A half smile formed on her face. "I knew he'd make it."

An ominous possibility pushed its way into Zane's thoughts. He squeezed her arm lightly. "What does Paul look like?"

"He's handsome." She let out a breathy giggle. "I think some of the girls had a thing for him. Most of the men we work with are old and wrinkly."

If it wasn't such a serious situation, Zane would've laughed. The sedative seemed to be working like a truth serum.

"What color hair did he have?"

Pageau frowned. "Don't you know?"

"Describe him for me."

She looked at the ceiling as if trying to recall the man's appearance. "He has wavy dark hair, and his eyes are as green as an Irish field."

Images of the dead body on the second floor flashed in Zane's mind. The man had seemed on the younger side, but his face had been so damaged that his own mother wouldn't have recognized him. Still, two things had been left intact—the man's shock of dark hair and his deep-green eyes.

Zane felt something lurch in his gut. Suppressing the dark feelings, he said, "You told me you that you knew he'd make it. What did you mean by that?"

Her eyes began to close. Either she was considering the question or she was succumbing to the effects of the sedative.

No, don't go to sleep. Not now. He gave Pageau's arm another squeeze, that one firmer than the last. She opened her eyes in response, and he repeated the question.

Her gaze went to the ceiling again. "Paul and I were the last ones."

"The last ones?"

She nodded. "Everyone else was gone."

Zane wasn't sure if she meant they had disappeared or were dead. She probably didn't know.

"We thought we were going to die. We hid," she continued. "After almost freezing to death outside, that was all we could do."

There was a pause, but Zane decided not to interject with another question. It was better to let her talk at her own pace.

"I remember Paul telling me that he was going to get help." She looked over at Zane. "Even though Parks was a long way off, he was going to try to make it there with one of the snowmobiles."

Zane frowned. "He left on a snowmobile?"

She nodded. "I think so. That was the plan anyway."

Poor guy never even made it out of the building.

Pageau grabbed his arm. "Please, let me speak to him."

Before he could answer, her eyes began to slowly close.

Zane was about to make one more attempt when someone cleared their throat behind him. He turned and saw Sunny standing inside the door.

"She needs to sleep," she said softly.

She was right. Zane stood, put the chair back against the wall, then made his way toward the door.

"How is she?" Amanda asked when he came out into the hall.

"Drowsy, but she has some memory of what happened."

"That's a good sign," Amanda said. "I'm sure more will come back later."

Zane looked at her. "Do you remember if one of the astronomers was named Paul?"

Amanda had an uncanny ability to memorize large amounts

of data, so he often leaned on her to regurgitate information from files.

She nodded. "Paul Strickland. Yeah, I'm pretty sure that's his name. Why?"

"Because he's the one we found on the second floor."

14

WITH A LOUD, dissatisfied grunt, Vince Stone threw the blankets off of his body then swung his legs off the side of the mattress. His bladder was about to burst, and he could've kicked himself for not taking care of business before going to bed. The bathrooms were in a completely different part of the station, and he was paying the price for the oversight.

A gust of wind wailed outside, rattling the sole window in his room. The storm seemed to be getting worse by the minute. The winds were so strong that Stone began to wonder if the building would hold up. According to Hawke, they could expect to deal with the nasty weather for at least another twenty-four hours, perhaps more.

It hadn't taken long for Stone to realize that Antarctica research stations were not places of great comfort even under normal conditions. On the contrary, they almost seemed designed to enhance suffering. At least the power was working, and they had decent food.

Shivering, he slipped on his boots. The sleeping quarters were on the second floor of the station, and the pathetic heating system barely worked to keep the space habitable. He guessed the temperature inside was somewhere in the forties, which meant that his walk to the other side of the building wouldn't be pleasant.

No one on the team enjoyed the frigid temperatures, but most seemed better able to handle it than he did. His dislike of cold temperatures could probably be traced back to his South Carolina roots. The coldest it ever got there was the upper twenties, and those only came around once in a blue moon.

Home would feel like a freaking tropical paradise right now.

Stone remembered reading that most researchers avoided coming to that godforsaken continent during the winter. Apparently, the Ellsworth astronomers hadn't gotten that memo.

Before leaving, he put on a coat and snatched his flashlight off the nightstand. In order to conserve energy, most of the overhead lights in the building were kept off. He wished they would change that policy because the lights seemed to add a small amount of warmth to the space.

After exiting to the hall, Stone closed the door behind him as quietly as he could. Sleep was going to be a valuable commodity for the next couple of days, which meant the last thing he wanted to do was wake someone else up.

He took the stairs down to the first floor then turned down one of the corridors that ran to the back. A minute later, he heard voices somewhere close by. He lifted his beam, which illuminated the corridor ahead. No one was in the hall, which meant the voices must've been coming from one of the rooms. *What are they doing down here at this hour?* Maybe it was Zane and Amanda coming back from the infirmary.

Ahead on the right, a faint glow spilled from a door that was cracked open. The voices seemed to be coming from there. Ordinarily, Stone would have kept going. After all, two people talking privately was none of his business. But there was something about their voices that seemed odd.

Curious, he thumbed off his flashlight and crept up to the

opening. When he closed to within a few feet, he realized what had seemed so odd about the conversation—the people in the room weren't speaking in English.

Stone could make out at least two speakers, a man and a woman. He wondered if the woman was Freja Larsen, the Danish woman. He didn't think so. Although he wasn't an expert on foreign languages, it sounded more like Russian or one of the other Slavic tongues. But even if it was Freja, he didn't know who was with her.

Anxious to see who was inside, Stone leaned forward to peek into the room. As he did, the floor creaked loudly under him. He cursed under his breath. He might as well have blown a tuba to announce his presence.

"Who's there?" the man called out, this time in English.

Reimer. What's he doing down here? Stone didn't much care for the arrogant scientist, and the idea of Reimer meeting in secret, speaking in some foreign language, made Stone suspicious. He had a good mind to go in and confront the bastard then thought better of it.

"Anybody there?" Reimer asked again.

"Go check," the woman whispered.

Her voice was familiar, but Stone couldn't quite place who it was.

"It's probably the wind," Reimer said.

As if on cue, a strong gale howled outside.

"See, what did I tell you?" the DARPA officer said.

"Close the door anyway."

Footsteps came across the room, and Stone pulled back out of sight.

A moment later, the door shut and the lock clicked.

15

Ellsworth Station

The Ellsworth team woke up the next day and went to work. Zane sent Vince Stone to the garage to conduct a thorough examination of the Hagglund vehicles. If the storm persisted and supplies ran low, they might be forced to take one of them back to Parks Station.

While Stone inspected the Hagglunds, Morgan, Reimer, and Hawke went to the communications room to see if any of the equipment could be repaired. The radios had received extensive damage, but Hawke believed they might be able to save some of the computer hard drives. It was thought that they might provide some clue as to what had gone on before their arrival.

After doing another sweep of the station with the SEALs, Zane, Amanda, and Freja went to the infirmary to check on Christine Pageau. They arrived just as Sunny Lee was finishing up another examination, that one even more thorough than the first. Once again, she was unable to locate any significant injuries. More good news was that Christine had woken alert and talkative, something Sunny attributed to rest and hydration.

The astronomer was already asking Sunny for solid food and to go for a walk. While hesitant to push things too fast, Sunny reluctantly agreed that a small amount of exercise and food might actually help the patient recover even faster. Even though Sunny was capable of walking Christine to the dining hall on her own, Zane and Amanda escorted them in case the patient needed help. Sunny had warned that Christine could experience moments of weakness, which in turn could lead to a sudden loss of balance.

Since she hadn't eaten for several days, team cook Brady Arnott prepared a light breakfast that included two pieces of wheat toast, one scrambled egg, and a glass of orange juice. Sunny cautioned Christine to take her time and chew the food thoroughly. She also told her to stop eating if she felt the slightest bit of discomfort.

After five minutes of eating, Christine wiped her mouth with a napkin and smiled. "I don't think I've ever enjoyed a piece of dry toast that much in my whole life."

"My culinary skills are legendary," Arnott said, his voice dripping with sarcasm.

Christine smiled.

"I was going to suggest you take a break, but it looks like you're doing fine," Zane said.

"I actually feel better now that I have a little food in my stomach," Christine said.

"Don't feel like you have to eat everything," Sunny reminded her.

Christine took a sip of orange juice then looked at all the faces around her. "I want to thank all of you for taking care of me."

"It's our job," Sunny said.

"No, I mean that." Christine looked at Zane. "Sunny told me what happened to Paul."

"I wasn't going to tell her at first," Sunny added. "But she kept asking for him, and if I didn't tell her that Paul never made it back to Parks Station, she was never going to relax enough to sleep." Sunny touched Christine's arm. "Your friend made a valiant effort to get help."

Zane nodded. It seemed as if the nurse had spared Christine the horrific details. "I only wish we could have gotten here sooner."

"How long have you been here at Ellsworth?" Christine asked.

"Less than twenty-four hours," Amanda said.

"I was in and out of it, so I wasn't sure."

"I assume at some point you heard us?" Amanda said.

Christine nodded. "Yes, I heard voices. Despite being a little delirious, I picked up little snippets of conversation, and I eventually realized you people had come here to help."

"Was that when you started tapping on the duct?" Zane asked.

"No, at first I tried to get out. That's when I realized that the grille wouldn't move. I suppose Paul turned the latches without thinking. Ordinarily, I could have smashed my way through, but after a day or two without food or water, I didn't have the strength."

"So you think you were in there for a couple of days?" Zane asked.

She shrugged. "I said a day or two, but to be honest, I don't really know how long it was. Once your mind goes, it's hard to keep track of time."

"Have you started remembering anything else about what happened here?" Amanda asked.

Sunny leaned in as though she was ready to cut off the questioning, but Zane held up a hand. As far as he was concerned, the patient was doing well enough to provide a few simple answers.

"It's mostly hazy," Christine said. "The only clear memories I have are right around the time Paul put me in the duct."

Amanda tried again. "You don't remember anything prior to that?"

"Bits and pieces, like the memory of a dream an hour after waking up." She paused. "I think I know why I'm having so much trouble remembering things. As Paul was helping me hide in the ductwork, he asked me how my head was doing. When I asked him what he meant, he said I had fallen and hit it on the floor."

Sunny frowned. "You never told me that."

"Sorry, I just now remembered it."

"I didn't find a bump," Sunny said.

"And I don't even remember falling," Christine said. "But that's what he said, and I don't think he would have any reason to lie."

Sunny nodded. "No, of course not. Anyway, not all head injuries come with a hematoma."

Christine frowned. "Hematoma?"

"It's a fancy term for goose egg."

"Last night, you told us that members of your team went down into the tunnels," Zane said.

"Yes, that's one of the things I do remember." A hint of fear flashed in her eyes. "That's when people started disappearing."

"I want to ask you one more thing," Zane said. "It's important because it may help us find any survivors. Do you have any idea how your colleagues got down to the tunnels?"

She gave him a blank look.

"Was it somewhere in the building, or was it outside?"

After a brief pause, she said, "I'm not sure exactly where it is, but I think they said something about the warehouse."

16

Delphi Headquarters
Arlington, Virginia

THERE WAS a soft knock at the door.

"Come in," Carmen said without looking up from her laptop. The door opened. "You wanted to see me?"

Carmen saved the document she was working on then looked up to see Keiko standing in the threshold. "Yes. Please come in."

Keiko was the world's most advanced humanoid. She had the appearance of an Asian woman in her thirties and could move, think, and speak in a way that blurred the line between human and machine. In an ironic twist, she had been recruited from an organization connected to criminal activities. During an operation against that organization, Keiko was eventually invited to join Delphi, something made possible by the ethics programming she had received from her designer, Ian Higgs, now deceased. Higgs also happened to be the father of Delphi operative Amanda Higgs.

Keiko crossed the room and eased into a chair on the other side of the desk. To that day, Carmen still marveled at the humanoid's fluid movements and cognitive abilities.

"Thanks for coming over so quickly," Carmen said.

"It's my pleasure. How can I help you?"

Talking with Keiko felt the same as interacting with the rest of Carmen's colleagues. She truly was a miracle of artificial intelligence.

Carmen closed her laptop and pushed it aside. "Have you been brought up to date on Operation Whiteout?"

"Yes. Dr. Ross gave me a brief overview yesterday. Knowing that you might need some assistance, he wanted me to understand the basics."

"Good. That will save me some time. Did he cover the information we received from Danish intelligence?"

"He did."

"Then I'm sure you're aware that there could be a mole on the team that's down at Ellsworth Station. Zane, Amanda, and Danish operative Freja Larsen are doing everything they can to identify the Russian asset on their end, and it's my job to support them in that effort. Anyway, I had hoped to be further along in that process, but I was sidetracked yesterday by a fire that needed to be put out."

"I assume you're referring to a metaphorical fire."

Carmen smiled. "Yes, a metaphorical fire. Like I said, I'm a little behind and could use your help. My goal is to obtain as much biographical information as I can then conduct an analysis to identify the most likely suspects."

"What specifically are you looking for?"

"First and foremost, possible connections to Russia or Russian intelligence. For example, I want to know if any of these people have traveled there in the last few years. It might also be helpful to know if any of them have an interest in Russian culture or speak the language."

"A logical strategy," Keiko said.

Carmen took a sip of her cold coffee then set the mug down. "I thought we could divide the list up. Since I have a number of connections in US intelligence, I thought I'd focus on the team members who hold the highest positions in government—Morgan Martini, Lucas Reimer, and Freja Larsen."

Carmen was about to continue when her phone buzzed loudly on the desk. She leaned in and read the name on the screen: *Sam Connelly*. Sam had previously worked for the NSA but had retired two years ago to start up a private cybersecurity company. His firm specialized in everything from network protection to the screening of potential employees using electronic data. While Carmen didn't care for Sam's methods, which were a little underhanded and sometimes even illegal, he was a wealth of information.

Carmen had called Sam the day before and asked him to look into the team members. He was a master of finding intel hidden in the secret corners of the Internet, including the infamous dark web.

Carmen gave the AI an apologetic glance. "I need to take this, Keiko."

"By all means. Do you want me to step outside?"

"No, stay right here. This may actually relate to what we're talking about." Carmen picked up her phone and answered. "Hey there."

"How is my favorite Italian American?" Sam asked.

"Your favorite Italian American has too much on her plate."

"Maybe I can help lighten her load a bit."

"*Meravigliosa!* That would be wonderful. What have you got?"

"Well, that depends. What have you got for *me*?"

Carmen frowned. They had already agreed to a very reasonable fee. Sam could be a little slippery at times, but she had never known him to go back on their verbal agreement. "What are you talking about?"

"Well, I've been able to pull up some really good dirt on one of these people you wanted me to look into. I mean, this kind of information should at least be worth a few drinks at Patsy's this Friday night."

Carmen shook her head. She shouldn't have been surprised. The man was an insatiable flirt. "If this information is as good as you say it is, then you'll have more than enough money to buy yourself a date. Besides, last I checked, you were seriously involved with someone."

"Let's just say we're in an open relationship."

Although she was normally up for playful banter, Carmen didn't have time to play games at the moment, even though Sam was more bark than bite.

"Don't worry. I'm only joking," he said after not getting an immediate response. "I gave up on going out with you a long time ago."

"I don't think you'll ever give up. Anyway, what do you have for me?"

"Well, it seems one of those people you sent down there has a little gambling problem."

"Lots of people like to gamble."

"True, but how many of them have to borrow large sums of money to fund their habit?"

"Who are we talking about?"

"DARPA guy."

"Lucas Reimer?"

"Correct."

"How do you know he's borrowing money? I assume he didn't run down to the local bank."

"One of his friends sued him for forty thousand dollars. I was able to get my grubby little digital fingers on the court papers that were filed, and they indicate that the friend loaned him the money to pay off gambling debts."

"So not only did he go into debt to fund his habits, but he never paid it off?"

"It would seem that way."

"What was the outcome of the case?"

"The plaintiff was awarded a judgment, then six months later, it was paid off and released."

Carmen frowned. "Wait a minute. So you're saying Reimer eventually got the money?"

"Either he paid it in full, or they worked out some sort of payment plan. Anyway, I'm still doing some digging to get all the details. Who knows? He may have borrowed from Peter to pay Paul."

Or from Russian friends with deep pockets, Carmen thought.

"By the way, I also checked his travel records, and it looks like he hits Atlantic City at least once or twice a month," Sam continued. "If he's good at this gambling gig, then he could've won enough to cover the debt."

"I must say, I'm impressed," Carmen said. "That's just the kind of information I was looking for. You keep this up, and I may meet you and your new girlfriend at Patsy's one night."

"Now we're talking." He laughed. "I'll see what else I can find for you."

"You're the best."

"I'll be in touch, hun."

Carmen set the phone on her desk and smiled.

"May I ask what that was all about?" Keiko asked.

"I think we may have gotten our first big break."

17

ELLSWORTH STATION

ON THE TEAM'S second day at Ellsworth, SEALs Colton O'Connor and Rod Cignetti had come up with a plan to provide around-the-clock security for the station. They would patrol the buildings together during the day then individually at night. Cignetti took the first evening shift, which ran from eight to midnight. When his shift was over, he told O'Connor he hadn't seen anything of concern. He also hadn't seen any sign of the missing astronomers.

When his shift began, O'Connor decided to go through the exterior buildings first. He despised the cold, so he wanted to get that part of it out of the way as soon as possible. Before leaving the building, he stopped in the foyer and pulled out a pack of Marlboro Lights. He tapped one of the cigarettes out then lit it with a cheap butane lighter. After two quick puffs to get it going, he opened the door and exited into the storm.

Outside, a strong gust of wind hit the SEAL like a bucket of ice water. Shivering, he shoved his gloved hands deep into his coat pockets. The conditions were bad enough without any wind, but the sudden gales made conditions almost unbearable. Even three or four layers of clothing did little to keep the cold from seeping in.

O'Connor paused at the top of the steps, the cigarette protruding from his mouth. He puffed in silence, watching the storm play out around him. The wind howled like a haunted choir, blowing clouds of snow and ice in every direction. At the moment, the station looked like a giant snow globe that had been shaken violently.

As he relished the taste of the cigarette, O'Connor's thoughts eventually turned to the dead body they had found the day before. The SEAL had been no stranger to violent scenes over the years, but the carnage in that room might have been the worst he had ever seen. The astronomer's wounds looked like they had been inflicted by a wild animal, which was odd since no predator on that continent could have been responsible.

But if not an animal, then what was it? Zane had speculated that a foreign government may have sent in an armed team to look for the anomaly. They'd probably tortured the poor astronomer to get more information. Then again, there were still some things that didn't add up. For example, O'Connor had come across several tortured individuals over the years, and all of them tended to have the same types of wounds: missing fingers, broken bones, and charred flesh. None of them had been haphazardly wounded like the man they found.

And that wasn't the only mystery. According to the others, before Christine Pageau's memory had gone spotty, she'd insisted the threat had come out of the tunnels. That meant that the anomaly might somehow be connected to the attack. If it turned out to be an alien ship as the government believed, that would mean the beings who'd crashed might be responsible for the astronomer's death. O'Connor found it hard to believe that the same extraterrestrials who had solved the mystery of intergalactic travel would feel threatened by a small group of unarmed scientists. Still, he found it interesting that the vicious attack had come so soon after Pageau claimed that members of the group had gone down into the tunnels.

O'Connor took two more puffs then flicked what was left of the cigarette into the air. As he watched the butt carried off by the wind, his eyes fixed on a dark object to the left of the main building. He frowned. As best as he could remember, it hadn't been there moments before.

As he continued to stare in that direction, he realized the object was moving. Whatever it was had come from the side of the main building and was heading for the garage.

What the...?

His pulse quickened as the dark figure floated across the frozen plaza. A roaring gust of wind kicked up a cloud of snow, temporarily blocking the view. Sliding his finger over the trigger of his rifle, O'Connor went down the steps then hustled toward the last place he had seen the silhouette.

A moment later, he saw movement ahead. That time, he could tell it was a person.

Who are you?

At first, he thought it might be Cignetti, but he quickly dismissed the idea. His exhausted partner had gone straight to bed. Besides, Cignetti wouldn't have come outside without radioing Colton first.

What about Vince Stone? Maybe the mechanic was going out to the garage to work on something, but that seemed unlikely too. He couldn't think of something more important than sleep. What could possibly be so important that it needed to be done when most of the team was craving sleep?

Then he remembered what Zane had said about a foreign government sending in a group of elite commandos. It could be a scout casing the station before an attack.

As the SEAL hurried to catch up, his quarry disappeared

around the side of the garage. O'Connor sprinted the remaining distance and turned the corner just in time to see the side door close. Before going in, he looked over his shoulder to make sure no one else was coming. Seeing nothing, he went to the door and opened it. The interior was pitch black. Whoever was inside hadn't turned any lights on. He found that strange.

Moving cautiously, he stepped inside. As he waited for his eyes to acclimate to the dark, footsteps echoed in the garage. Squinting, he saw a tiny spark of light. The intruder was walking past the parked Hagglunds, their silhouette backlit by the soft glow of a device.

O'Connor frowned. *Is that a satellite phone?* He didn't think so. Everyone knew the phones weren't working with a storm overhead. He didn't think it was a radio, either, since they could've used it in the main building.

Concerned, O'Connor walked toward the light. As he drew closer, he could see the person was wearing a hooded parka, but their face was turned in the opposite direction.

Once he was ten yards out, he noticed that the light came from the flashlight app of a phone. The person had placed the phone on the table and was holding another device up to their right ear. *A radio.*

He asked himself the same question as before—But why come out here to use it?

It was time to get an answer.

O'Connor aimed his M16 at the person's back and spoke in a firm voice. "I need you to put your hands up slowly."

The person in the parka tensed but didn't otherwise move.

"I said put those hands up where I can see them," O'Connor said, this time louder.

Finally, they complied. Seeing no signs of weapons, O'Connor moved around to the left. He found it interesting that the person hadn't identified themselves yet. Either they didn't realize who he was and were scared, or it was someone who had come to the station from the outside.

As O'Connor circled his target, he eventually saw a familiar face peering out at him from inside the parka's hood.

He lowered his weapon. "Good grief. You had me thinking we were under attack."

"I apologize." The person slid the radio back in their pocket. "It's just me."

"What are you doing out here anyway?"

Still silent, the person removed their right hand from the coat. O'Connor flinched. A pistol was pointed at his chest.

The SEAL took a step back. "What the…?"

He tried to lift his rifle but was too late. The muzzle of the pistol flashed twice, and his world faded to black.

18

AT FIRST, Zane thought the knocks on his door were a part of a dream. That wouldn't be unusual. His dreams were often quite vivid. But as the knocks grew louder and more frequent, he slowly realized they were very much a part of reality.

He opened his eyes and grunted a response, "Who is it?"

"Cignetti. I need to speak with you."

"About what?"

"We have a problem."

Over his years in the field, Zane had heard that phrase hundreds of times. In some cases, it meant there was a small challenge that needed to be overcome. But there was something about the tone of the SEAL's voice that indicated it was more than that. Something was urgently wrong.

Zane flipped off the covers and put his feet on the floor. "Come in."

Cignetti entered and closed the door behind him.

"What's going on?" Zane asked.

"Colton is missing."

How? A wave of concern rippled through Zane's body. There

couldn't be many benign explanations for the disappearance of a highly trained Navy SEAL.

"You're sure about that?" Zane said.

"I'm positive. I need to show you something. It's outside, so you'll need to put on some clothes."

Still groggy, Zane quickly dressed, making sure to pull a balaclava over his head. He would have preferred to have put on a few more layers, but time was of the essence. For the moment, he would just have to tough out the cold.

"When was he last seen?" Zane asked as they exited the room and started down the hall.

"When he started his last shift, which was from midnight to four."

"What time is it now?"

"It's five thirty. I woke up about a quarter to five and realized Colton had never come to get me."

Zane looked at him. "Why didn't you come get me then?"

"I wasn't initially concerned. Sometimes he likes to take a longer shift to smoke a few cigarettes. Which is fine with me because I like to sleep." Cignetti led Zane down the stairs and across the foyer. "Anyway, I tried to radio him and got no response. That's when I knew I had a problem."

"Going forward, let me know when there is the slightest concern about something. If something happens, it's all on me."

"Sorry. I just wanted to look around before I raised the alarm. I figured he might've turned his radio off. Anyway, Freja was in the dining room reading something, so she offered to help look for him. We found something."

"Where?" Zane asked as the SEAL opened the front door.

"The garage."

As they stepped outside, Zane quickly pulled up the hood of his coat. The storm was still raging, perhaps even worse than before. He was glad he had taken the time to at least put on the balaclava. The last thing he needed right now was to have his face frozen.

The overhead lights were on inside the garage when he and Cignetti entered. Freja stood on the other side of the space, hands on her hips. She was staring at something on the ground but looked up as the two came toward her.

"We started our search outside," Cignetti said. "I figured if anything had happened to him, it would be out here. We didn't find anything in the supply facilities, but we did find a clue here."

Freja squatted and pointed to the floor. "I almost missed this when we came through earlier."

Zane leaned in, hands on his knees. A dark smudge stood out against the soft gray concrete. It was about three or four inches long and was as wide as a pencil. The operative had been around enough spilled blood to know what he was looking at. Still, it was a garage. There were probably fluids all over the place.

He looked at Freja. "You think it's blood?"

She nodded. "I tested a sample on my finger. It wasn't completely dry, and I could swear I detected a faint copper smell."

"You were able to smell copper on a tiny dab like that?" Zane asked.

She shrugged. "My family used to tease me because I have an almost superhuman ability to detect scents."

Cignetti clicked on a flashlight and directed the beam at one end of the line of blood. "Take a look at that."

Zane leaned in and squinted down at it.

"It's smeared," Freja said.

"Maybe someone stepped on it," Zane said.

"That's possible, but I also found a few other faint streaks close by," she added. "I think someone was trying to wipe it all up and missed a spot. Without forensics, it's going to be difficult to know what happened. And we certainly aren't going to be able to determine whose blood it is, assuming it is blood."

We already know whose blood it is. Zane straightened and crossed his arms. "I assume you didn't find any weapons?"

Cignetti shook his head. "This is a garage. The perpetrator could've used a tool they found out here."

"There was a pocketknife in one of the drawers," Freja said. "But it looks clean. Besides, if someone went through the trouble of wiping up the blood, they certainly wouldn't have left the murder weapon lying around."

Zane stared at the trace amounts of blood on the floor. If O'Connor had been injured, he wouldn't have stopped to clean up either. Besides, if he'd been injured in some accident, the SEAL would have gone straight back to the main building or radioed his partner.

"Assuming someone attacked O'Connor, who would it be?" Cignetti asked.

"That's a good question," Freja said.

She gave Zane a look. He guessed they were thinking the same thing—that the perpetrator was the Russian mole. At the same time, they couldn't rule out an outside team sent down by a foreign government.

As he considered the possibilities, Zane remembered Cignetti saying he had found Freja reading something in the dining room when he'd gotten up. *What was she doing downstairs at five in the morning?* Even if she hadn't been able to sleep, she could've read in her room. Despite the strange behavior, Zane found it hard to believe that the Danish operative was the mole. She'd been the one to bring them the information about the mole in the first place. Not only that, but if she had killed the SEAL, the smart move would've been for her to go straight back to her room.

Then there was Rod Cignetti. His story seemed awfully convenient. After all, no one could question him saying he had been asleep until five. If Cignetti was the mole, perhaps O'Connor had caught him in the act of doing something. It was also true that a well-trained SEAL knew how to kill.

"What now?" Freja asked, pulling Zane out of his thoughts.

"We need to lock this whole place down as quickly as possible," Zane said. "A killer is out there somewhere, and we need to find them before someone else dies."

19

Zane gathered the team in the dining hall for an emergency update. Team cook Brady Arnott served up a breakfast of eggs, yogurt, and hash browns, but no one seemed interested in their food. Instead, their attention was focused on Zane and Freja, who had just shared the news that Navy SEAL Colton O'Connor had been missing since going on patrol around midnight. Understandably, their reaction was a combination of shock and fear.

"You don't know what happened to him?" Reimer asked after they had finished, his words more an accusation than a question.

"No, we don't," Zane said. "But I'm not going to sugarcoat it. We suspect foul play."

"This is ridiculous," Reimer said, his voice dripping with incredulity. "You have no idea what happened to him, yet you tell us his disappearance is related to foul play."

Zane had endured about as much as he could of Reimer's mouth. "Apparently, you weren't listening. I said we *suspect* foul play."

"So what makes you think that?" Martini asked. "Was there any tangible evidence that he was hurt or killed?"

Zane considered how best to answer her question. He and

the rest of the security team—Amanda, Freja, and Cignetti—had decided not to share the news about finding blood in the garage. That way, the only other person who would know the details about the crime scene would have to be the killer. Divulging certain pieces of evidence gathered too soon would put the investigation at a disadvantage if the killer was in their midst.

Zane cleared his throat. "It's because there isn't a good natural explanation for him to be missing."

"What about the storm?" Sunny asked.

"What about it?" Freja asked.

"You said he was on patrol," Sunny said. "I'm sure at some point he went outside. Maybe he tripped and hit his head. Believe me, a person can die out there within minutes."

"It's a fair point," Zane said. "But we spent several hours going through those buildings and the area around them. As best we can tell, he isn't out there."

"Maybe he heard something or saw something that caused him to wander too far from the station," Hawke said. "Sometimes, there is so much snow blowing around that it's difficult to get one's bearings. If he couldn't see the mountains, then he may not have been able to fix a point of reference."

"And if that's true, then he might still be alive," Sunny said.

Zane nodded. "We considered the possibility that he may have left the station and gotten lost. Other than foul play, it's really the only thing that makes sense."

"So what are you going to do about it?" Reimer said.

"The winds seemed to have calmed a bit in the last hour, so we're going to conduct a wider search when this meeting is over," Zane said. "But while it's always good to hold out hope, it's still hard to envision Colton O'Connor getting lost. The man is a trained SEAL, and in my opinion, it's extremely unlikely that he would get so disoriented that he couldn't find his way back."

"I'm not sure we trust your opinion anymore," Reimer said.

"Why didn't you have people patrolling in pairs? I'm starting to think you're not up for this."

A surge of anger rippled through Zane. Fortunately, Cignetti spoke before he could.

"If that's what you think, then your problem is with me," the SEAL said. "I'm the one who came up with the patrol plan."

"So you thought it was smart to have one man watching over the entire station?" Reimer asked.

"I guess you didn't notice, but there are only two of us, and we both need to sleep at some point," Cignetti said. "If we had a whole squad out here, then we'd certainly work in pairs. Hell, I might even send out three at a time. Look, Colton and I have guarded many installations over the years, and I can't even count the number of times we've guarded an outpost alone. It's what we do."

"And yet now, he's missing," Reimer said.

Zane noticed Cignetti's jaw clenching. The soldier was disciplined, but the DARPA officer was about to push him over the edge. At some point, Zane realized he might be forced to intervene.

"Assuming there was foul play, what do you think happened?" Hawke asked.

"Unfortunately, we don't have an answer yet," Freja replied.

"There is no way to know what happened to O'Connor, so all we can do is continue to search for him," Zane said.

His answer was technically true. They would likely never know the full details of what had gone down in that garage, but Zane would put money on the SEAL no longer being alive.

"We were told that other countries might want access to that anomaly," Sunny said. "Is it possible some sort of hit team was sent down here?"

"We can't rule that out," Zane said.

"If it's a hit team, then why don't they just attack us all?" Martini asked.

Zane didn't want to get off in the weeds, but he realized he needed to answer to put everyone at ease. "Who knows? They may not have sent a large contingent. And if that's the case, it's safer to target us one at a time."

Looks of concern spread around the room.

"Who's to say one of us isn't responsible?" Hawke asked.

Brady Arnott frowned. "Why would someone in our group kill one of the men protecting us?"

Hawke shrugged. "Maybe they want access to whatever is down there in that ice. They might be working with the hit team Morgan referred to."

"Have you people lost your minds?" Reimer said. "You're sitting around like a bunch of amateur detectives while a soldier is out there somewhere, waiting for us to come find him. We should be looking for him."

"What a convenient change of subject for you," Stone said in a voice loud enough for everyone to hear.

All eyes turned toward the mechanic, who was a man of few words.

"What's that supposed to mean?" Reimer growled.

"We were just talking about someone working on the inside, and you changed the topic," Stone said.

"So what?" Reimer asked.

"I find that interesting in light of your little private rendezvous the other night."

Reimer's face reddened. "What on earth are you talking about?"

"You thought the two of you were alone, but I heard you," Stone said. "I was right there. Heard it with my own ears."

A shocked silence fell over the room. Neither Zane nor anyone else seemed to know what Stone was talking about, but it was pretty clear that he was pointing the finger at Lucas Reimer.

Even though Zane didn't like the idea of coming to Reimer's

defense, he needed to know more. "Vince, what do you mean, you heard something?"

Stone pointed at Reimer. "I'm talking about him and some woman speaking in some foreign language last night. I went to use the bathroom and heard them whispering in a room on the first floor."

Reimer and another woman were alone and speaking in a foreign language? Zane felt the hairs on the back of his neck stand on end.

"You're so full of it," Reimer said. "Have you been drinking?"

Stone looked at the faces around him. "And I'm willing to bet that woman he was with is right here in this room."

There was a nervous exchange of glances at each table.

Reimer stood. "You lying son of a—"

"Who was it?" Stone yelled. "Tell us who you were with!"

Martini put a hand on Reimer's shoulder, coaxing him to sit. She then stood herself and spoke in a trembling voice. "I was with Lucas last night." She looked at Stone. "It was me you heard in that room."

Reimer turned to her. "Morgan, that's none of their business."

"But there is an innocent explanation," she continued. "Lucas and I have been studying Russian for a while now. We were in the same language class last spring, and we've been practicing together ever since."

She was met with blank stares. Zane didn't buy one bit of her story, and no one else seemed to either.

"You must realize how strange this sounds," Amanda said. "The two of you happened to be in the same language class? And then you decided the best way to practice your language skills was to hide in a room together in the middle of the night?"

"It won't sound so bad once I tell you the whole story," Martini said. "Lucas and I have worked on many of the same projects, so over time, we became friends. The government encourages those who are involved in national security to learn a foreign language. They'll even pay for any classes you take. Anyway, at one point, I told Lucas I wanted to learn Russian, and he told me it was something he had been considering as well."

"Another very convenient explanation," Stone said.

"Do you want me to show you the emails I got from the language lab?" Martini asked. "Or the expense voucher I turned in to my supervisor?"

"Why Russian?" Amanda asked. Zane could see what she was angling at. He'd been about to ask the same thing.

"Easy," Martini replied. "Our country's biggest national security threats are currently coming from two countries, and I'd be willing to bet you can guess which ones those are. I thought Chinese would be too difficult to learn at my age."

"Then tell us why the two of you chose to do this in secret last night," Freja said. "Why not just practice in your room or in the dining hall?"

"Because we knew how it would look," Martini said. "We all know there are other countries that would like to get their hands on what's hidden under this station, so we both just thought it would look odd for the two of us to run around the station speaking a foreign language." She waved her hand to indicate the whole room. "I mean, look at the reaction we've gotten right now."

Zane tried to digest the information with an open mind. On the one hand, her explanation made sense. Then again, if they were so concerned about being caught speaking Russian, it was something they could have shared early on. He wasn't convinced by the explanation as to why they had gotten together in the middle of the night.

"We'll talk about this later," Freja said to Morgan. "And yes, I would like to see proof that you took that class."

There was an uncomfortable silence as tense looks were exchanged between team members. Zane had to take control before the situation devolved further.

"We need to start our search, so I'm going to end the meeting," Zane said before anyone could bring up another concern. "I'd suggest all of you get something to eat. We're going to come up with an enhanced security plan by the end of the day, and we'll share it with you at dinner. For now, I want everyone to travel in pairs whenever possible."

Hearing no response, Freja said, "We'll be back in touch as soon as we have more information."

Muted conversations followed.

Freja stepped closer to Zane and lowered her voice. "Well, what do you think?"

"I think we have our first two suspects."

20

AFTER CHATTING with Freja for a few minutes, Zane left the dining hall and headed up to his room. With the storm in a temporary lull, he wanted to see if his satellite phone had a signal. Getting help was now their number-one priority. He doubted the phone would work, but he had to try.

If he couldn't get a signal, he would just have to find another way. They had one dead body and a missing special forces operator. To Zane, the disappearance of Colton O'Connor was particularly disturbing. He had been chosen for the critical mission because he was the best of the best. And if he could be taken down, it meant they were up against a skilled and cunning adversary.

Zane also had a bad feeling about Patrick Rider, who they still hadn't heard from. Hopefully, he had cut his losses and flown the chopper all the way back to Parks Station. If Rider had managed to make it, there was a good chance he would get in touch with the US government. If not, he could at least assemble a rescue team to travel to Ellsworth in vehicles capable of operating in the worst of weather.

But what if Rider never made it back to Parks? In that case, there were at least two ways the trip may have played out, and neither was good. In one scenario, Rider decided to set the chopper down and hike back to Ellsworth. Hawke seemed to think his partner could do that without a problem. Zane wasn't so sure. The wind chill had made conditions three or four times worse than usual. Most found the cold unbearable even with four or five layers on. The body did warm up when walking, but even that could be an issue if Rider got sweaty. In those conditions, sweat could be lethal.

The other scenario was one in which the chopper crashed due to high winds. Zane didn't like to think about it, but he knew it was a real possibility. Even a large helicopter like an Agusta Westland 139 would struggle to remain airborne in a storm like the one gripping this part of Antarctica.

After entering his room, Zane went straight to the tiny bedside table where he kept a few personal items. If he couldn't get a signal, he would get dressed and head back downstairs to meet the others and look for O'Connor. While it was the right thing to do, Zane also knew their chances of finding the SEAL were slim to none, and slim was looking less likely by the minute. At least they could say they did everything they could.

Zane opened the top drawer of the bedside table. Inside were several items—a compass, a map of the station, a pocketknife, and a flashlight. But no satellite phone. His pulse quickened. He yanked the other two drawers open. Both were empty.

He cursed under his breath. He had always been good about keeping track of his gear, so he knew he hadn't misplaced it. Before he jumped to any conclusions, he needed to check with Freja Larsen and Rod Cignetti. Even if his was lost or stolen, both of them had satellite phones.

Freja was helping Brady Arnott clean up the kitchen, so Zane tried Cignetti first. He removed his radio and pressed the large button on the side. "Rodfather, this is Samson. Do you read?"

There were several seconds of static before Cignetti's voice finally came through the speaker. "I'm here. You ready to head out?"

"Just about. Hey, do you happen to have your sat phone with you?"

"Yes, why?"

Zane exhaled. If someone was trying to steal all their phones, at least they hadn't managed to get their hands on Cignetti's yet. "Can you check for a signal? The storm seems to have lightened a bit, so maybe we'll get lucky."

"Copy that. I'll go get it and check before I go down to meet you."

Zane frowned. "Go get it? I thought you had it on you."

"Not actually on me, no. It's in my backpack."

"And where is your backpack?"

"In my closet."

An ominous feeling crept over Zane. "Can you grab it and check the signal now?"

There was a brief pause before an answer came through. "Roger that. Hang on a sec."

Zane hoped he was making too much out of the whole thing. In all the hoopla surrounding O'Connor's disappearance, he might have simply misplaced his device. He didn't think so, but stress and a lack of sleep often made people do things they wouldn't ordinarily do.

Zane's worst fears were realized when Cignetti's voice came through a half minute later. "I don't understand it. I'm certain I put it in my bag. Let me go back to the dining hall. Maybe I—"

"Don't bother. I think we have a problem. I was certain I put mine in the drawer next to my bed, and now it's gone."

There was a long pause. "So what are you saying?"

"I'm saying someone took our phones. They're trying to cut off our communication with the outside world."

"What about Freja's phone?"

"I don't think she has her radio with her right now, but I'll go find her and have her take a look. In the meantime, see if you can find Stone."

"I don't think he has a phone."

"No, not for that. If the Hagglunds are in working order and there is enough fuel, then I want the two of you to take one of them back to Parks. It may be our only hope of getting help."

"What about Rider?" Cignetti asked.

"I don't think Rider made it."

* * *

ZANE, Amanda, and Freja sat around a table in the dining hall, their expressions a mixture of shock and concern. Freja's satellite phone was missing as well, which meant there was no hope of making contact with Parks Station.

Zane looked at Freja, who was sitting across from him. "You're sure it's not somewhere in your room?"

"One hundred percent positive. I turned it upside down."

"Did you take it anywhere?" Amanda asked.

Freja shook her head. "There isn't a signal, so there was no need to."

Amanda nodded.

Zane lowered his voice. "It's pretty clear our mole is starting to take action."

"What do you think their overall objective is?" Freja asked. "It would be nice if we could somehow anticipate their next move."

"I've actually given that some thought," Zane said. "I think they're trying to soften up the target for an attack."

Freja's brow furrowed. "What do you mean?"

"Let's assume our theory is correct, and we're up against a foreign government," Zane said. "As I mentioned before, I don't think they have a large contingent down here. If they did, they would've already moved against us. That means the mole is trying to do everything they can to diminish our capabilities.

Take out one or both SEALs then eliminate our contact with the outside world."

"Then they'll call in their team," Amanda finished.

Zane nodded. "I had always assumed the mole's job was to simply report on intelligence—the number of armed personnel on our team, the type of weapons we were using, the timing of patrols, and so on. This asset is taking more of a proactive role than I imagined."

There was a minute of silence as each person was lost in their own thoughts.

"We'd better hope Rider made it to Parks," Amanda finally said.

"Between the three of us, I don't think we can count on him for help," Zane said.

Freja's brow furrowed. "You don't think he made it?"

"I don't know if he did or not, but we have to make plans as though no help is coming."

"What about the shortwave radio?" Amanda asked. "Does Hawke think it can be fixed?"

"He and Arnott are up there working on it now," Zane replied. "But he told me not to expect a miracle. Whoever destroyed all the equipment did a pretty thorough job. At this point, our best hope is to send one of the Hagglunds to Parks."

"Who are you going to send?" Amanda asked.

"Stone and Cignetti. In fact, they're looking the vehicles over right now to make sure at least one of them is in good working order."

"I don't necessarily disagree, but why would you pick them?" Freja asked.

"Stone needs to be in the vehicle in case there are engine problems along the way."

"What about the SEAL?" Freja asked. "What if we're attacked while he's gone?"

"She has a point," Amanda said before Zane could answer.

"We have one SEAL missing already, and you said yourself that an attack could be imminent."

"I said it could be." Zane shook his head. "And my theory about the attack was just that, a theory. But you make a fair point. The problem is that I don't want Stone out there alone. For all we know, the enemy could launch an attack on the vehicle, which is now our only hope of getting help."

"I'll go with him," Amanda said a half minute later.

Zane frowned. "I don't think that's—"

"It makes the most sense to send me," Amanda said. "Cignetti is a soldier. I'm not. He'll be needed here."

"The mole could alert the people he or she is working with," Zane countered. "That vehicle could be ambushed."

"I know how to use a rifle. Besides, I just thought of something. When we leave, we'll take a winding route, and we won't share it with the others."

Zane had to admit that it was an excellent idea.

"We're all assuming that Stone isn't the mole," Freja noted.

"If he is, then he probably won't agree to go," Amanda said. "The mole wants to be here."

"He could be planning to kill whoever is with him," Freja countered.

"We'll make sure I'm the only one with a weapon." Amanda turned to Zane. "I can do this."

There was a cautious pause.

"I'm open to it," Zane finally said. "Give me some time to think it over."

Freja leaned forward and put her elbows on the table. "A lot of our problems would be solved if we could just figure out who the mole is. That said, I want to hear what the two of you think in terms of who it might be."

"We have at least two prime suspects," Amanda said.

"I have a hard time believing that Reimer is a Russian asset," Zane said.

Freja lifted a brow. "Why not? No offense to your military, but he seems like a despicable human being. Not to mention him sneaking around to practice his Russian, the very language of the country that could be behind all of this."

"The fact that he's such a jerk is the very reason I don't think he's who we're looking for," Zane said.

"Explain," Freja said.

"I'm no counterintelligence agent, but my gut tells me a mole would lie low and play along. If I was infiltrating a group, the last thing I'd want to do is stir the pot and draw attention to myself. Reimer doesn't seem to have a problem putting himself front and center."

"Unless he's employing reverse psychology," Amanda said. "In that case, you're thinking exactly the way he wants you to."

"Trust me. I'm watching him," Zane said. "I just ultimately think it's going to be someone else."

"What if there are two assets?" Freja asked. "What if he and Morgan Martini are working together? I don't know about you, but I still don't buy this BS story they cooked up."

"It is odd, I'll give you that," Zane said. "Has Morgan shown you the proof they were taking the class?"

She shook her head. "Not yet. To be honest, she probably did though. I don't think she would have offered proof if she hadn't."

"Agreed."

"Speaking of Reimer and Martini, where are they?" Amanda asked.

"In the warehouse at the back of the building," Zane said. "They took Christine Pageau back there to look for access to the tunnels. Morgan is determined to start looking for the anomaly."

Amanda frowned. "Is that a good idea for Christine to be so active so soon?"

"I hope so," Zane said. "Sunny gave her the green light, and we all know how cautious she can be. Apparently, dehydration was about the only thing Christine was dealing with, and that's been corrected."

Zane was about to say something else when a voice crackled through his radio. "Samson, you there?"

Cignetti. They must have finished examining the Hagglunds.

Zane picked up the radio and responded. "Samson here. What's the good news?"

"I'm afraid I don't have any."

A frown tugged at the corners of Zane's mouth. "What's going on?"

"I don't know how else to put this, but it looks like both vehicles have been sabotaged."

Zane's frown deepened. "What's wrong with them?"

"The batteries are gone."

Zane swore softly.

"But that's not the only thing," Cignetti said. "It also looks like some engine hoses were cut. We might be able to fix the hoses, but these babies won't work without batteries."

Zane thought for a moment. "I know this is a long shot, but take a look around the building to see if our saboteur tried to hide them in the snow."

"Roger that."

After signing off, Zane set the radio back on the table then looked at the two women sitting across from him. "I hate to say this, but it looks like we're stranded out here."

21

AFTER FINISHING HIS CIGARETTE, Vince Stone stepped inside the garage and closed the door behind him. The interior wasn't heated, but it still felt better than being out in the wind. As he turned around, he saw Rod Cignetti coming toward him.

"I just talked to Watson," the SEAL said. "He wants us to make a quick sweep of the area around the buildings. He thinks whoever tampered with the vehicles may have tossed the batteries outside."

"Sorry, but we ain't gonna find those things," Stone said. "They're probably buried a quarter mile away."

"I hear you, but it can't hurt to look. The person may not have had much time."

Stone nodded. "I guess that's true."

"I think it's time we gave you a little protection." Cignetti pulled a pistol out of his coat and held it out. "This is my spare. An HK45C. You know how to use it?"

Stone smiled. "I spent five years of my life in the US Army, so that won't be a problem."

"No offense. Just needed to be sure."

"None taken. I would've done the same." Stone took the gun

THE ANOMALY

and examined it. The Heckler & Koch had been modified with light-gray paint, the perfect camouflage for operations conducted in the snowy terrain. "Very nice. I'm used to a nine-millimeter Beretta, but this will do."

"Do you have a flashlight?"

Stone patted his pocket. "Yep."

After the two stepped outside, they were hit with a strong gust of wind. Stone shivered and swore under his breath. The lull in the storm seemed to be coming to an end, which was going to make their search even more impossible.

"I'll start here and work my way around back." The SEAL waved a gloved hand toward the two storage buildings that stood just to the west. "Why don't you start on the other end, and we'll meet at the back."

"And if we don't find anything?"

"Then we'll expand the search."

Stone nodded but said nothing. He had hoped this would simply be a brief look around the buildings. He still didn't think there was much of a chance they would find the missing batteries.

Cignetti saluted him. "See you in ten."

"Copy that."

After putting the pistol in his coat pocket, Stone thumbed on his flashlight and walked quickly down the front of the buildings, turning left at the end. As he started down the side, a cloud of swirling snow was kicked up by strong winds. Even with the flashlight, he could only see about ten feet ahead of him.

All Stone could do to continue was focus on the task at hand. He directed his beam toward the side of the building, looking for any irregularities in the snowdrift that was gathered there. As far as he could tell, there was no sign of digging. It all looked smooth. And that was the problem. If the batteries had been placed there several days before, they would undoubtedly be covered by then. The only real way to search would be to dig through all of it, and that was something he wasn't going to suggest.

While Stone understood the need to find the missing batteries, he wondered if this search was a good use of their time. With both vehicles out of commission, he believed they should simply set up a defensive perimeter inside the main building and wait for help to arrive.

He had been impressed with the way that Hawke and Rider had handled the big chopper on the flight to Ellsworth. Their performance gave him faith that Rider would find a way to get back to Parks Station. And even if he didn't, at some point, the government would send help. Their team was supposed to check in with Washington regularly, and the silence coming from Antarctica would eventually move the authorities to action. He just hoped the help wouldn't come too late.

As he neared the rear of the building, he heard a sliding noise somewhere ahead. Nobody else was supposed to be near the garage but them. His heart beat a little faster, and he turned his flashlight off. If someone was out there, he didn't want to draw attention to himself.

Hearing no further sounds, he eased up to the corner and peered down the back of the building. A strong gust blasted him in the face. Frozen air stung the area around his eyes like hundreds of hypodermic needles.

As he waited for the wind to die down, the sliding noise sounded again. The movement was slow and stealthy. *Is it a person or something mechanical?* The sound had been too muffled to tell. The howling storm also made it difficult to tell which direction it had come from.

His concern growing by the minute, Stone pulled the pistol out and chambered a round. At least he could defend himself if something was out there.

He wondered if he should use the radio to contact Cignetti then decided against it. Talking would only give his location

THE ANOMALY

away. He supposed he could back away and radio him from a safe distance, but that didn't sit well with him either. Stone had never been one to shrink from danger, and he wasn't about to now.

Keeping his gun at the ready, Stone stepped around the corner and edged along the back wall. The swirling snow was worse on that side of the building, making it even more difficult to see than before. If someone rushed him, he'd have only seconds to react.

Something slid across the snow, and now it only seemed to be about fifteen or twenty yards away. Stone lifted the pistol with both hands and continued. Soon, the hairs on the back of his neck stood on end. Just ahead, he saw a dark shadow hunkered against the back of the building. It quivered like a predator that was about to pounce.

What the hell?

The dark shadow moved in his direction, gliding across the ice. His heart racing, he took aim. Then he lowered it again as the object coming toward him took on a familiar shape.

Stone cursed under his breath. *A freaking trash can.*

It was a good thing he hadn't fired because that would surely have brought Cignetti over. *Talk about embarrassing.*

He put his gun away, grabbed the can, then dragged it over to the building. He noticed two other cans standing against the back wall. Both were partially buried in the snowdrift, and next to them was a slight depression, which was where he guessed the third can had been. He found it strange that only one had been knocked out of place by the wind.

Seeing no lid in the vicinity, Stone set the can in the depression and pushed it down as hard as he could. He then began to kick snow around its base to keep it from blowing away again. On the third kick, his boot hit something solid. Whatever he'd hit was about a foot to the left of the can. He stopped and squinted in the dark at his feet. A sense of hope rushed through him. Maybe it was one of the batteries. As Cignetti had said, maybe they'd needed to make a quick getaway, and stashing them close by had been their only option.

Stone turned on his flashlight and directed the beam toward his feet. The cone of light illuminated an object protruding from the drift. It looked like a half-buried artifact from an archaeological dig.

Reaching out, he used a gloved hand to brush away the snow. Soon, more lines of the object began to appear. The shape was familiar, but for some reason, it wasn't registering. He furrowed his brow at the dark fabric that looked like the lower edge of a knit cap.

Seconds later, Stone scraped away the final layer of snow and ice. He gasped and recoiled.

Two human eyes stared back at him.

22

ZANE, Amanda, and Freja were just wrapping things up in the dining hall when Cignetti radioed them with the news that Colton O'Connor's body had been found. Zane was shocked that they had discovered it so quickly. Then again, the killer probably hadn't had much time to dispose of the corpse.

The three operatives wasted no time heading for the garage. They found Cignetti and Stone standing over the body, which had been laid out on the floor.

Somber silence filled the space. Cignetti's eyes were fixed on the deceased soldier, his expression a mixture of sadness and shock. On the battlefield, there wasn't time for quiet reflection, but there in the garage, the SEAL's emotions bubbled to the surface. He and O'Connor had shared more than military service —they had also been close friends.

Zane came over and stood next to Cignetti. "I'm sorry."

The SEAL nodded. "He was a fierce warrior and one heck of a human being."

Zane squatted next to the body. As Cignetti had reported, there were two bullet wounds to the forehead, one toward the left temple and the other dead center.

The location of the wounds revealed something interesting. Usually, a professional would execute the victim by shooting the chest first then the head in a classic double-tap technique. A shot to the chest, the easier of the two, would incapacitate the victim. That gave the shooter more time to aim accurately at the head. In this instance, there was no blood on the chest. Instead, both were to the face. That seemed to indicate the killing had taken place at close range. There was no need to aim at the chest first when the target was standing a few feet away.

Zane used a finger to trace the wound on the forehead. "Nine millimeter."

Cignetti nodded, already pulling himself together. "No doubt about it."

Zane looked up at him. "Are you using a nine?"

"No, I use a forty, and my backup is a forty-five." Cignetti frowned.

"He gave me his forty-five," Stone said.

Cignetti frowned. "Why do you ask?"

Zane stood. "No disrespect to either of you, but this seems like an inside job."

Cignetti nodded.

"If this was someone inside, it could mean they brought an unauthorized pistol with them," Freja said.

"What about some other group that might be out there?" Amanda asked. "After all, he was on patrol."

"Both shots were executed at close range, so this was probably someone he knew," Zane said. "Or the killer surprised him. I'm leaning toward the former though."

"That storm makes it almost impossible to see more than a few feet, so it's possible the killer could have gotten pretty close outside," Stone said.

Amanda gave Zane a questioning look. They had previously agreed to keep the information about the smeared blood on the garage floor a secret, but Stone hadn't been in the loop. Zane wondered how much he should say, if anything. His gut told him that the mechanic wasn't the mole. Not only that, but Cignetti had said it was Stone who'd discovered the body. If he was the killer, it wouldn't make sense for him to lead them to the very body he'd hidden.

"We believe O'Connor was killed right here in this garage," Zane finally said.

Stone frowned. "How do you know that?"

"Because we found traces of blood on the floor in here shortly after Colton went missing," Zane said. "And there was no good explanation for it being there. We decided to keep it a secret until we gathered more information."

Stone nodded but still seemed a bit irritated that he hadn't been told.

"We need to find the nine millimeter that was used to kill O'Connor," Amanda said.

"That shouldn't be too hard," Cignetti said. "We'll put everyone in the dining room then conduct a thorough search of their rooms."

"I think we need to be more subtle right now," Zane said. "My guess is, the person doesn't have the weapon in their nightstand. If it were me, I'd hide it in another part of the building. That way, it couldn't be linked to me if someone stumbled across it."

"They may have even stashed it outside somewhere," Freja said.

Zane looked at Cignetti. "But you're right, when we get the chance, we do need to look in some of the sleeping quarters. It would be stupid not to. The killer may be confident that no one will come looking."

"When can I start?" Cignetti asked. "We need to find Colton's killer."

"Morgan Martini and Lucas Reimer are supposedly busy searching for access to the tunnels. If they're still out doing that, you can start with them."

23

AMANDA WAS SITTING at the desk in her room when she heard the sound of the door open behind her. She turned to see Sunny enter, a white mug in hand. "Is that coffee?"

"I told you I was an addict."

"I can't do caffeine at night."

"It's actually decaf." Sunny walked over to the bottom bunk and sat down. "Even an addict like me can't do regular this late."

"We have decaf?"

Sunny nodded. "Brady found a couple of cans in the pantry. There isn't much left. If you want some, you'd better get down there quick."

"I'm good, but I may go down for some water. That pasta we had for dinner made me thirsty."

"It made me thirsty, too, but it was *so* good."

Two hours earlier, the entire team had gathered for a dinner of seafood fettuccine Alfredo, garlic bread, and salad. It was a simple but delicious meal. Amanda wasn't sure what Arnott had put in the sauce, but it might have been the best she'd ever had.

"It's amazing what that guy can do all by himself." Amanda closed the laptop before Sunny could see that she was reading through the bios of the team members. "One of my colleagues is Italian, and at times, she can be a little critical of what some people try to pass off as a dish from her home country. I don't think she would've had any complaints tonight."

"Don't let me keep you from whatever you were doing." Sunny propped a pillow against the wall, leaned against it, and picked up her Bible. "I'll just sit here and read."

"You're fine." Amanda scooted her chair around to face her. "To be honest, I'm tired of looking at all that information. I'm starting to get a headache."

A strong gust howled outside, rattling the window.

Sunny pulled a fleece blanket over her legs in response. "So what exactly were you reading?"

Amanda rolled her eyes. "You know. Just some boring security material."

"Did you hear they found the way down into the tunnels?" Sunny asked.

Morgan, Reimer, and Pageau had discovered the entrance during their search of the warehouse. While looking behind one of the station's generators, Reimer noticed a hatch on the floor. The hatch gave access to a set of stairs, which in turn led to a large rectangular room that had been cut out of the ice. Inside were several rows of shelves containing items that suggested the space had been used as a natural freezer at some point in the past. But outdated pantry items weren't all they found. The big discovery came when Christine Pageau located a small opening at the rear of the room. That turned out to be the access point they were looking for.

Once they found the tunnels, Reimer had wanted to start the search for the anomaly right away, but Zane had put that off for at least a day. The passages were dark and treacherous. Any group going down would need the appropriate gear. But Zane had shared with her the other reason he was reluctant to begin the search. He feared a group of foreign commandos might be hiding down there, waiting to take action when given the signal by the mole."

"I did hear that," Amanda said.

"Pretty exciting, don't you think?"

"It is. For a while there, I was starting to wonder if they really existed."

"So when are you guys going down?" Sunny asked.

"Zane told us to get a good night's sleep and be ready to go down as soon as tomorrow morning."

"I'll stick with nursing," Sunny said. "Dark and creepy places aren't my thing."

Silence fell over the room. Sunny slid on a pair of reading glasses and looked down at her Bible.

"Speaking of your career, I take it you like what you do?" Amanda finally asked.

"I truly love it." Sunny looked at Amanda over her glasses. "I've always been fascinated with the human body. I just love to think about how all its different pieces work to keep us alive and healthy. As David says in the Psalms, we are 'fearfully and wonderfully made.'"

"I love that verse. So I take it you wanted to study medicine from a young age?"

Sunny nodded. "Yes, and I have my mom to thank for that. When I was a little kid, she bought me a book on the human body by Isaac Asimov. I must have read it a dozen or more times. I've read a lot of very sophisticated medical material over the years, but none of it has ever grabbed me the way that book did."

"Asimov is great," Amanda said. "I read some of his works too."

"*Fantastic Voyage* was another one of my favorites. I know this sounds crazy, but I think it's interesting how in some small way, that book has become a reality." Sunny shot Amanda a knowing grin. "Please don't misunderstand me. I know we can't shrink people and put them in a little submarine, but we *are* able to send tiny cameras into people's bodies. Just recently, a team of German scientists developed a camera that's so small it can be injected into the bloodstream."

"I saw the headline." Amanda smiled. "I love listening to people who are excited about what they do. I can see it in your eyes."

"Looking back, I can see God's hand in my career," Sunny said. "He gave me an interest in the human body, and now I'm able to use it for His glory."

"How so?"

Sunny thought for a moment. "First of all, I get to help people heal. It's an act of service that I truly enjoy. But to be honest, the best part about it is that I get to share my faith, even with those who are close to death. I've been around lots of dying people, you know, and some of them are literally hours away from their appointed time."

"I've never shared my faith with someone who is dying," Amanda said. "Are most receptive?"

"It differs from person to person. God will usually make it clear when I'm supposed to speak. I just tell the person that God is ready to forgive their sins if they trust in His Son, Jesus Christ, who died on the cross for them. I make it clear this isn't about trying to get religious or trying to perform good works. I often use the thief on the cross as the perfect example of someone saved by grace. There wasn't time for the thief to get baptized or do good deeds, and yet Jesus assured the man he would go to paradise upon his death."

Amanda was unable to suppress a smile. "I love hearing how God orchestrates the little details of someone's life."

The two spent the next fifteen minutes discussing Amanda's career—her background in archaeology and her current work for Delphi. Amanda managed to describe the fundamentals of her job without giving away any sensitive information. Sunny seemed to understand the need for secrecy and didn't push her for more details.

Once they were done, Amanda stood. "Well, my throat is parched. I'm going to go grab some water. Can I refill your mug for you?"

"I think I'm good. Thanks though."

Amanda slipped out into the hall and closed the door behind her. As she went toward the back stairwell, she reflected on her conversation with Sunny. Up until then, they had both been caught up in the operation and hadn't had a chance to speak on a deeper level. But after sharing their faith and a little on where life had taken them, Amanda realized it hadn't been a coincidence that they had ended up in the same room.

When she reached the first-floor atrium, Amanda saw a light on in the communications room. On the other side of the glass, Niles Hawke appeared to be working on something, likely the shortwave radio. It was a comforting sight. Since the Hagglunds were out of commission, the radio might be their only means of making contact with Parks Station.

Amanda stuck her head in the door. "Hey."

Hawke flinched at the sound of her voice.

"Sorry," Amanda said. "Didn't mean to startle you. You're up late."

"Trust me, I'm knackered. But it needs to be done."

"Making any progress?"

"No," he said grimly. "But you know what they say, 'Hope springs eternal.'"

She nodded. "I wish I could help, but electronics aren't my thing."

"Technically, they're not mine either, although I probably know a little more than most."

"Hey, I'm headed down to the kitchen for a water. Can I grab you something while I'm down there?"

He thought for a moment. "Well, I may be up for another hour or two, so I might fancy a cuppa if you have time to make it."

Amanda's brow furrowed. "A cuppa?"

"Sorry, that's my British slang coming out. A cup of tea, if it's not too much trouble."

"It's no trouble at all."

"Thank you. I think there is some Earl Grey in the same cabinet as the coffee."

After telling him she'd be right back, Amanda entered the hall that led back to the dining room. The farther she got from the atrium, the darker it became. That and the howling wind outside made her skin crawl. Freja Larsen and Rod Cignetti were currently on patrol, but she didn't see any sign of either.

A minute later, Amanda crossed the dining room and entered the kitchen. A sole light glowed under the cabinets to her left. Sunny had probably left it on when making her coffee.

As Amanda walked toward the cabinets for the tea and kettle, a groan sounded from somewhere close. She froze.

She wondered if it had only been the wind when she heard another groan. The sound seemed to come from the room at the rear of the kitchen. *Definitely human.* She worried that Freja or Vince might be hurt.

Aware that danger might be close by, Amanda scanned the kitchen for a weapon. Her eyes soon fell on a cutlery set on a nearby counter. Careful not to make a noise, she went over and pulled out a chef's knife. It wasn't as good as having a gun, but the large blade could do plenty of damage in close quarters.

Now armed, she eyed the doorway at the back of the kitchen. As best she could remember, the back room housed the refrigerator and freezer. She couldn't think of a good reason anyone would be back there. Once again, her mind went back to Freja and Cignetti. Perhaps one of them had been ambushed while on patrol then hidden in the tucked-away room.

Gripping the knife tightly, she passed through the doorway. Immediately, she heard a noise to her right. Turning in that direction, she saw two figures writhing in front of a freezer compartment. The arms of the combatants encircled one another as they wrestled.

Reacting on instinct, Amanda brought the knife up and moved quickly in their direction. About halfway there, she stopped. From where she stood, she could see the movements of the two combatants more clearly now. Shock rippled through her. They weren't *fighting*. They were making out. The groans had been those of pleasure as the man and woman wrapped each other in a passionate embrace.

As the two continued to kiss and press against one another, Amanda realized who they were. She slipped out without making a sound.

24

THE NEWS that Niles Hawke had been killed came to Zane in the same way that the news about Colton O'Connor had—an urgent knock on the door from Rod Cignetti. When Zane swung the door open and saw the SEAL's face, he knew immediately that something horrible had taken place.

According to Cignetti, he and Freja had been on patrol when they noticed a lamp had been left on in the communications room. Conscious of the need to save energy, Freja stepped inside to turn it off. That was when she discovered the pilot lying facedown on the floor with a bullet wound to the head. Concerned that the perpetrators might be close by, Cignetti and Freja had made a quick sweep of the second floor but had found nothing to indicate the killer or killers were still around.

Once Zane was dressed, the two went immediately to Amanda's room. Zane slipped inside and managed to wake her without disturbing Sunny. After giving her the news, he told her to meet them in the communications room as soon as she was able.

Zane wanted to learn as much as he could before the others woke and started pointing fingers at one another. The last time someone was killed, the meeting had spiraled out of control. Vince Stone had flat out accused Lucas Reimer of killing Colton O'Connor. Angered by the accusation, Reimer then claimed Stone was trying to divert attention from himself. The DARPA scientist reminded everyone that it was Stone who had found the SEAL's body buried in the snow, and he had only been able to do that because he was the one who had put it there.

When Zane and Cignetti arrived at the communications room, Freja was standing just inside the door, her arms folded across her chest and her eyes fixed on the body. While she appeared calm, it was clear from her expression that she was deeply troubled by Hawke's death.

She turned toward them when they entered. "I got to know Niles a little bit since coming down here," she said, her eyes wet with emotion. "I'm an avid skier, and I soon found out he was too. As we shared a few stories, we realized we had skied many of the same slopes in Europe. We even talked about getting together when his tour down here ended." She looked at Zane. "So yeah, this one hurts pretty bad."

Zane nodded. "Heck of a guy. Worked around the clock to get this equipment fixed."

"He was first class," Cignetti said.

"Yes, he was," Freja said.

What made the whole thing even more depressing was that Hawke's friend Patrick Rider was likely dead too. A rescue team probably would have arrived by now if Rider had made it back to Parks Station. And even if he was alive out there somewhere, he was likely holed up in a mountain cave, his chances of survival shrinking with each passing hour.

Zane felt an overwhelming sense of sorrow at the sudden dark turn of life. Rider and Hawke had simply been asked to transport the team, and both men had paid with their lives.

Cignetti looked at Freja. "Have you found the bullet casing? Might be nice to have if we ever pinpoint a suspect."

She shook her head. "No, and I don't think we will. This person is a professional, so I'm pretty certain he or she would have picked it up."

"A professional? They forgot to turn off the light," Cignetti said.

Zane squatted next to the body, which had been rolled onto its back. A single bullet wound painted the center of Hawke's forehead red. The pilot's eyes stared into nothingness.

"Another nine millimeter," Freja said.

Zane nodded. "O'Connor and Hawke were likely killed with the same gun." He leaned in for a better look at the wound. "Even if you had a protractor and a felt-tip marker, you couldn't have marked that more perfectly in the center of his forehead."

"Looks like he was shot at close range, too, which means he knew the killer," Cignetti said.

Zane stood. "And yet I still don't think we can rule out someone coming in from the outside. The atrium was dark, so he wouldn't have seen them approach. They could have slipped in and shot him the minute he turned around." Zane looked at Cignetti. "But you're right. I think the most likely scenario is that the killer could approach because Hawke felt comfortable around them."

"You mentioned it could be someone from the outside," Freja said. "How did they get in? The tunnels?"

"We have to consider that possibility," Zane said.

"There could be a whole team down there," she added.

Zane nodded. "I agree. Which is why we need to get down there—"

He was cut off by the sound of approaching footsteps. Seconds later, Amanda appeared in the doorway, and her gaze went straight to the body.

"Another nine millimeter to the head at close range," Zane said.

After staring at the body for a few more seconds, Amanda

looked at Zane. "I didn't tell you this earlier, but I was here last night. I brought Niles some tea."

Zane frowned. "What time was that?"

She shrugged. "I'm not sure exactly. Eleven maybe?"

"Did you notice anything strange?" Freja asked. "Did you see anyone else walking around?"

Amanda hesitated, and Zane noted a flash of something in her eyes.

"No, I didn't see anyone else," she said. "I was on my way to the kitchen and popped my head in to see if he needed anything. He said he'd like a cup of tea, so I made that for him and brought it back."

"Did he mention talking to anyone before you stopped by?" Zane asked.

She shook her head. "No. When I came back, he just told me a little bit about the repairs he was trying to make. To be honest, I didn't understand most of what he said."

There was still something in Amanda's expression that Zane found a bit odd. He could tell she had seen something, but for some reason, she wasn't sharing it. Maybe she couldn't figure out whether it was important or not. Or maybe she didn't want to share it in front of Cignetti, who hadn't been briefed on the possible presence of the mole.

Zane turned to Freja. When they locked eyes, he nodded at Cignetti, hoping she understood the subtle message. "Do you know where the gurney is?" he asked her.

"Of course."

"Do you mind grabbing it while I check around for the casing?"

"I don't mind at all." Freja looked at Cignetti. "Can you give me a hand? I may have a little trouble getting it up the stairs."

The SEAL nodded.

They had stored the other two bodies in one of the station's storage buildings. The cool temperatures inside the building allowed the bodies to remain in a preserved state. Zane hoped this would be the last corpse they would have to put there.

"We'll be right back," Freja said.

Once they were gone, Zane turned to Amanda. "Okay, now tell me what you saw."

"Actually, I was telling the truth," Amanda said. "I didn't see anyone up here. But I did see two people in the kitchen."

"Who?"

"Lucas Reimer and Morgan Martini."

"Sounds awfully late for dinner."

"They were nibbling on something, but it wasn't food."

Zane's brow furrowed. "I don't understand."

"Sorry, it was a joke. I guess none of this is funny. They were back near the freezer, making out."

That wasn't what Zane had expected to hear. He knew the two were close, but he had no idea they were having an affair. "What did they say when they saw you?"

"They didn't. It was dark back there, and they were too caught up in what they were doing. I probably could've done a few cartwheels, and they wouldn't have noticed."

He exhaled. "First they're alone practicing Russian, now this."

"It's pretty bizarre behavior if you ask me," Amanda said.

"More odd for two people to have a late-night rendezvous then go upstairs and shoot someone in cold blood."

Amanda nodded. "Unless only one of them was involved in the shooting. In fact, if one of them is the killer, they might have seen the little make-out session as the perfect alibi."

"That's an excellent point," Zane said. "Let's think about this. After the two finished up their little tryst, they probably would have come up the back stairs. And when they did, they would have noticed Hawke working on the radio."

"The mole then could have gotten their gun and come back to do the deed."

"Correct. The last thing the mole wants is for us to reestablish communication with Parks Station."

Silence fell over the tiny room.

"So what are we going to do?" Amanda finally asked.

"We're going to go have a little talk with our two little lovebirds."

* * *

ALTHOUGH THE DINING hall certainly didn't look like an interrogation room, the scene still had the feel of something straight out of a crime drama. Zane and Amanda sat on one side of a dining room table like a couple of hardened detectives with their poker faces on. Reimer and Martini sat across from them, their expressions like those of suspects who had been accused of something they didn't do.

The whole thing had started benignly. Zane had asked the two to come down to discuss the tragic death of Niles Hawke. What he hadn't told them was that they were suspects. After giving them a brief overview of what had happened, Zane had begun to ask a series of basic questions on what they'd seen or heard, if anything, before Hawke's death.

Then, about five minutes in, the questions grew more pointed. And with that, the mood at the table darkened. Tension and anger began to boil beneath the surface.

"I'll ask you one more time," Zane said after a long moment of silence. "Were you in the kitchen at any point since dinner last night? Someone told me they saw you there, and according to them, you weren't there to freshen your coffee."

His face turning a deep shade of red, Reimer stood and slammed his palms on the table. "How dare you accuse me of murder!"

"No one's accused you of anything," Zane said in a measured tone. *At least not yet.*

"Don't play games," Reimer roared. "You're trying to say I killed Hawke."

"No. I just asked a simple question about where you were, and for some reason, you don't want to answer it. Or maybe I *do* know the reason."

Reimer leaned in, a jagged vein rising on his forehead like a river on a map.

Martini put a hand on Reimer's arm. "Lucas, please."

He shrugged her hand off. "You're just trying to deflect blame from your own pathetic performance." He pointed a finger at Zane's chest. "It's been one embarrassing mistake after another. First, you allowed that pilot to fly out of here right as that storm hit. The poor guy probably didn't last thirty minutes in those conditions. And if he's dead, it's because you didn't have the guts to stop him."

"That's not what happened," Amanda said. "Hawke and Rider were the ones who came up with the idea. They're the experts on local conditions, so we deferred to their expertise."

Ignoring the comment, Reimer kept his gaze on Zane. "Then we find a dead astronomer, his body mauled like something out of a horror movie. What's your response to that? You send soldiers out to patrol on their own. That SEAL's death is on—"

"A smart person might think you're trying to throw us off the scent with all this smoke you're blowing," Zane said, cutting him off.

"You ignorant bastard!" Reimer roared. "I'll have your job when we—"

"It was me," Amanda blurted. "I saw both of you in the room behind the kitchen."

Reimer fixed his gaze on her then slowly settled back into his seat. An awkward silence fell over the room. Zane had wanted to avoid saying who had seen them, but he was glad that Amanda had decided to speak up. Having the eyewitness present made an event much harder to deny.

"There is something we need to tell you," Martini finally said. Reimer turned in her direction. "Morgan, don't—"

"No. We have to tell them. We have to tell them because we did nothing wrong."

Reimer opened his mouth to say something then stopped himself when he saw Martini wasn't going to be deterred.

"Lucas and I have been seeing each other for a while," Martini said. "It started during the language class we took together." She looked at Amanda. "And yes, we were together last night, but I can assure you that we had nothing to do with the death of Niles Hawke."

"I appreciate your honesty, but why come down here?" Zane asked. "Surely, you know how this looks."

"Neither of us could sleep with all the wind, so we came down to get a snack and talk. That's the honest truth." She paused for a moment. "Then one thing led to another."

"How long were you there?" Amanda asked.

"Not long," Martini said. "Maybe a half hour or so, then we decided to go back to our rooms. We didn't want to be seen together at such a late hour, so Lucas went up the front stairs. I waited a few minutes then went up the back."

Zane found it interesting that they had gone up separately.

"Was Hawke in the comms room when you walked by?" Amanda asked.

Martini hesitated before answering. "Yes. In fact, I spoke to him briefly."

"About what?" Zane asked.

"This is ridiculous," Reimer said. "We're done here."

Martini put a hand on his arm again. "He told me what he was doing, and I thanked him for working so hard to get us out of this mess. I truly meant that."

Reimer glared at Zane. "He was doing more to get us out of this than you."

"Look, that's all there is to it," Martini said.

Reimer rose from his seat again. "Let's go."

This time, Martini stood with him, and Zane didn't try to stop her.

25

NOT ONE TO SIT AROUND when faced with the threat of an attack, Zane knew it was time to move. They needed to search the network of tunnels underneath the station. Although he felt reasonably certain O'Connor and Hawke had been killed by the mole, he couldn't rule out the possibility that the perpetrator was hiding in the tunnels, coming up at opportune moments to pick them off one at a time.

Zane had decided to only take two with him—Freja and Cignetti. The smaller number would allow them to travel with stealth and speed as they searched for hostiles. Their primary goal was to locate any threats, but they would also keep an eye out for signs of the anomaly.

After briefly going over the details of the mission, Zane led his teammates to the warehouse. The stairwell leading down into the ice was located behind the massive generators lined up at the rear of the space. When they arrived, Zane realized he would need to restrict access to that part of the building once they returned. Not only would it limit access to the tunnels, but it would protect the generators, which were crucial to their survival. He feared they could be another target for sabotage.

After all, the mole had already disabled the Hagglunds. Losing power would be even more disastrous.

"Let's do this," Cignetti said as he grabbed the trapdoor's handle and lifted the hatch.

Zane turned on his flashlight then led them down the set of crude steps made with old two-by-fours. Once they were safely at the bottom, he pulled the light cord to his left. A single bulb flared to life at the center of the space, illuminating a large room with walls of solid ice. A dozen rows of shelves stretched into the distance. Although most of them were bare, a few items had been left behind by the previous research team.

Zane had already been through the room once, so he only glanced down one of the aisles.

"Hang on," Freja said.

Zane looked back to see her pluck something off one of the shelves. It looked like a brown lump sealed inside plastic wrap.

"I don't even want to ask what that is," Cignetti said.

"And if you did, I'm not sure I'd have an answer," she said. "I guess it's meat." She held the package close to her face. "Someone wrote 'January of 2008.' I'd say it's a little past its fresh date."

"I didn't realize you two were so soft," Zane said. "It's vacuum sealed, so it probably tastes the same as the day it was brought down here."

Freja put it back on the shelf. "In that case, I'm sure Brady can cook it up for you to sample tonight."

"I think I'll pass," Zane said as he began moving again.

"I don't think Sunny has enough antibiotics to keep you alive if you ate that," Cignetti said.

When they reached the far end of the room, Zane led them over to the fissure in the back wall. Its jagged appearance suggested it had formed due to something like an earthquake. Zane wondered if that same event had also caused the small building to sink, which in turn had led to the discovery of the anomaly.

"When you said there was an entrance to the tunnels, I pictured something different," Freja said.

Zane peeked through the fissure. "It's tight, but it does get quite a bit wider on the other side."

Zane turned sideways and slipped through the gap. Once he came out into the tunnel, he swept his flashlight in every direction. The passageway was eight or nine feet high, with enough width for three or four people to walk abreast. The ice walls were mostly smooth, but the floor was textured, making it ideal for walking.

As he waited for the others to join him, a cold settled in his bones, only it didn't seem to be related to temperature. While not a big believer in the supernatural, he had experienced moments in which he had sensed the presence of evil in a place. This was one of those times. Something was lurking in the tunnels. He was certain of that.

Fortunately, all three of them were prepared. Cignetti carried an M4 rifle, while Zane and Freja carried pistols. Each of them also carried a tactical knife and an extra set of batteries. Getting lost in a tunnel without a source of light had been one of Zane's biggest concerns. Losing the ability to see in a maze of tunnels could quickly turn deadly.

After Freja came through, she put a gloved hand against the ice wall. "Beautiful."

Cignetti came through behind her and moved his beam around the space. "No wonder one of the buildings sank. This ice is like Swiss cheese. I'm surprised the whole station hasn't been swallowed by some sinkhole."

"I thought about the same thing," Zane said. "But this particular tunnel seems to move away from the building and toward the mountains."

"I'm guessing we'll see more. They probably run in all sorts of directions," Freja added.

Zane nodded. "You might be right."

"Which way do we go?" Cignetti asked.

Zane directed his flashlight beam to their left. "If you take the tunnel in that direction, you'll eventually hit a dead end." He turned around and pointed the beam in the other direction. "Reimer said we should go this way. According to him, the tunnel seems to go on indefinitely."

"Let's check it out, then," Cignetti said.

As the three began moving down the passageway, Zane made a mental note to keep track of their surroundings. Although he had no formal training in spelunking, he did know the importance of remembering such details as distance traveled, turns taken, and anything else that might help them find their way out if they got turned around. If they encountered any crossing tunnels or forks, things could get confusing very quickly.

About twenty yards in, the tunnel took a sharp left turn. From there, it continued straight for a while before finally curving to the left once again. After the second turn to the left, they began to encounter a few offshoots, all of them smaller than the path they were on. For the moment, Zane continued along the main route.

"It seems like we're going in a circle," Cignetti said.

"If so, then we may end up back where we started," Freja said.

Cignetti ran his beam across the smooth tunnel wall. "Everything looks the same down here."

"That's why I'm not taking any of the side tunnels," Zane said.

"What exactly are we looking for?" Freja asked.

"Bullet casings, food, trash, that sort of thing," Zane answered. "Anything that might indicate commandos are operating down here."

"I've been thinking about what they might do if they decide to attack," Cignetti said. "They might decide to hit us from both sides. One group makes a feint attack on the main building. We respond to that, then another group comes up through the tunnels to hit us from below."

"That would actually be brilliant," Freja said. "Assuming they have enough manpower to carry it out."

"It's a good point," Zane said. "We'll take care of our weak underbelly when we get back. For starters, I want to move one of those generators over the trap door."

"Those things weigh a ton," Cignetti said.

"I think we can slide them into place," Zane said. "There isn't any locking mechanism on the trap door, so putting something heavy over it is really our only option to stop someone from coming up."

Freja pointed her beam straight ahead. "I think the tunnel is getting wider."

Zane examined the walls on either side. She was right. Not only was the passageway wider, but the ceiling was higher as well. He also felt a very slight movement in the air, almost like a draft coming in from somewhere.

A few minutes later, Cignetti held up a hand, bringing the others to a halt. "Something is on the ground at twelve o'clock," he whispered.

Zane's eyes narrowed. About thirty yards away, a lone figure was stretched out on the ice. *An enemy sniper? If so, why hadn't they fired?* Cautious, Zane instinctively reached for his pistol.

"Who or what is that?" Freja asked.

"I think it's a body," Cignetti whispered back.

"Alive or dead?" Freja asked.

"They're not moving, so I'm thinking the latter."

"Agreed," Zane said. "Let's have a closer look."

Guns at the ready, the three advanced. Soon, their flashlight beams converged on what was clearly a body. Dark-pink ice crystals spread out underneath it. A chill ran down Zane's spine as his mind flashed back to the astronomer in the room on the second floor, his body ravaged in a similar manner.

"White-and-gray camouflage," Freja said as they drew within

a few feet. "And those boots are standard issue for the Russian military."

She was right, but Zane's focus was on the man's body. One leg was bent at an awkward angle, and there was a stub where the man's right arm should've been. Adding to the macabre scene, the man's face had been ripped into a mangled mass of flesh, bone, and tissue. His appearance was so distorted that Zane doubted a family member would be able to identify him.

Zane knelt next to the body. "You sure he's Russian?"

"Positive. I'm very familiar with their gear. Almost all Russian soldiers wear the same brand of boot."

"Then our suspicions were right all along," Zane said.

She nodded. "It would seem so. We probably should search him for—"

"Hey!" Cignetti called, his voice echoing down the tunnel.

Zane stood and looked around. The SEAL wasn't anywhere to be found.

"There," Freja said.

Zane followed her gaze. Just ahead, the tunnel took another sharp left. The soft glow of light peeked around the corner.

"Come take a look at this!" Cignetti shouted after not getting a response.

Zane strode toward the sound of his voice. After taking the turn, he saw Cignetti's silhouette about twenty yards ahead. The SEAL was standing perfectly still, the beam of his flashlight trained on something in the distance.

When they finally came up beside him, Freja gasped. Directly ahead, the tunnel opened into a much larger space. It was so massive that the beams of their flashlights couldn't reach the ceiling.

Zane stepped forward for a better view, but Cignetti grabbed his arm. "Easy, partner. I wouldn't do that if I were you."

Zane looked down. Several feet away, the tunnel floor

dropped off into a deep chasm. If he had taken another two or three steps, he would have gone over the edge.

"Next time, it might be a good idea to point something like that out first," Freja said.

"Sorry," Cignetti said. "If it makes you feel any better, I almost went over it myself."

Freja pointed her beam down into the chasm. "How deep is it?"

"I wonder if we can get to the other side," Zane said.

"Actually, that's the other thing I wanted to show you." Cignetti swung his flashlight to the right, illuminating what appeared to be an ice bridge. "I believe that will take us there."

"It's beautiful," Freja said as they edged toward it.

"I can't tell if it's a natural formation or a man-made structure that got iced over with time," Cignetti said.

Freja walked up to the start of the bridge. "It looks natural to me."

Zane kneeled and directed his beam at some dark crystals on the ice.

"Blood?" Cignetti asked.

Zane stood. "Looks like it."

"Which means that commando probably came through here," Freja said. "He must have come across the bridge to get away from whatever killed him."

Zane looked toward the other side of the bridge. "I'd love to know what's over there."

"The cavern looks like it goes on forever and ever," Freja said.

"I think I know what's over there," Cignetti said in a thoughtful tone.

Zane looked at him. "What are you thinking?"

"Our experts said they believe the anomaly is an alien spaceship," Cignetti replied. "Well, if they're right, I think we may have just found our crash site."

26

VINCE STONE WAS ready to leave that godforsaken place and never return. Although he had endured some difficult circumstances while serving his country, none of those deployments compared to being holed up in an Antarctic research station during a winter storm. With no rescue team on the way, it felt like being trapped in a nightmare set on an endless loop.

Stone had experienced extreme cold before. He'd had to shower when there was no hot water available and sleep on the ground outside without a blanket. He had even been ordered to shovel snow for hours with temperatures in the teens. But none of that compared to trying to survive a winter storm in Antarctica. It was the kind of cold that could take your life in minutes.

Still, the frigid temperatures weren't the main reason he was so desperate to leave. After all, inside the main building, the cold wasn't all that bad. What bothered him most was the evil he had sensed from the moment they had touched down at the station.

Stone's now-deceased grandmother, a kind Christian lady from Florence, South Carolina, had once told him that she could sense a demonic presence in certain places. He had laughed it off at the time, attributing it to her old age and what he'd believed was overzealous religious fervor. But then, there at the bottom of the world, Stone realized his grandmother had been right all along. He *could* feel something sinister in the atmosphere. It was like a scent, only one of a spiritual nature. And the discovery of the astronomer's mangled body had only confirmed that the feeling had been right.

Something was out there, and it was waiting for the right opportunity to wreak havoc in the station once again.

Rattled by the growing sense of doom, Stone had decided to conduct one more search for the missing batteries. If he could locate them, then they might be able to get back to Parks Station. Without a way out, the body count would continue to rise. He felt it in his bones.

After leaving the dining hall, he hustled up the back stairs to his quarters. He needed to get dressed before meeting Brady Arnott, who had agreed to help him search. They would first focus on the exterior buildings. Although those had been searched before, it still seemed like the most likely place to find the ditched batteries.

Stone had just arrived on the second floor when he noticed light spilling out of the cracked door to Reimer's room. He had been keeping an eye on the DARPA officer ever since hearing him speak Russian two nights before.

Even though the light was on, Stone knew the room was unoccupied, and that was because he had just seen Reimer, Martini, and Christine Pageau in the dining hall. The three had been deeply engrossed in a conversation about the possibility of extraterrestrial life.

Stone stopped at the open door then glanced back over his shoulder. There was no one in the hall behind him, nor could he hear anyone coming up the stairs. He considered going inside and having a look around. Reimer was a Russian spy—no one was going to convince him otherwise. And if Reimer was the mole, then he had probably hidden the pistol somewhere in the room.

It didn't take long for Stone to make up his mind. A quick look couldn't hurt. The rooms were small and sparse, which meant he could probably accomplish the task in less than five minutes.

After taking a final look down the hall, he opened the door. As he suspected, it was empty. He slipped inside, closed the door behind him, then went over to the bedside table and turned the lamp off. He then pulled out a tiny penlight that was attached to his key chain and flicked it on. If someone came down the hall, he would quickly plunge the room into darkness.

Stone opened the wardrobe. Inside were several shirts, two coats, three pairs of shoes, and a few other personal items. Seeing no sign of the pistol, he closed the wardrobe and went over to the two pieces of luggage stacked in the corner. Once again, he found nothing of interest.

Frustrated, he straightened and exhaled. If Reimer had brought a gun, he must have hidden it somewhere else in the building. It made the most sense not to hide something incriminating in his own room.

Before leaving, Stone decided to take one last look around to see if he'd missed anything. As he swept the penlight's beam across the bed, he noticed the sheets and blankets were piled in a messy clump on top of the mattress.

Mattress.

He frowned. Hiding a weapon there would be the ultimate cliché, but he had to look. He stepped over to it, lifted the mattress with one hand, then used the other hand to direct the beam into the space underneath. *Nothing.* As best he could tell, the gun wasn't—

He froze, his eyes fixing on a black rectangle tucked in a gap between the bed frame and the wall. He lifted the mattress as high as he could. Although it was hard to tell exactly what he was looking at, it sure seemed like a gun.

He set the penlight on the box spring then leaned into the gap and reached out as far as he could. After feeling around, his fingers finally closed around the adhesive-backed grip of a pistol.

His heart beating faster, Stone pulled the gun out and examined it with the penlight. It was a Glock 43. With a barrel length of about three and a half inches, it was one of the smallest pistols in the Glock family. Single stack with a six-round capacity. Nine millimeter.

Nine millimeter. Both victims had been killed with that same caliber weapon.

Stone felt the hairs rise on the back of his neck. *This is it.* It was all the proof he needed to bring the hammer down on Reimer.

As he went to slip the gun into his pocket, he heard footsteps in the hallway and making their way toward the door. At first, he thought it might be Arnott, but they had agreed to meet in the foyer.

Panic seized every muscle in Stone's body. He clicked off the penlight in case someone had seen it through the crack under the door.

Suddenly, the footsteps stopped. In the dreadful silence, Stone's eyes darted around the room, searching for a place to hide. Unfortunately, there weren't any good options.

Then, right as he was about to duck into the wardrobe, the door swung open.

27

BEFORE RETURNING TO THE STATION, Zane and Freja searched the Russian commando's clothing for anything that might shed some light on who he was and how he had come to be in the tunnels. Unfortunately, they were only able to find a few basic items—a half-empty pack of cigarettes, a small butane lighter, two spare magazines, a pocketknife, and a compass. They also found a flashlight a few feet away, its batteries dead.

Their big break came a few minutes later when Cignetti found an MP-443 Grach pistol against the tunnel wall. They hadn't seen it when they'd first come through because they had been so focused on the man's horrific injuries. The gun's magazine was spent, indicating the soldier had fired all its rounds during the battle against his attacker.

Freja confirmed that the MP-443 was one of several handguns used by the Russian Armed Forces. And since the deceased soldier had been chosen for that critical mission, she believed he was likely a member of Spetsnaz, the elite special operations arm of RAF.

Once they finished examining the body, Zane and Cignetti moved it into a nearby alcove. Zane had respect for the bodies of fallen soldiers, but under the circumstances, it was the best they could do. He noted the location so they could retrieve it later once help arrived and the station was secured. Until then, the low temperatures would keep the corpse in a preserved state.

On the way back to the station, Zane reached out to Amanda by radio. He told her to get Stone and meet them in the dining hall in order to discuss what they had found. She pressed him for details, but he told her to wait until they were all together. He didn't want to have to repeat the story several times, and he also knew that if he shared a little information then, she would only want more.

"I wasn't able to find Vince," Amanda said after the group gathered in the dining hall.

Zane looked up from the table where he, Cignetti, and Freja were sitting.

"He wasn't in his room?" Cignetti asked.

Amanda shook her head.

"Did you try to reach him by radio?" Freja asked.

"Several times," Amanda replied. "And there's something else. I also haven't been able to locate Reimer."

"What about Morgan?" Freja asked.

"She's in her room and claims she doesn't know where either man is."

A frown tugged at the corners of Zane's mouth. It was too strange for both Stone and Reimer to be missing. That hardly seemed like a coincidence. His thoughts went back to the interrogation that had taken place earlier in the day, and a tiny flame of concern flared inside him. Reimer had been livid when he and Martini had left. If he was the mole, then perhaps he feared being exposed and had left the station.

"Did you check the exterior buildings?" Cignetti asked.

"That was next on my list, but I figured I'd come here first in case they happened to be here too."

Zane could understand Reimer's disappearance, but he found

it hard to believe the mechanic was somehow involved. It had been Stone who had reported on the late-night conversation between Reimer and Martini. Perhaps he had made it up.

Zane was about to ask Amanda a question when Freja let out a startled noise.

Cignetti stood. "What the...?"

Zane turned to see Reimer walking toward him. His arms hung awkwardly at each side, and his face was as pale as the snowy terrain outside. As he came closer, Zane realized someone else was behind him. That someone was Stone.

"Tell him to put it down," Reimer said through clenched teeth.

It was then that Zane realized Stone had a pistol pressed against Reimer's back.

Zane stood. "Vince, he's right. Lower the weapon."

Stone shook his head. "Ain't gonna happen."

"It isn't a request," Zane said firmly. "Put it away."

Apparently emboldened by the presence of others, Reimer turned his head slightly and spoke in a loud voice. "You heard him. Put it down!"

Stone held the pistol in the air. "Have you seen this before?"

Zane focused his gaze on the weapon, a small semiautomatic.

"He's a crazy bastard!" Reimer yelled.

Stone waved the pistol around. "I found it under this clown's mattress. He's the one who's been killing our people. I've been trying to tell you that, but you wouldn't listen."

If true, it was a damning discovery. Still, Zane thought it odd that a professional would hide his or her weapon under their own bed.

"He's lying," Reimer said, the vein on his forehead bulging again. "I caught him planting it in my room. He's trying to frame me."

Stone gave a little chuckle. "Have you ever noticed he always has a convenient explanation for everything that happens? I find him speaking a foreign language in the middle of the night, and he claims he was just doing homework. And now I find a loaded weapon in his mattress, and he has the nerve to say I planted it."

Reimer fixed his gaze on Zane. "You know what kind of security checks we went through when we came down here. Every square inch of my luggage was checked on three different occasions. Not once did they find a weapon."

Zane had to admit that he had a point. He, Amanda, and Freja had gone through one before boarding the CIA charter at Joint Base Andrews, then a second screening at Puntas Arenas. The third check had come shortly after they landed at Parks Station.

"That's a straw man," Stone said, keeping the pistol aimed at Reimer. "No one ever said he brought it down here."

Reimer angled his head back to glare at the mechanic. "Then how did it come into my possession?"

Stone looked at Zane. "Whoever killed that researcher left a gun for Reimer to pick up when he arrived. I'm willing to bet he has other weapons stashed around this place."

Zane knew they could test the validity of those claims later. For the moment, he needed to defuse the situation. "Vince, I need you to put down that gun. We're all armed, so Lucas isn't going anywhere."

Stone hesitated for a long moment before finally lowering the pistol.

Zane looked at Reimer. "As for you, you're going to be confined to your room until we get this sorted out."

Reimer's face reddened. "You can't order me to—"

"I can, and I just did," Zane snapped. "You're lucky I'm making this voluntary."

Reimer opened his mouth to say something then decided against it.

"Now listen carefully to what I'm about to say," Zane continued. "If we find any further evidence against you, or if you violate the restrictions I'm going to put in place, then we'll lock you up under twenty-four-hour guard."

Reimer said nothing.

Zane looked at Cignetti. "Take him up to his room. And make sure to check his person for weapons before leaving him there."

"Roger that."

Once they were gone, Stone came over and set the gun on the table. "Glock 43."

They didn't have the resources to worry about fingerprints, so Zane picked it up. He had shot the 43 many times. The diminutive nine millimeter was a popular concealed-carry weapon. It was easy to hide and very reliable.

"I think you're making a big mistake," Stone said. "You and I both know that man is working for the other side. What more evidence do you need?"

"You may be right, but my gut tells me the guy is just an annoying blowhard." Zane held up the Glock. "Did you find a suppressor?"

Stone shrugged. "No. So what?"

"The mole would have one," Zane said. "There is zero doubt that Hawke was killed with a silenced weapon. If he hadn't used a suppressor, then we all would've woken up."

"Anybody can cobble together a homemade silencer with any number of things, including plastic bottles." Stone crossed his arms. "Besides, he could have hidden the suppressor somewhere else. I'd bet my retirement account that this dude has stuff stashed all over the place."

"As I said, you may be right," Zane said. "It's why I've confined him upstairs. We're going to conduct a detailed search of his room and the entire building, and if we find anything, I'll lock him up."

"This ain't the US judicial system," Stone said. "This is the wild frontier. He should be locked up until proven innocent."

Freja looked at Stone. "You said someone must have left the gun here at the station for Reimer to find when he got here."

Stone nodded. "That's the only thing that makes sense."

She nodded at the pistol. "This is a Glock, which the Russian military doesn't normally use."

"Who said this other group is Russian?" Stone asked. "We could be up against the Chinese. Heck, it could be a private corporation that wants to get its hands on whatever is down there."

Zane and Freja exchanged a glance.

"I think it's time we filled all of you in on something we found in the tunnel," Zane said.

28

AFTER TELLING Amanda and Stone about the discovery of the dead Russian commando, Zane decided it was time to call the entire team together for a meeting. With lives on the line, it was his duty to let them know what dangers they were facing. The only person not invited to the meeting was Lucas Reimer. Zane had briefly considered including him then realized that would be a huge mistake. If Reimer was the mole, he didn't need to know about what they had found, nor did he need to know the team's plans going forward.

Upon learning that her lover had been confined to his room, Morgan Martini continued to proclaim his innocence. She reminded Zane that she and the DARPA officer had spent most of their waking hours together, and she had never seen him do anything hinting at subterfuge. In an attempt to convey a sense of fairness, Zane told her that he and Cignetti would conduct an extensive search of Reimer's room that afternoon. If they found no further evidence of wrongdoing, he might loosen some of the restrictions.

Once the remaining team members had assembled in the dining hall, Zane and Freja gave them a detailed description of the discovery they'd made in the tunnel. They left nothing out, including the horrifying condition of the Russian soldier's body. Up until then, Zane had seen a confident resolve on the faces of the team members. Even after the murder of their two colleagues, there had been a collective resolve that they needed to work together to survive. But after hearing that another body had been disfigured, the first hint of fear began to creep into some of their eyes. They seemed to realize that there were two enemies out there, and one of them was terrifying beyond words.

As Zane monitored the group's fearful reaction, he noticed there was one exception. While Morgan Martini had certainly been alarmed at the news of another mangled corpse, that concern quickly melted away when she learned about the discovery of a large cavern. Like Cignetti, she was convinced it could be the crash site. She insisted that another team be sent down immediately, one that included both herself and Lucas Reimer.

"I think it would be irresponsible to go on some exploratory mission under these circumstances," Sunny said after hearing Martini's suggestion. "If something happens to you, the rest of us will be left to fend for ourselves."

"We aren't going to send everyone down," Martini countered.

"But why even risk a few lives when help should be here soon?" Sunny asked. "Wouldn't it be prudent to wait?"

"I still haven't seen this help everyone keeps talking about." Martini hesitated as if choosing her next words carefully. "I know this is hard for some of you to hear, but Patrick Rider didn't make it. He's dead, and all of you need to deal with that reality."

Sunny fixed her gaze on Zane, begging him to speak up.

"First of all, help will come eventually," he assured them. "Even if Rider didn't make it, we've missed all of the check-ins with DC. That alone will trigger a rescue operation."

Martini shook her head. "Then where are they?"

"First, they would have to mobilize a new team," Zane replied.

"My guess is, that's already been done. At this point, they're probably waiting for the storm to run its course. It would be impossible to fly choppers in this weather. They could probably get here in all-terrain vehicles, but even that would be a treacherous journey."

"So we're going to pass up this opportunity to search for what could be the greatest discovery of our lifetime?" Martini asked.

"No. We do need to go down for another look. First and foremost, I want to make sure there aren't more enemy combatants hiding in the tunnels."

"What about the anomaly?" Martini asked. "We were sent to this station to safeguard whatever technology might exist down there. That means we can't let the Russians find it before we do. Who knows? They may have access already."

While he didn't mention it, Zane was almost certain they didn't need to worry about the enemy beating them to the prize. If the Russians were already in possession of alien technology—assuming it even existed—then they would have already told the mole to cease his or her operations to avoid exposure.

"We'll keep our eyes open for any signs of the anomaly, but the safety of our team will be my priority," Zane said.

"I agree that our security is important," Martini said. "But we were tasked with securing any technology that might be buried in that ice, and we always knew there might be others trying to get to it first. In that sense, nothing has really changed."

"I shouldn't have to remind you that two of our people have been killed, not to mention most of the previous research team is either missing or dead," Zane said. "No one knew we'd be facing such a dire situation."

Martini crossed her arms. "I don't think we can just set aside our primary objective."

"We're not going to," Zane said. "As I said before, we'll keep our eyes open for anything that might be of interest. You have my word on that."

"Then I need to be on the team that goes down there," she insisted. "It's my area of expertise."

"If we determine the ice bridge and cavern are safe, I promise I'll take you down."

"What about Lucas?" Martini asked. "He needs to be there too."

"We'll determine that later," Zane said.

"If there is something important in that cavern, then he doesn't need to be there," Stone said.

"Why not?" Martini glared at Stone. "Oh, that's right. Because you framed him for something he didn't do? I'm starting to think *you're* the one we need to worry about."

Stone stood. "You little bitch. How dare you—"

"Knock it off," Zane said. "I'm not going to tolerate these arguments that do nothing to advance our agenda."

A stifled silence fell over the room.

"Who are you taking down this time?" Christine Pageau finally asked.

"I'm going to take Freja and Rod down again," Zane said. "Only this time, we'll be better equipped."

"I have some experience climbing," Pageau said. "My skills might be useful in getting across that bridge."

Zane looked at Sunny for approval, but she gave him a very subtle shake of the head.

"It's too dangerous," Zane said to Pageau. "Besides, I have some climbing experience myself."

"And I do as well," Cignetti added.

Zane asked if anyone had any questions before adjourning the meeting. He was anxious to start the search of Lucas Reimer's room.

Brady Arnott came toward him as everyone got up to leave. "Do you want me to go down with you in the morning? I feel like I haven't been any help."

"Thanks, but I think we'll be fine. I want you, Amanda, and Vince up here in case something happens."

"If you change your mind, let me know." Arnott started to walk off then turned back again. "Oh, I almost forgot to tell you something. I had some extra time today, so I went through the previous cook's office."

Zane raised an eyebrow. "The cook had an office?"

"He wasn't just the cook. As best I can tell, he was their logistics guy too. He ordered their supplies, that kind of thing. Anyway, as I was going through his filing cabinet, I found a laptop in the bottom drawer. It was underneath the hanging folders, almost like it had been placed there so that no one else would find it."

Zane's brow furrowed. "Was there anything useful on it?"

"Unfortunately, the screen lock is enabled. I was a bit of a computer whiz in high school, so I'm going to see if I can find a way around it. I doubt I'll find anything of value on there, but I guess you never know."

"The fact that he had tucked it away makes me think it might be important." Zane was curious to see the laptop for himself, but he had other more pressing priorities. "Thanks for looking into it for me. Let me know what you find out."

29

Zane, Freja, and Cignetti stood on the near side of the ice bridge, staring across the expanse. Like so many structures in the underground world of Antarctica, it wasn't clear how it had formed. If some ancient explorers had built it, then ice might have gathered on the structure over time.

"It didn't look all that bad from where we were standing the last time," Freja said. "Up close, it looks pretty intimidating."

Zane ran the beam of his light across the bridge's surface. She was right. It would be a dangerous trek, although much of the ice seemed textured enough to walk on. They would simply have to take their time.

Cignetti looked at Freja. "Are you sure you're okay with this?"

"I'm fine. Remember, I'm from Denmark. Danish kids see worse than this going to the bus stop."

Cignetti smiled. "Then we'll let you lead the way."

"As long as we stay away from the edge, I think we can get across without a problem," Zane said.

"Assuming it doesn't get worse," Cignetti said. "We can only see about a third of it."

Zane nodded. "Just remember, we brought our gear for a reason. Use it if you have to."

Fortunately, each Antarctica station was stocked with some basic equipment for traversing the icy terrain or climbing the local mountains. Zane had gathered ice axes and several lengths of strong rope to help them make their way across the bridge. He was particularly glad they had the axes. Those would come in handy if one of them started slipping toward the edge.

Cignetti squatted and pointed his flashlight down at the ice. "Here's the blood I mentioned before."

The cone of light illuminated several small patches of dark-pink crystals clumped together in different spots across the ice bridge, forming a trail.

"It looks like the soldier may have been wounded before crossing the bridge," Freja said.

If Freja was right, the Russian soldier must have been attacked somewhere in the cavern. Wounded and dripping blood, he had fled across the bridge and into the tunnel. Once there, he had been overtaken by his attacker and killed.

While the explanation made sense, Zane still had questions. *How did he survive the first attack?* Zane wondered if his gun had been effective against whatever the threat was. He looked down at the crystals again. Given the nature of his wounds, it seemed like there would be much more blood on the bridge. Something didn't add up, but Zane couldn't yet figure out what it was.

"Are we ready?" Freja asked, pulling Zane out of his thoughts.

Cignetti rose to his feet. "Let's do it."

"I'm guessing the bridge is about a hundred yards long, so take your time," Zane said. "No need to rush."

The sides of the bridge looked slicker than the center, so they decided to walk down the middle in single file. Cignetti went first, followed by Freja. Zane brought up the rear. Each person held their flashlight in one hand and their ice ax in the other.

Zane reminded them to keep low and use the pick as an anchor if they found themselves slipping.

They had only traveled about twenty yards when Cignetti stopped. "Take a look at this."

Freja and Zane came up behind him.

"What is it?" Freja asked.

"The trail of blood goes off to the right," Cignetti said, moving the beam of his light in that direction.

As Cignetti said, the frozen trail of crystals veered away from the center of the bridge. As they approached the right edge, he could see a series of bizarre ruts carved deep into the ice. The marks looked like they had been made by a set of massive claws. Zane shook his head. Maybe the marks were from some large piece of climbing equipment. But again, they *did* look like they belonged to an impossibly large animal.

Freja muttered something in Danish.

Cignetti focused his beam on the marks. "What is that?"

"I have no idea," Freja said.

"Well, we can rule out your theory about our victim in the tunnels dripping blood as he came off the bridge." Cignetti followed the trail of blood crystals from the start of the bridge to the claw marks. "Looks like it was something else's blood, and they retreated toward the cavern, not the other way around."

"It looks like our soldier wounded his attacker," Freja said. "Then the attacker fell off on their way back."

"Or the attacker had the victim's blood on its feet," Zane offered.

Freja looked at him. "*Its* feet?"

Zane used his flashlight beam to highlight the grooves along the edge of the ice. "A human certainly didn't leave those."

Freja shook her head. "There aren't any animals I know of that would make such a mark."

"None that have been recorded," Zane said.

"You think it's some new species?" Cignetti asked.

Zane shrugged. "Every year, we hear about the discovery of new plants and animals in more temperate zones. Why not down here?"

The three stood in silence, shaken by the possibility that there was a new species of predator prowling in the dark network of tunnels. Even though Zane had proposed the theory, he wasn't sure it made sense from a biological standpoint. He didn't think there were any food sources to sustain a large predator down there. The only food was on the surface, and that was limited to a few pelagic birds and penguins. He kept sorting through the different possibilities until Freja pulled him out of his thoughts.

"Zane." Her voice was urgent.

He looked up to find her standing perfectly still, her gaze fixed on him. There was fear in her eyes.

"Something wrong?" Zane asked.

"I'm..." was all she could manage to say.

"She's slipping!" Cignetti said.

Zane looked down to see her feet sliding toward the side of the bridge as if drawn by some unseen force. It was like watching someone on a moving walkway in an airport, only in slow motion.

"I need help," she said, her voice frantic.

"Crouch down." Zane tried to keep his voice even. "Drive your pick into the ice."

Freja kept her eyes locked on him. "I don't think I can."

"You can do it. Just go slow and easy."

While the bridge looked flat, Zane could see then that it was sloped slightly in that section. The surface of the ice was also smoother than before. It was almost like trying to stand on top of a giant ice cube.

Freja started to lower into a crouched position. "I'm falling."

Realizing he needed to act, Zane moved slightly toward her. As he did, he noticed his boots were sliding as well. His heart beating faster, he raised his pick and slammed it down against the surface of the bridge. The sharp blade buried deep into the ice, steadying him.

He reached out with his free hand. "Grab me."

"Zane, I—"

"Grab it!" he shouted.

She reached out, their hands clasping. Zane had felt somewhat stable before, but her additional weight was now pulling him in her direction. If his anchor didn't hold, then they would both go over the edge. They needed an additional anchor.

"Use your ax, Freja!"

She lifted it, but doing so caused her body to tilt awkwardly. As she began to fall, she swung the pick in a downward arc. The position of her body caused the blade to hit at a bad angle, which prevented it from digging into the ice.

Zane's heart raced as both began to slide toward the edge. Then he saw movement in his peripheral vision. Another hand reached out and clasped Freja's wrist. *Cignetti.*

With both of their anchors in place, the men were able to begin the process of pulling Freja to a safer spot. Zane's muscles burned as he held the anchor with one hand while pulling her with the other. Times like this made him thankful for spending all those hours in the gym. Someone with lesser strength would have never been able to pull it off.

Soon, the three of them were back on the flat portion of the ice bridge. The three were then able to catch their breaths minutes before finally making their way to the safest part in the center.

"Well, that was fun," Freja said.

"You want to rest for a few more minutes?" Zane asked.

She shook her head. "No. If I sit here and think about what happened, the fear will set in. I'm not going to let that happen."

Cignetti smiled. "That's my kind of lady."

30

MUCH TO THEIR RELIEF, the rest of the journey across the bridge was uneventful. As it turned out, where Freja had nearly fallen was the most precarious spot. The rest of the bridge was relatively flat and worn, like a frozen road that had been driven over for several days.

After making it to the other side, the three stopped to take in their surroundings. The scene was awe inspiring. The cavernous space seemed to go on forever. Their flashlights danced over hundreds of glittering ice columns rising from the cavern floor, their sizes ranging from a few feet wide to as much as twenty.

"It looks like we stepped onto the surface of another planet," Freja said.

Cignetti pointed his flashlight toward the columns closest to them, which were darker than the rest. "What are those?"

"Stalagmites," Zane said. "At first, I thought they were all made of ice, but some must be minerals."

"How do we even search a place this large?" Freja asked.

"I say we choose one side and take it around the circumference of the space," Cignetti said.

Zane swept his beam to the right, which seemed to be the side they were closer to. The towering cavern wall loomed at the periphery of the light. "Let's start over there."

They were on a slight rise, so the three made their way carefully to the bottom. Once there, they turned right and walked past the first row of the stalagmites. All of them were twisted into oddly shaped forms that looked like ghoulish sentinels.

"*Jord*," Freja said as they continued on.

Zane looked at her. "Your what?"

She laughed. "No, *jord*. I don't know the exact word in English. There's some dirt here."

Zane looked down. As she had indicated, the surface they were walking on was a strange mixture of ice, rocks, and soil. "I did a little reading about the Earth's crust here in Antarctica," he said. "There is a top layer of ice, and under that is terra firma. We're probably in the transitioning between the two."

After reaching the perimeter, they turned and followed the wall left. Unlike the cavern floor, the walls looked like they were solid ice with the occasional stone or boulder mixed in. There were also a number of openings in the wall, from small fissures to large gaps. Some appeared to be the entrances to small tunnels.

"Sound carries extremely well in here, so at least we'll know if something is coming toward us," Cignetti said.

"That's a pleasant thought," Freja said. "It's always nice to know when you're about to be killed."

"If predators were hunting down here, I think we'd know about it by now," Zane said.

They continued until they reached the other end of the cavern. Although there was no way to measure how far they had traveled, Zane guessed it was at least half a mile long, maybe more. The three then marched across the back wall and turned left at the corner, which took them back in the direction of the ice bridge.

Almost immediately, Zane noticed that this side of the cavern was different. The ceiling was lower here, and it was broken and fractured in places. If a spaceship had crashed down, then this was the more likely place to find it. Even so, Zane hadn't seen anything that suggested the presence of a craft. There were no pieces of debris, nor were there any ship fragments sticking out of the ice. Just a field of stalagmites surrounded by ice.

Five minutes later, Cignetti came to a halt and ran his flashlight over the wall to their right.

"See something?" Freja asked.

He stared at one particular spot on the wall. "Yes and no."

"I don't understand," she said.

The SEAL leaned close to the ice and turned his head, putting his cheek against the wall as he pointed his light down the length of the wall. It was almost like he was looking for some sort of imperfection on the surface.

A few seconds later, he pulled back. "Take a look, and tell me what you see."

Confused, Zane stepped forward and pressed his face against the wall's surface. Like Cignetti, he directed his beam down its length. After studying the view for a few seconds, he stood up straight again.

"Well?" Cignetti asked.

"All I see is a flat sheet of ice," Zane answered.

"Precisely."

"You're going to have to cut to the chase," Zane said.

"It's too flat, almost like a piece of sheet metal," Cignetti explained. "I've studied the sides of this cavern the entire time. There is no other section like this one."

The more he thought about it, the more Zane realized the SEAL was right. The wall had been curvy and grooved everywhere else. But along this stretch, it was as smooth as Sheetrock.

Zane nodded. "I see what you mean, although I'm not sure what the significance is."

"It's not just in one spot." Cignetti waved his beam back and forth. "This entire section is as flat as a pancake."

"In a place with this many natural formations, you're going to run into a lot of odd shapes, but you're also going to find some flat surfaces," Freja said. "It would be like me going to a park near my home in Copenhagen. You'd find some weird-looking icicles, but you'd also find a flat sheet of ice on the lake."

"You're making my point," Cignetti said. "You'd expect to find flat ice on the surface of something that's already flat, like a lake, a driveway, or the roof of a car. This is a vertical wall."

"So you're saying that there is something flat behind this wall?" she asked.

He nodded. "I think it's possible."

Zane unhooked his ice ax. "Well, there is only one way to find out."

Cignetti pulled his equipment out as well. In moments, the two began hacking away at the wall's frozen surface. Unlike an ice cube, the ice here was opaque and granular like the frost that lined the sides of an old freezer.

A half minute later, Zane's adze chopped off a large chunk of ice, exposing another flat surface, which was also white. He tapped it once with the handle, which produced a distinct echo. *Metal.*

The three looked at one another, startled by the familiar noise.

Cignetti leaned in and brushed the flat white surface with a gloved hand.

"Oh, my." Freja's hand moved to her mouth.

Zane followed her gaze. "What?"

"His glove," she said. "Look at what happens when he moves it around."

"She's right," Cignetti said, his voice tingling with excitement.

When Zane couldn't tell what they were talking about, Freja invited him to where she was standing. He went to her side and fixed his gaze on the wall.

"Okay, do it again," Freja said.

The SEAL reached out and ran his hand across the wall. As he did, the metal surface under the glove turned from white to the same gray as his glove.

Hit with a thought, Zane placed the ax handle against the surface. Almost immediately, the metal transitioned to black.

"Camouflage," Cignetti said. "This thing, whatever it is, has the ability to change its outer skin to match its surroundings."

"This is beyond human technology," Freja said. "We found the alien ship."

31

ALTHOUGH HE WOULDN'T HAVE DESCRIBED himself as one of them, Brady Arnott had been known as the ultimate geek in high school. Prior to discovering a love for culinary arts, he had immersed himself in technology. He was an avid gamer and the guy everybody went to when their phone or PC needed to be fixed. He had even learned how to hack into private servers, which was something he didn't advertise a lot.

With those skills, getting through a lock screen on a PC was like taking candy from a baby. It only took Brady twenty minutes to get into the laptop of his predecessor, a man named Daniel Rasmussen.

With the device now at his disposal, Brady thought about where to begin his search. There was no way to send data from Ellsworth, so it wouldn't do any good to look through the cook's emails, direct messages, or social media posts. Instead, he started on the folders stored on the device. Although a long shot, he hoped to find something like a diary. The laptop had been hidden in the filing cabinet, which could be an indication Rasmussen had taken some private notes.

Unfortunately, Brady found nothing of value. From the documents on the local drive, he learned the names of the team before, as well as the recipes they preferred. All of the notes on them were ones any cook might have. A thorough man, Rasmussen had even kept a list of the various foods the researchers were allergic to.

Next, Brady began going through Rasmussen's photographs. Not only did the man love to take pictures, but he'd been meticulous in the way he'd organized them. Every single image was saved to a specific folder with a descriptive label. Interestingly, he found one file labeled "Monique." It contained several dozen photographs of one of the female astronomers, and most appeared to have been taken without her knowledge. *What a creep.*

He also found a folder labeled "Farewell Party." It had been created fairly recently, dated about a month before Operation Whiteout began. After opening it, he discovered fifty-six images and three videos. As best as he could tell, the multimedia files documented a party that had been thrown to celebrate the end of the astronomers' stay in Antarctica.

Brady started with the videos. The first two were filmed by Rasmussen as he walked around the dining hall, asking the party attendees if they liked the various food items that had been served. It was clear that most of the team had been drunk, as the conversations often ventured toward racy topics or silly nonsense.

When Brady double-clicked on the third video, he realized it was slightly more serious than the previous two. It appeared to show a ceremony that had been held at the end of the party. Lead astronomer Kristoff Pettersson asked each of the scientists to share a little bit about their time at Ellsworth Station. He encouraged them to relay a few funny stories, but he also wanted them to tell how the research might change the future course of their careers.

About midway through the video, Pettersson introduced one

of the female researchers then asked her to come up. As the others applauded, the woman stood and walked to the front.

A frown tugged at the corners of Brady's mouth as he watched her join Pettersson. For a moment, Brady assumed he must have misunderstood what Petterson had said. Confused, he rewound the footage and played it again.

A chill ran down Brady's spine. *Impossible.*

His heart beating faster, he wondered what he should do with the information he possessed. Zane and the others weren't due back for a few hours, so at that point, there wasn't much he could do. His gut told him not to trust anyone but Zane. There could be some kind of conspiracy going on. Since he was currently in the previous cook's office, it would probably be best just to hang out there until the team returned. Then and only then would he share the shocking contents of the video.

He closed the laptop and took off his headphones. Immediately, he sensed a presence in the room. Someone must've followed him to the room and managed to slip inside while he was going through the files.

He stood and slowly turned around. A figure was at the door, their face just outside the glow of the lamp.

"Who's there?" Brady asked, even though he thought he already knew the answer.

The person stepped into the circle of light, their face now visible. A gloved hand came up holding a black pistol tipped with a silencer.

Brady tried to think of something to say that might get him out of the situation alive. But he knew that it would be an act of futility. He had discovered the truth, and the person standing inside the door wasn't about to let him live.

Two muffled pops sounded in the room, and Brady felt the coldness of death overtake him.

32

AFTER RETURNING TO THE STATION, Zane scheduled a mandatory meeting in the dining hall. The only ones not in attendance were Lucas Reimer and Brady Arnott. Reimer was still confined to his quarters, and Zane couldn't find the chef in any of the rooms on the first floor. Zane wasn't overly concerned about Arnott. He had probably chosen to work on the laptop in a place he wouldn't be seen upstairs or perhaps in the garage.

Once everyone else had assembled, Zane and Freja gave a detailed briefing of their trip to the cavern. That time, Zane kept nothing from the group. They told the team about the discovery of what appeared to be claw marks on the ice bridge, though they did stress that the grooves could have come from climbing equipment.

Then, like two professors unveiling the results of a very important research paper, the operatives shared Cignetti's discovery of the strange metallic surface on the cavern wall. They described how the material had changed color to match its surroundings, a built-in camouflaging feature that had presumably allowed it to escape detection.

Once they were finished, a stunned silence fell over the room.

Zane surveyed the faces staring back at him. Most didn't seem to know what to say. It was one thing to hear about some anomaly in the abstract. It was another to have it confirmed by eyewitnesses.

Martini finally broke the silence, her lips quivering with excitement. "I can't believe it. It's the ship. We found the ship."

"Let's not get ahead of ourselves," Zane said. "We still can't rule out some secret test flight conducted by the Russian or Chinese governments or even a private company."

She shook her head. "It's too far under the surface, and that sort of technology doesn't exist yet on our planet."

"How can you be so sure?" Pageau asked.

"Our intelligence community monitors these things," Martini replied. "And while we don't have as many human assets as we'd like, we *do* have the best electronic surveillance in the world. If something like this was in the works, we'd know about it."

"I think she's right," Cignetti said from his seat. "That craft is buried deep in the ice. That means we can be pretty certain it's been there for at least a couple of decades and probably much longer than that."

Martini nodded. "And this isn't the sort of technology that could have been developed in the seventies or eighties."

The room went quiet again as each person digested what they had just heard. Although Morgan had made some good points, Zane still didn't think they could rule out technology developed by a foreign power. Just because the ship was far beneath the ice didn't mean it had been there for decades.

"There is something else we need to mention," Zane finally said. "There is a large mound of rocks along the same wall as the metal plate. We believe those rocks were pushed up when the ship crash-landed."

"Think about how tough the ship's exterior must be," Cignetti said. "If this had been your typical commercial aircraft, the nose of the plane would collapse on impact and explode in flames.

When this one came down, its nose cut into the ground like a spear piercing soft soil."

"Which explains the rock getting churned up," Amanda said.

Freja nodded. "And why the ship came to rest so deep underneath the surface."

"So is it safe to assume the section you found was probably the rear of the craft?" Amanda asked.

"That's what I'm thinking," Cignetti said.

"You told us that only about thirty or forty feet of the exterior was exposed. If that's the case, it's unlikely we'll be able to get inside."

"It's too early to say," Cignetti replied. "We'd certainly like to look around that rock pile. Unfortunately, we all started to get short of breath. While I don't think we were in danger of passing out, the low oxygen levels down there make it difficult to work for very long. On this trip, we wandered around the perimeter of the cavern. The next time, we'll go straight to the site."

Zane looked at Stone. "We'd like to cut out a section of that camouflaged exterior. If nothing else, at least we can take that back to be studied. Any chance we can make that happen with the tools we have?"

"At a minimum, we'd need a power saw to cut through something like that," Stone said. "But I'll see what I can find."

"This was a crash landing, so maybe we'll find some pieces that broke off," Zane said.

"Other than the dead soldier, was there any sign of human activity down there?" Amanda asked.

Zane shook his head. "No, although I must admit, we stopped looking after we found the exposed metal."

"The entire Russian team could've been taken out by whatever killed that soldier, but we can't assume that," Freja added.

"It's hard to understand how large that place is unless you go down there yourself," Cignetti said. "We're talking half a dozen or more football fields. On top of that, there is a sea of stalagmites.

A whole platoon of commandos could hide in there, and we probably wouldn't know it unless we conducted a grid search."

"That's not comforting," Amanda said.

Zane took a sip of his water then set the bottle down. "Everything Rod said is true, but I honestly don't think anyone else is down there. At least, not at the moment."

"So what *did* kill that soldier?" Stone asked.

Zane and Cignetti exchanged a glance. Zane knew it was a question that would come up, but despite their efforts, they didn't have an answer beyond speculations.

Freja was the first to reply. "We don't know, but I have my own theory."

Stone frowned. "And what is that?"

"I think something came off of that ship."

A wave of chatter went through the group as they discussed the likelihood that something had survived the crash then escaped into the tunnels. Despite the chilling possibilities, Zane didn't see fear on the faces around him. The team had been hardened by the sight of the mangled astronomer, and there seemed to be a common resolve to get to the bottom of his death, even if it meant facing that same threat themselves.

"So you're saying whatever killed that man is still down there somewhere?" Stone's voice carried over the others.

"Remember those marks we saw on the bridge?" Zane replied. "We think it's a sign this thing—whatever it is—went over the edge. And if it did fall off, there is no way it survived."

"Couldn't there be more than one?" Stone asked.

Zane nodded. "There could, but we saw no signs of life down there of any kind."

"I need to be on the next team that goes down," Martini said, pressing the issue. "And Lucas too."

Zane frowned. "I'm not so sure he—"

"Lucas *has* to be there. Technology is his area of expertise."

Zane would need to think about that. While he and Cignetti

hadn't found any incriminating evidence in Reimer's room, the idea of letting the man participate in an excursion that could reveal technological secrets currently seemed a bridge too far.

Seeing his hesitation, Freja leaned in close and whispered, "I understand your concerns, but I think we can make it work. He won't be armed, and we can make sure he doesn't have access to any samples we collect."

Zane considered her remark. It was a fair point. Without a weapon, Reimer wouldn't be a threat to the group. And while he'd be able to see the craft, any samples he might collect could be confiscated until he was completely cleared of wrongdoing.

He turned to Martini. "Okay, we'll bring him along. But we're going to do it my way. He'll have some restrictions."

She nodded. "I understand. I don't think you'll regret having him with us. Lucas is a treasure trove of knowledge when it comes to these things."

Zane checked his watch. It was already six o'clock, so he brought the meeting to a close. He had asked Arnott to prepare something that morning in case the work on the laptop carried into the evening, so pans of lasagna were waiting in the fridge. He told everyone to help themselves.

Aside from the anomaly, that device was a top priority. Although it might not contain anything useful, Zane hoped to at least get some indication of what had happened just before their arrival. Perhaps some of the astronomers had set out for one of the other stations. Or maybe they were hiding somewhere in the tunnels. Unfortunately, Pageau's memory was still foggy. He'd have to wait to hear back from Arnott for more clues.

As the team got up to leave, Zane wondered if he had made the right decision about Reimer. While he still had a hard time believing the DARPA scientist was a mole, he also couldn't rule it out. At this point, only time would reveal the truth.

33

THE NEXT MORNING, Zane led a six-person team down to the crash site. He, Freja, and Cignetti were joined by Morgan Martini, Lucas Reimer, and Vince Stone. Martini and Reimer were brought along for their extraterrestrial expertise, while Stone was placed in charge of taking photographs and collecting samples. Even if they weren't able to obtain a piece of the ship's metallic exterior, they would at least obtain video documentation of how it worked.

Once again, Zane asked Amanda to remain at the station. She wasn't happy about being excluded, but she recognized the importance of having at least one operative on the surface. Zane promised to include her if a third trip was organized.

After making their way across the ice bridge, the group went straight to the area where the ship's exterior was exposed in the cavern wall. Martini and Reimer wanted to see the camouflaging tech in action, and Zane wanted to document it on film. Once again, Cignetti placed various objects against the metal, and the skin transitioned to a matching color. Martini and Reimer marveled at the metal's ability to adjust to its surroundings in the blink of an eye. The only time the artificial intelligence seemed to get confused was when several objects of diverse pigmentation were placed on the surface. In that case, the metal would default to a medium gray.

Unfortunately, Stone had been unable to find a tool that would cut the substance, which meant they would be unable to collect a sample. But even if they did have a saw or some other tool, Zane doubted it would work on the ship. If extraterrestrials could develop a substance with camouflaging technology, then it was almost certain they had also made it impenetrable.

After spending an hour studying the metallic substance, the group began the tedious task of searching the mound of rocks a short distance away. Zane hoped to find an opening in the debris that would give them access to other parts of the ship. If the ship was damaged, then they might even be able to get inside. As far as Zane was concerned, that would be the ultimate victory. Untold technological advancements might be hidden onboard.

The sheer size of the cavern was the biggest obstacle. The area near the ship was almost half the size of a sports arena, with around a thousand rocks and boulders stacked almost to the ceiling. Searching them all would drain them physically, particularly in light of the limited oxygen in the cavern.

It was decided that Zane, Freja, and Cignetti would climb to the top of the stone pile and search the area closest to the ceiling. If they found nothing there, they would slowly make their way down. Meanwhile, Stone, Martini, and Reimer would begin at the bottom and work their way up.

Zane gave everyone a few final instructions then began his ascent. He took his time, being careful to step on rocks that looked like they were firmly in place. The last thing he needed was to take a nasty fall and hit his head or twist an ankle.

After reaching the top, he turned and looked back down. He almost wished he hadn't. While he wasn't particularly bothered by heights, the distance from the cavern floor was unsettling.

One slip would have sent him bouncing off unforgiving surfaces and jagged edges.

Setting his sudden fear aside, the operative got to work. He used one hand to steady himself while the other directed his flashlight beam into every nook and cranny. He was certain there had to be a way to get through to the ship. Whatever had killed the Russian commando had attempted to flee back across the ice bridge. Its direction indicated that it had come out of the ship.

"I found something!"

The distant shout pulled Zane out of his thoughts. *Cignetti.* About fifty yards away, the SEAL was waving his flashlight beam back and forth to get everyone's attention. There had been an urgency to his voice that suggested he might have uncovered the path they were looking for.

"Coming," Zane called out.

He could also see Stone, Martini, and Reimer making their way up the slope.

As Zane began moving in Cignetti's direction, he tried to suppress his excitement. Even if they had found a way through the debris, that didn't mean they would have access to the interior of the ship. Realistically, it might take days before they finally found a way to get inside.

Freja had already arrived when Zane got there. Reimer and the others arrived soon after that.

"So what did you find?" Freja asked.

Cignetti directed the beam of his flashlight into a narrow gap between two large boulders. Zane came alongside him for a better look. Just past the gap, a passageway ran downward at a forty-five-degree angle, ending at a point about twenty feet away.

Freja looked at Cignetti. "Have you been in?"

Cignetti nodded. "I just got back. That passageway takes a sharp turn to the right then runs for another twenty or thirty feet. I thought it was a dead end until I went all the way down.

There was another exposed section of the ship's exterior at my feet."

"That's all good," Martini said. "But we've already found an exposed section of the ship's skin."

"That's not the only thing I found. There is an opening in the armor, and it's big enough for us to get through."

Reimer made an excited sound in his throat.

"So you could see inside the ship?" Stone asked.

"Yes, but I wasn't exactly sure what I was looking at. A corridor maybe?"

"Well, what are we waiting for?" Reimer asked. "Let's go."

Cignetti and Zane exchanged a meaningful glance. Both men had seen the two mangled bodies and knew that whatever had ripped them apart had likely come out of the ship.

"We'll go in," Zane finally said, his eyes moving from face to face. "But hear me loud and clear. If I deem it's too dangerous to continue, we're all coming out. No exceptions."

Stone nodded. "You won't have to tell me twice."

Zane set his gaze on Reimer. "That's especially true for you. Disobey my orders, and you'll be placed in protective custody."

After some hesitation, Reimer nodded.

"The crevice is tight, so we'll have to go down single file," Cignetti said.

With that, he entered the gap, with Zane right behind him. Stone, Martini, and Reimer followed the operative in, with Freja bringing up the rear. As Zane squeezed into the passageway, he realized the route through the debris was going to be more uncomfortable than he thought. Angular rocks jutted out from the floor, many of which had sharp edges. After reaching the bottom, they went right at the turn and followed Cignetti to the end.

The SEAL crouched and directed the beam of his flashlight toward the floor, illuminating a section of the craft's exterior. Based on what they had been told, Zane had expected to see a tear that had been caused by the crash. Instead, he saw a square opening that looked like it had been placed there on purpose.

"It's a hatch," Martini said.

"Can you see anything?" Freja asked as she came up from the back.

Cignetti sat on the edge of the opening, his feet dangling into the gap. "I'll drop inside and have a look around."

"Want me to lower you down?" Zane asked.

"It's not far. I'll be fine." Cignetti put his flashlight in his coat pocket then slid the rifle over his shoulder and offered it to Zane. "But you can hold this."

The operative took it from him.

"I'll also need some light," Cignetti said.

Using his free hand, Zane directed his flashlight through the opening. Although he couldn't see much, he could tell that the floor in the corridor below was a dark gray.

While holding onto the edge of the opening, Cignetti lowered his legs through the hatch and dangled for a couple of seconds before finally letting go. After landing, he pulled out his flashlight and swung it in both directions. "All clear."

Zane passed the SEAL his rifle, maneuvered into position, then dropped into the corridor below. The floor covering was surprisingly soft yet firm enough to provide support.

Once everyone came down, Zane aimed his beam down the corridor. Arches of dark metal punctuated the passageway at regular intervals. He wasn't sure what he had expected, but the ship's interior—at least that part of it—seemed rather mundane.

Stone pulled out his camera and went to work taking photographs. Reimer and Martini bent down and used their fingers to push on the soft floor covering.

"I guess this is what we have to look forward to in the future," Martini said.

"It feels sort of like epoxy," Reimer said before standing up.

"Which way do we go?" Stone asked.

Cignetti pointed his flashlight to the left. "Not that way."

Zane followed his gaze. About twenty yards away, the corridor ended in a pile of rock, rubble, and debris.

"If that's the front of the ship, then it's probably been flattened like a pancake," Stone said.

"Even extraterrestrials can't build ships able to withstand the Earth's crust," Martini said.

Left with no other options, the group began walking in the opposite direction, which Zane believed was toward the rear of the ship. As they passed under each arch, it glowed a soft green. It reminded Zane of the lights that came on when he walked through the freezer section of a grocery store.

Although it was difficult to tell under the layers of clothing, Zane believed the ship's interior was slightly warmer than the cavern. The higher temperature could be due to an advanced heating mechanism, or it might simply feel warmer due to the lack of a draft inside.

"Giant night lights," Stone said.

"Either the ship still has power, or it's some sort of stored solar energy," Reimer said.

As they continued, other passageways opened on their left. Since they likely led toward the ship's interior, Zane turned left into the next one they came to.

Immediately, Reimer and Freja began to cough.

"There is some kind of chemical in here." Stone attempted to wave the haze away from his face.

"Well, we know it's not from the crash," Martini said. "This ship has probably been down here for decades, if not centuries."

Zane frowned and sniffed at the faint odor in the air. It smelled chemical but unlike anything he had ever encountered before. Maybe something had spilled during the crash. If so, he found it odd that it would linger for so long.

A minute later, the hall opened into a larger space. Zane suddenly found himself standing on a grated metal catwalk suspended in the air. As best as he could tell, the walkway stretched across a massive wall overlooking a huge bay.

The others soon joined him, pointing the beams out over the catwalk's railing.

After taking in the view, Morgan Martini put her hand to her mouth.

34

AMANDA HURRIED down the darkened stairs. She wanted to check on Brady Arnott. Zane had told her that Arnott was working on a way to get into the previous cook's laptop. Although boredom had played a role in her decision to go looking for Arnott, she was genuinely curious about what the laptop might contain. It had been hidden away, which could mean it held secrets that might finally shed light on what had happened in the days leading up to their arrival.

After making it to the first floor, Amanda entered the hall to her left. She wasn't sure where the previous cook's office was, but she believed it was on that side of the building. She would just have to look around until she found it.

She had just started moving down the corridor when the distant sound of footfalls reached her ears. They were soft and stealthy like the footsteps of someone who didn't want to be heard.

She stopped. "Brady?"

There was a brief shuffling then silence. A confused frown tugged at the sides of Amanda's mouth. Surely, the person had heard her call out. She thought about pulling out her flashlight, but her instincts told her not to.

"Brady, is that you?"

Once again, there was no response.

She waited, her eyes straining to see who or what might be out there. She didn't see any movement, but she did see a faint bar of light spilling from underneath a door on the left. Was someone in there?

Sensing something was off, Amanda drew her pistol and stepped to the door. It would be embarrassing if Arnott was inside, but she wasn't going to take any chances. Better to be laughed at than be ambushed.

Reaching out with her left hand, she turned the knob slowly. Once she was sure the bolt had disengaged, she yanked the door open and entered with her gun raised.

A single lamp glowed on a nearby desk, revealing a tidy office with no one inside.

Nothing. Exhaling, she put the gun away then closed the door behind her. She didn't see a laptop on the desk, so perhaps it was Arnott she had heard out in the hall. Maybe he'd had his headphones on. She had seen him wearing them while cooking.

As Amanda stood at the door, the distinct smell of cleaning solution filled her nostrils. Inhaling deeply, she realized it was coming from the floor. Crouching, she saw the faint gleam of moisture on the tiled surface.

Goosebumps spread across her arm. Someone had been wiping the floor.

A series of facts flashed through her mind in quick succession. A locked laptop hidden in a filing cabinet. Arnott's absence. The footsteps in the hall. Suddenly, she realized what had likely happened. Somehow, the mole had learned that Arnott had discovered the laptop and its possible secrets. According to Zane, Arnott had first told him about it after their last group meeting in the dining hall. Amanda wondered if the mole had overheard the two of them talking.

She considered her next move. If she hurried, she might be able to catch up with whoever she had heard earlier. Besides her, there were only three others in the building—Brady Arnott, Christine Pageau, and Sunny Lee. Arnott was probably dead, which left only two suspects.

Sunny Lee. Amanda found it hard to believe that Sunny could be the killer, and yet it was Sunny who had suggested they room together. The nurse could've been angling to get close to a member of the security team. A sick feeling twisted Amanda's stomach. *Did she make the whole thing up about being a Christian to get me to let my guard down?*

Amanda pushed the thought aside for the moment. Though Christine Pageau had been trapped in the vent when they'd arrived, she couldn't immediately rule her out. First, Amanda needed to find the two women. Once she did, she might be able to study their reactions and figure out who was guilty.

As she turned toward the door, she noticed something sticking out from underneath a bookcase. It looked like one corner of a picture frame. It looked out of place in an office that seemed so neat and organized.

She crouched and pulled the frame out. Inside was a posed photograph of seven people standing on a manicured lawn. Based on the architecture of the buildings in the background, it looked like the picture had been taken on a university campus.

"Seven people," Amanda whispered to herself.

Seven was the number of astronomers who had been stationed at Ellsworth.

Her gaze went to the bottom of the photograph, where a month and year were printed. As best she could recall, the date would have been just before the astronomers had been sent down to Ellsworth.

Amanda scanned the faces in the picture. Something didn't

seem right, so she went through them again, this time more carefully. She noted their hair, their features, and their height in comparison to the others.

Suddenly, her blood ran cold.

Someone was missing from the picture.

35

THE TEAM STOOD in stunned silence as they took in the breathtaking view. The catwalk on which they stood was positioned along the high wall of a chamber so large that their flashlight beams just barely touched the other side. It felt more like a building than it did a spaceship.

Zane had studied hundreds of UFO reports over the years, and one came to mind in that moment—the Phoenix Lights incident. Twenty-five years ago, photographs and film footage of the phenomenon poured in, showing a triangle of lights that hovered over several cities across the southwestern United States. The distance between each light suggested a craft of gargantuan size. Some reports had called the ship a floating city.

A natural skeptic, Zane had initially assumed the size of the famous UFO had either been distorted by camera angles or manipulated by software. But he'd eventually come to believe the craft was every bit as large as the witnesses had said it was. After all, hundreds of people had seen and photographed the lights, and it would be absurd to think that they had all conspired to doctor the images.

Zane wondered if his team had uncovered the same type of

spacecraft as the one documented in Phoenix. Due to its size, perhaps they were standing inside the mother ship of a larger fleet. If it was, then the room they were in was probably a hangar for smaller craft—the discs and cigar-shaped UFOs that had often been seen dipping in and out of sight.

"What the hell is that?" Stone asked, his flashlight pointed downward.

Zane leaned over the rail. Directly below them, half a dozen metal catwalks were attached to the wall at regular intervals. Each one probably corresponded to a different deck level of the ship. At the very bottom, a thick layer of fog floated in the air, masking the floor. It was an eerie sight.

"I guess we know where the haze came from," Cignetti said.

Reimer pointed. "There is some sort of apparatus down there."

Martini leaned farther over the rail. "Where?"

"To the left."

As Zane continued to watch, he was eventually able to make out a few light-green disks in the swirling fog. Each one seemed to be attached to a long pipe that ran from left to right. His curiosity piqued, Zane let his flashlight run toward the center of the room. It was then he realized there were numerous rows of piping.

Stone turned to Reimer. "You're supposed to be the expert. Want to tell us what we're looking at?"

The DARPA scientist shook his head. "From up here, your guess is as good as mine. We're at the back of the ship, so maybe it's the engine room."

"So we agree to let you come with us, but now you're saying you don't have a clue what we're looking at?" Stone looked at Zane. "What's he even doing here?"

"In case you didn't know, no one has ever documented the interior of an extraterrestrial craft," Reimer said, his voice tinged with anger. "Once we go down, I'll examine any—"

Stone stepped up to him, their noses almost touching. "Then I repeat, if you can't tell us anything about this ship, then why exactly are you here?"

Cignetti stepped forward and put a hand on Stone's chest.

"That's enough," Zane said.

Stone glared at Reimer then slowly stepped back.

"Lucas, you said we were at the back of the ship," Freja noted. "What makes you think that?"

"Because we traveled in the opposite direction of the collapsed area," Reimer said.

"If I had to guess, I'd say the ship's bridge was completely destroyed," Martini said. "That could mean there were no survivors."

Cignetti ran his flashlight over the piping. "You have technology that can take you from one galaxy to another, then your ship crash-lands like an old jalopy."

"As a mechanic, I can tell you that no technology is foolproof," Stone said. "If you build something, it can break."

"It didn't have to be a malfunction of the technology," Martini explained. "Any number of things could have brought this ship down. It's possible they were attacked by a competing group of extraterrestrials. Or the ship could have been hit by a meteorite after entering Earth's atmosphere."

Zane looked at Freja, who had been silent the entire time. "See something?"

She shook her head. "Just trying to figure out what those circles are."

"We'll never figure it out from up here," Zane said. "I think it's time we go down."

"Agreed," Reimer said.

Zane realized it might've been the first time the researcher had ever agreed with him.

"I'm a little concerned about that fog," Cignetti said. "We don't know what it is, and the fumes could be harmful."

"Since we're not dead yet, I'm assuming it isn't toxic." Zane shrugged. "That said, we do need to be careful. If any of you experiences respiratory problems, let me know right away, and we'll evacuate."

After getting nods of understanding, Zane turned and led the group down the grated walkway. Fortunately, there was a set of stairs close by, which they descended single file. Cignetti went first, his rifle up and ready. The steps zigzagged back and forth between the different levels like a fire escape at the back of an old building.

Once they arrived at the bottom, Cignetti led the group slowly through the haze. Zane didn't like the fact that their visibility was limited, but there was no way around it. If they wanted to examine the bay's contents, then they were going to have to take a risk.

Seconds later, a large object materialized in the haze. The green disks they had seen from above were actually the top of a long tubular structure that was suspended in the air. A small metal pipe connected each tube to the larger pipe that ran from one end of the room to another.

"What the hell…?" Cignetti muttered.

"This isn't the engine room," Reimer said.

As they came closer, more details began to emerge. The tubes were made primarily of metal, with one glass window about two-thirds of the way up. The entire structure was large, perhaps twelve feet high and about four feet wide.

Cignetti ran his light to the left. "There's a whole row of these things, and they're all connected to the main pipe."

Zane kept his gaze on the closest one. The bottom of the window was at eye level. He guessed it had been put there to allow the user to monitor what was inside. Zane wasn't sure he wanted to find out what that might be.

Stone approached the nearest tube and trained his flashlight beam on the window. "Look at that."

Zane came alongside him, his gaze fixed on the glass. A milky fog swirled behind it. It looked a little like the fog in the room, although much thicker. There was also a thin film of moisture on the inside of the glass, indicating the fog was some kind of liquefying gas.

Cignetti looked at Reimer. "What are we looking at?"

The DARPA scientist took a step closer. "It looks like some kind of chemical processing unit, but to be honest, I don't have a clue."

"There's a handle." Cignetti pointed along part of the contraption. "I think the whole side of this thing is a door."

Zane ran his beam across the unit. As the SEAL had noted, the entire side of the tube facing them was constructed like the door of a car. The glass window made up the top half of the door, with a metal plate below constituting the other half.

"It has a handle," Stone said.

"I don't recommend opening it," Freja said.

Martini stepped forward and put her hand on the tube. "At first, I thought these might be used to store the fuel that runs the ship, but now I'm not so sure." She hesitated as if unsure how much she should say. "But the more I think about it, the more it seems like some kind of vessel—"

Before she could finish, something dark moved on the other side of the glass.

Freja stepped back, and Cignetti lifted his rifle.

As they watched, a scaly limb pressed against the glass for a brief second then disappeared. Zane wondered if the creature had somehow sensed Martini's touch.

"That thing is alive," Stone said.

"As I was saying, I think these are specimens of some kind," Martini said.

Zane looked at her. "Specimens?"

She nodded. "It's possible this ship was used for biological research, which means these containers may house species they picked up in other parts of the galaxy. Isn't it fascinating?"

"Fascinating isn't the word I'd use," Freja said.

Before anyone could stop him, Reimer reached up and tapped on the glass. Immediately, the tube shook slightly.

"Are you crazy?" Stone shouted.

Zane grabbed Reimer's arm and yanked him back.

"You people need to relax." Reimer shrugged off Zane. "They wouldn't build something that the creature could just break out of."

Stone glared at him. "Relax? I think we all know something escaped from one of these containers."

"It would explain the state of the two dead bodies," Freja said.

As the others continued to talk, Zane heard the faint clank of metal in the distance. As best he could tell, it had come from somewhere above. Moving slowly so as not to draw attention to himself, he turned and looked up. Unfortunately, it was too dark to see anything, and he wasn't about to use his flashlight. If they were being followed, then it would be better if whoever—or whatever—it was didn't know he was on to them.

Turning to the others, he said, "Let's get going. At some point, we may find it hard to breathe, and I want to cover as much ground as possible."

As they moved down the row of tubes, Zane noticed they all seemed to be constructed in the same manner, but each came in various sizes. Some were well over ten feet tall, while others were less than five feet.

Freja stepped closer to Zane and whispered, "Do you smell that?"

They both came to a stop, and he inhaled through his nose. The faint chemical smell they had encountered earlier was getting stronger.

He nodded. "I think it's the same scent as before."

"I think it's a spill."

"A spill of what?"

Freja was about to reply when Cignetti shouted from somewhere ahead. It was then that Zane realized they had fallen behind. The two rushed forward to find the others standing in a semicircle.

Zane and Freja came alongside the group and joined their beams with the others. The fog was even thicker there, and Zane soon realized why. Just ahead, the doors of two tubes had been left ajar, and a pool of dark liquid seeped underneath them.

Suddenly, his thoughts went back to the dead astronomer and the dead Russian commando. Two victims. Two empty tubes. Assuming one of the two specimens had perished in the fall from the ice bridge, that left the other unaccounted for.

Zane remembered the metallic clank he had heard just minutes before, and a chill ran down his spine.

36

Russian officer Konstantine Zaretsky watched the Americans through squinted eyes. Across the space, their flashlight beams looked like tiny lightsabers waving back and forth in the fog. As the Russian commander continued to watch, the beams eventually clustered together then disappeared down what appeared to be a large corridor leading out of the bay.

Zaretsky exhaled, finally able to relax after the close call a few minutes earlier. One of his men had accidentally banged the barrel of his rifle against the metal railing. While it wasn't loud, it had been enough to draw the attention of the leader of the American team. Although the man had tried to be inconspicuous, Zaretsky had seen him react.

Ordinarily, he would've welcomed a gunfight with the Americans. After all, he had seven men who were armed with AK-74s. In most scenarios, that much firepower would quickly overwhelm a lightly armed opponent. But in this case, Zaretsky's team would have been at a distinct disadvantage. Not only would they have been exposed on the catwalk, but the Americans would have been able to take cover in the swirling fog.

Zaretsky felt a certain sense of satisfaction at the success he and his men had achieved. The first Spetsnaz team that had been sent to Antarctica had disappeared. The cause of that disappearance might never be known, but he believed they had gotten lost in the tunnels or had fallen into one of the many chasms. Whatever the reason, they had failed.

Although he tried to maintain some modicum of humility, Zaretsky had a feeling that he and his men would be celebrated when they returned to Russia. Despite operating in some of the worst conditions possible, they had managed to destroy all the communication devices at Ellsworth Station and shoot down a helicopter, keeping the Americans isolated and stranded. But now they had grasped the ultimate prize—they had found the alien ship, a discovery that would give his country a treasure trove of advanced technology.

It was true that they had received help from their asset, a brilliant individual who had infiltrated the American team. But it was Zaretsky's men who had done all the dirty work. They were the ones who had established a base camp in a grubby cave. They were the ones who had slept on the cold floor. They had even managed to survive on MREs and water.

He was convinced their monumental efforts wouldn't go unnoticed. With any luck, they might even be given an audience with the Russian president, a man who had a deep appreciation for tough people who got results under tough conditions.

Still, he had to admit the discovery of the spaceship had come about through a combination of hard work and good fortune. It all started when his men had discovered the underground tunnels and a massive cavern filled with stalagmites a couple of days before. From the moment he set his eyes on it, the Russian officer believed the cavern was linked to the anomaly.

In a stunning twist of fate, Zaretsky and his men happened to be in the cavern when the Americans crossed the ice bridge for the first time. The mole had informed him that the American team would be exploring the tunnels that day, but it was not known precisely where they would be. Hidden in the sea of stalagmites, they'd witnessed the Americans uncover something along one of the walls, although they hadn't known what it was until they'd received a report from their mole later.

Tipped off by their asset, the Russians had been ready when the American team had come down to the cavern a second time. Unaware they were being watched, the Americans did what Zaretsky and his men had been unable to do and found a way into the alien ship. He'd been humbled when the Americans had made the discovery first. At the same time, the Russian officer knew any successful mission involved a few lucky breaks.

His thoughts turned back to the situation at hand. The Americans had left the bay, which meant he could now enact his twofold plan. He would split his team up. One group would track down and eliminate the Americans, who they no longer needed now that his men had access to the ship.

The other two men would stay behind to help him examine the tubes. As a high-ranking officer, Zaretsky understood a fair amount of English, and he had overheard the Americans say that live specimens were being held in the cylindrical containers. It was imperative that they collect a few of the smaller creatures to take back to Russia. It would undoubtedly be the greatest biological discovery of all time, and he would be the one to get the credit.

He clicked on his flashlight and pointed it at the nearby stairs. "We're going down to the floor. If any of you makes another noise, you'll be shot." He let his gaze move from one face to the next. "Is that understood?"

Heads nodded in quick succession.

"Good. Let's go."

They went down the stairs in single file. After they reached the floor, Zaretsky gave the orders to four of his men to wipe out the Americans. He told them to keep their lights off and approach with stealth. He also made it clear they were to take out the long-haired American and the SEAL first. *Cut off the head of the snake, and the body will die quickly.*

Once they were gone, he led the two other men, Nikolai and Anton, over to the first row of tubes.

Nikolai aimed his beam at the window of the nearest container, which was about ten feet in length. A murky haze swirled on the other side of the glass. "What's in there?"

"Animals," Zaretsky said. "We're going to take a few back with us."

"What kind of animals?" Anton asked.

"We won't know until we open it up."

Before Zaretsky could stop him, Nikolai reached out and knocked on the glass. A second later, the container shuddered violently, and a dark shadow moved in the haze behind the glass.

Nikolai backed up, a string of expletives spewing from his mouth.

Anton lifted his rifle defensively.

"Idiot!" Zaretsky barked. "Don't touch it until I say so."

"Yes, sir."

After the shaking stopped, Zaretsky stepped closer, his gaze running up to the top of the container. "This one is too big. Let's find one small enough for transport."

37

PISTOL IN HAND, Amanda slipped up the stairs. Before doing anything else, she wanted to check Christine Pageau's room. If she wasn't there, then Amanda would search the entire building one room at a time. She also needed to find Sunny and make sure she was safe.

Amanda was still in shock over the discovery of the mole's identity. She had always assumed the person had traveled with them to Antarctica. Instead, Pageau had been waiting for them at the station, probably planted there by the Russians. Although risky, it was a brilliant move that'd allowed them to have someone on the inside who could knock off the Americans one at a time. Amanda grimaced as she thought about everything Pageau had learned. The Russians were certainly in on every detail about the anomaly as a result.

As Amanda arrived on the second floor, a troubling question entered her thoughts. Maybe Pageau was who she claimed to be. But before Amanda could second-guess herself too much, she remembered the evidence. The photograph had shown the entire astronomer team right before their departure to Antarctica, and Pageau was not among them.

In the end, it wouldn't hurt to make the woman prove that she was indeed the highly decorated astronomer. Amanda just needed to make sure it didn't escalate into a violent confrontation. What a tragedy it would be if one of them ended up getting hurt or killed based on a false accusation.

As Amanda approached the woman's room, she noticed a soft glow spilling out from underneath the door. That didn't necessarily mean someone was inside, but she would definitely need to proceed with caution. If the mole suspected that Amanda knew the truth, then she might be waiting to ambush her.

Amanda paused outside the door and considered her next move. If she ambushed Pageau, Amanda would have the advantage of being hidden in the dark corridor. Then again, there was no telling how long it might take for the woman to come out. It could take hours. She wasn't about to wait that long. The situation needed to be resolved right away.

Her plan set, she grabbed the knob and twisted it. After counting to three, she shouldered the door open and entered the room with her pistol in the air. The woman who Amanda believed to be the mole was sitting at a desk on the other side of the bed, staring at her laptop screen. When she heard Amanda come in, she spun around and let out a startled gasp.

"Get your hands up!"

Pageau froze. "What in the world is—"

"I said get those hands up!"

She lifted her arms slowly. "Okay, okay."

Amanda came around to the other side of the bed to check for a weapon in the woman's lap or underneath the desk. Satisfied nothing was there, she told Pageau she could put her arms down.

"Thank you," the impostor said. "Now, do you mind telling me what's going on?"

The woman seemed genuinely confused, but Amanda knew it was likely the well-refined act of someone who was used to explaining her way out of tight situations. After all, if she had been chosen for that mission, then she had to be one of Russia's elite covert operatives—a person who spoke flawless English and could probably match skills with anyone in Hollywood.

"Where have you been for the last half hour?" Amanda asked.

"Isn't it obvious?"

"Answer my question!"

The woman exhaled then turned and gestured at her laptop. "As you can see, I've been right here at my desk. Not that it's any of your business, but I've been reading through some of the research I conducted this winter." She forced a laugh. "Do you want to see when I logged in?"

"Are you telling me you haven't left this room at any time in the last half hour?" Amanda asked.

"This is ridiculous." Pageau shook her head. "I did get up once to use the restroom. Other than that, I've been right here."

The restroom was on the first floor. Amanda furrowed her brow. Maybe that was who she had heard going up the stairs a few minutes ago.

Pageau's eyes widened. "Wait a minute. You think I'm the mole, don't you?"

Amanda decided it was time to lay her cards on the table. "I saw the photograph."

After a few seconds of silence, the woman asked, "What photograph?"

"You know exactly which one I'm talking about."

"I honestly have no clue."

"I'm talking about the photograph you tried to hide under the bookcase."

"Now *you* sound like a crazy person."

"Crazy?" Amanda asked. "If I'm crazy, then tell me why were you missing from the official team photograph that was taken just before coming down here?"

There was a long pause before a hint of understanding flashed in Pageau's eyes. "Okay, at least now I understand your confusion. There's a perfectly good reason for that." She briefly rubbed her face before continuing. "Robert Lang and I were last-minute additions to the team. Two members of the initial group had to step down. One had a death in the family, and the other was battling a serious illness."

Amanda had to admit the answer had been delivered quickly. Then again, it was also possible the woman had been ready for that very question. "Sounds like a convenient excuse to me. I never read anything about that in the material we were given."

Pageau let out a sigh. "Okay, I think I know how I can sort all this out. I have some photos on my phone that show me interacting with the group. Eating with them. Drinking with them. Once you see, you'll understand what a horrible mistake you've made."

"Where's your phone?"

"I think it's in my dresser. To be honest, I haven't really looked at it since you guys arrived."

Amanda considered what the woman had just said. If she did have photographs of the group together, then it would completely rule her out as a suspect. Amanda doubted the Russians had placed a spy in academia.

Amanda nodded at the dresser. "Get it out, and we'll take a look."

The woman stood and walked over to it on the other side of the bed. Amanda kept her eyes trained on the contents as Pageau rummaged through her clothing. Coming up empty, she closed that drawer and opened the next one down.

A few seconds later, she said, "Here it is. Let's see if it still has some juice. Otherwise, we'll need to find a charger."

Throughout her adult life, Amanda had possessed the ability to see things play out in slow motion whenever faced with a life-threatening situation. She didn't know if it was a biological trait or a gift from God, but it had often enabled her to act with greater speed than others could under similar circumstances. What happened next was one such moment.

Before the woman took the phone out of the dresser, Amanda noticed she had taken a small but telling step to her left. Amanda's sixth sense sounded a warning bell.

The confirmation came seconds later when Pageau's hand came out of the drawer in that tell-tale slow motion. The woman's fingers clutched something bulky and matte black, and Amanda's brain moved at warp speed, registering the semiautomatic pistol.

Knowing what was about to take place, Amanda dove to her right, firing twice as she dropped behind the bed. While it had possibly saved her life, the quick move had also caused her to miss her target. Although unable to see the result, she knew instinctively that her rounds had gone wide right.

In that brief instant, the woman had also taken action. She had brought the pistol up with stunning speed and had managed to squeeze off two rounds of her own. Two operatives. Two instinctive reactions.

Amanda hit the floor as the room echoed with gunfire. A searing burst of pain cut through her shoulder like a hot poker. Ignoring the sensation, she rolled up against the bed, her pistol at the ready.

Footsteps thumped out of the room and down the hall. For the moment, the impostor had chosen to retreat.

Now that she was no longer in danger, Amanda felt the pain in her shoulder. The injury was even worse than she'd thought. The impact from the fall must have dislocated it.

She started to get up then froze when she saw a pool of blood spreading across the floor underneath her.

38

AFTER BRIEFLY EXPLORING the first bay, Zane and the others entered a wide corridor on the other side of the space. While the specimen containers were interesting, Zane wanted to explore as much of the ship as possible in the time they had left. Martini and Reimer hoped to find the ship's propulsion system, which could provide the biggest technological boon of all.

As they continued down the dark hall, Zane couldn't shake the feeling that they were being followed. First, there had been the dull clank that'd come from one of the suspended walkways. Although the ship was resting in an unstable environment, he doubted the shifting of rocks outside would produce the sound he had heard.

But the noise wasn't the only thing that concerned him. For the last half hour or so, he'd had the distinct feeling of being watched. After all his experience in the field, he had learned to trust his gut on that.

Unfortunately, they were in a poor tactical position to do much about it. They were moving farther and farther away from the exit, so unless they found another way out, their only escape route had been cut off.

He doubted the surviving specimen would've waited that long to attack. If they were dealing with Russian commandos, they were likely outnumbered. Subterfuge would be the key to getting out alive. They did have one advantage—in all likelihood, the enemy didn't know that Zane was aware of their presence. That being the case, they were probably overconfident. And if they were overconfident, then it might be possible to lure them into a trap.

Struck with an idea, Zane slowed his pace and looked down. The charcoal-colored floor was made of the same epoxy-like material as the one in the bay. He swung his flashlight over to the wall, which seemed to be constructed of solid metal. *Perfect.*

After letting the others get ahead of him, Zane walked over to the right side of the corridor. Reaching into his pocket, he pulled out the small stainless steel water bottle he always kept with him. He unscrewed the top and finished what was left. He then laid it on the floor, positioning it perpendicular to the wall.

His plan was simple. If they were being followed by Russian commandos, then they would likely split up before heading down the corridor, with each group walking close to either wall. If they did, there was a good chance one of the men would accidentally kick the bottle into the steel wall. That alone would alert Zane to their presence.

Satisfied the bottle was properly positioned, he stood and hurried after the others. The flashlight beams were now a good fifty yards away. He briefly considered sharing his suspicions, but after giving it some thought, he decided to wait. He had no concrete proof that they were being followed, and it was probably best not to cause undue stress.

When he finally caught up with his team, they were entering another type of bay.

"I think we hit pay dirt." Reimer's eyes were glazed with excitement.

"How so?" Freja asked.

"This looks like the engine room." Reimer's face broke into a broad smile that seemed unusual for a man that was often so tightly wound.

Zane took in their surroundings. Throughout the space, massive cylinders ran from the floor to the ceiling. Each one was a conglomeration of glass tubes, metal pipes, and an assortment of other components.

"I think you're right." Martini squeezed her lover's arm then moved toward the nearest cylinder, her flashlight splashing across its surface. "All this piping could be the delivery system for the ship's fuel."

Vince Stone took out his camera and started photographing the equipment from several different angles.

Freja approached the cylinder's base and studied a clear glass plate mounted on top of a metal arm. "Anybody know what this is?"

Reimer went to her side. "It looks like a screen."

"As in computer screen?" Freja asked.

Ignoring her question, Reimer pressed a finger against it. There was a brief hum, then a string of characters appeared inside the glass. To Zane, it looked like one of the futuristic devices depicted in science fiction films.

Martini's eyes widened. "It's alien script. We're looking at some sort of message."

"Can you read it?" Freja asked.

Reimer and Martini shook their heads.

The characters being displayed didn't look like any Zane had ever seen before. The closest thing he could compare them to was hieroglyphics, although even that wasn't a perfect fit.

"I think something's happening," Martini whispered.

New lines of characters appeared below the first. Soon, the lines of script scrolled by so fast they couldn't keep up. It was like looking at the spinning fruit in a slot machine.

"I think it's booting up," Reimer said.

Although fascinating, Zane was beginning to think Reimer had made a big mistake in bringing the system to life. Unauthorized use of the equipment could potentially trigger some sort of internal defense mechanism.

As everyone watched in silence, Zane heard the distant *ping* of metal on metal.

He stiffened.

The trap. Someone had knocked the water bottle into the wall.

Zane looked at the faces around him. As best he could tell, no one had heard the noise except for him. Careful not to draw attention to himself, he backed away from the others then ran his flashlight beam up the nearest wall. As he suspected, there was a catwalk about thirty feet above them. Unlike the other bay, there appeared to be only one there. Fortunately, one was all he needed.

"Want to tell me what's going on?"

Startled, Zane turned to see Freja had come up behind him. He had been so focused on the catwalk that he hadn't seen her approach.

"I know you stayed behind earlier," she continued, her voice low. "I think you found something. Want to tell me what it was?"

Zane realized he couldn't keep it a secret any longer. "We're being followed."

Freja frowned. "And you didn't tell me?"

"I wasn't sure until just now." Zane told her about the first noise in the first bay then the trap he'd set.

She cursed under her breath. "I wish you'd mentioned it to me sooner."

"You're right, I should have."

"We need to get out of here." She pointed her flashlight toward the other side of the bay. "There has to be another exit."

"We can't leave—at least not yet."

"You just told me they're about to come in," Freja asked.

"They are, and that's exactly what we want them to do."

39

FOLLOWED BY HIS MEN, Konstantine Zaretsky walked down the second row of specimen containers, stopping at each one to tap on the outside and peer through the glass. As best he could tell, the animals seemed to be in three different levels of cryogenic sleep. Unlike the first creature, some didn't move at all when the container was disturbed. He presumed those were in the deepest level of sleep or had died. Others moved slightly when the containers were tapped, revealing some level of consciousness. Then there was a third group that reacted violently to any form of stimulus.

His goal was to find a smaller specimen that was at the deepest level of sleep. They would take it out of the tube, and if it didn't look dangerous, they would attempt to transport it back to their base camp without killing it. If the animal looked deadly, then they would kill it on the spot. Even a dead one could be studied.

As they continued down the row, Zaretsky wondered how each of the animals had been collected. He guessed the aliens had tranquilized them with some advanced type of gun or electroshock weapon before containing the incapacitated animals inside one of the tubes filled with a liquefied gas.

Zaretsky couldn't understand why some of the animals seemed to be more awake than the others. If the ship had been down there for a long time, some of the liquefied gas might have been leaking out. That or it was only effective for so long. It was also possible some of the animals had died.

As he neared the end of the row, he stopped at a container that was about six feet long. It was the shortest one they had encountered so far. He stepped up to it and banged on the side with the palm of his hand. The tube didn't move. He banged on it harder, but there was no response.

It was just what he had been looking for. The animal inside was either dead or unconscious.

Hoping to get a glimpse of the specimen, Zaretsky stepped closer and put his flashlight against the glass. Amid the swirling gas, he saw what appeared to be the leg of a very large insect. He smiled. It wasn't what he had expected, but it certainly fit the profile of what he was looking for. After all, how dangerous could a bug be?

He looked back at his men. "Let's open this one up."

Nikolai and Anton hesitated. The two were normally fearless, but there was something about the containers that had put both of them on edge.

"Did you not hear me? Get moving!"

"You want us to just open the door?" Nikolai asked.

Zaretsky stroked the stubble on his chin as if taking the question seriously. "Let's see. No. Let's just stare at it for a few more minutes. Maybe take a few photographs through the glass."

Nikolai paused, clearly confused as to how he should take the comments.

"Of course we're going to open it, you imbecile!" Zaretsky shouted.

"What if it attacks?" Anton asked.

Zaretsky shook his head. "Take a look at the thing's leg. It looks like a grasshopper. Are you telling me you're scared of an insect?"

"I just want to know what we should do if it comes at us," Anton said. "Are we allowed to shoot it, or does it need to be taken alive?"

Despite his rising anger, Zaretsky had to admit it was a fair question. Even a giant insect could have sharp mandibles or claws. It was also possible that the specimen was venomous. "If it comes after you, then feel free to shoot. It's better if we take it alive, but even a dead specimen will be valuable."

The two seemed to relax after hearing his answer.

Nikolai looked at Anton. "I'll open it while you cover me."

Anton backed away and lifted his AK-74, which had a flashlight strapped to the barrel.

Despite his outward bravado, Konstantine took a few steps back and drew his pistol as well.

With everyone set, Nikolai grabbed the door handle and pulled on it. It didn't budge.

Anton pointed with his rifle. "There's a button to the right."

Nikolai leaned in and pressed it. A loud click followed, indicating the lock had disengaged.

"Open it already!" Zaretsky ordered.

Nikolai grabbed the handle and pulled the door open. There was a hissing sound as the unit's seal broke. A billowing cloud of fog spilled from the opening like a newly opened box of dry ice.

The haze was so thick that Zaretsky was already having trouble seeing what was going on. "Step away until it clears."

Nikolai backed away but was immediately swallowed up by the cloud.

A growing sense of concern rose inside Zaretsky. The container and the area around it were completely shrouded by the cloud of gas. At this point, he couldn't tell if the specimen was still inside or if it had come out. If it snuck past them, it would be impossible to catch in the thick haze. But there was another more ominous possibility—if it sensed danger, the creature's instincts might tell it to attack.

Zaretsky's thought's turned to the spindly legs he had seen earlier. They weren't particularly large, but the outer hide looked tough. He also didn't know what was at the end of those legs.

As they waited for the haze to clear, a series of strange *clicks* came out of the swirling fog. At first, Zaretsky thought the sound was electronic, perhaps something related to the container's operating system. But the longer he listened, the more he realized it was being made by the creature they had just released.

"What the…?" Anton's voice trembled beside him.

Zaretsky looked, but he couldn't see him. "What is it?"

There was no answer.

"What is it?" he tried again.

"I can't see anything," Nikolai called from the fog.

His heart beating faster, Zaretsky slowly backed away. As he did, his eyes caught movement higher up. A grotesque silhouette appeared at the top of the container. The haze cleared momentarily, revealing long, single-jointed legs and an abdomen that was the size of a large piece of luggage. It looked like a giant spider emerging from its funnel web.

His hands shaking, Zaretsky tightened his grip on the pistol.

"I don't have a good angle," Nikolai called. "Shoot it!"

"Shoot what?" Anton said. "I can't see anything."

Zaretsky watched in horror as the creature leaped from its perch. A surprised scream echoed from somewhere in the mist, although it was impossible to tell who it had come from. He wanted to help, but he'd lost sight of both men and the creature. If he fired his pistol, he was just as likely to hit one of his men.

Two shots rang out, followed by the sound of shattering glass.

"Help me," Anton cried out. "Help me!" A blood-curdling scream was followed by the sound of something snapping.

Zaretsky realized it was time to retreat. If he could somehow make it to the stairs, then he might be able to get up above the fog. He would then attempt to shoot the creature from there.

Turning, he ran through a gap in the first row of containers. As he did, his foot caught a metal ridge on the floor. He tumbled through the air, his flashlight and gun sailing in different directions. He landed hard then rolled several times.

After catching his breath, he managed to rise on one elbow. There were several more screams behind him, then only silence. The fog had dispersed enough that he could see the three flashlight beams, all of them level with the floor. He would need one to find the stairs.

As he considered his options, something moved in the fog, backlit by the glow of the nearest flashlight. Legs. Long ones.

Zaretsky felt the hairs rise on the back of his neck as the giant arachnid moved toward him. A moment later, the *clicking* began again, the same clicking that preceded the other attacks.

His heart hammering against his chest, the Russian officer got to his feet then bolted into the darkness.

40

AMANDA TOOK her time going down the stairs. The last thing she needed to do was lose her balance and take a hard fall. Fortunately, the bullet had only grazed her right shoulder. Still, she had lost a lot of blood, which in turn had brought on a light-headedness that was getting worse with each passing minute. Although it probably wouldn't kill her, it had certainly impaired her ability to move and think.

Ordinarily, she would have gone straight to Sunny to have the wound treated. But the mole was on the loose, and Amanda was the only one who could stop her.

After reaching the bottom of the stairs, she paused for a moment to catch her breath. The wound was more painful than anything she had experienced before. Getting shot in real life was nothing like what she'd seen in the movies. The actors always pretended to suck it up and go about their business like nothing had happened, but Amanda's shoulder burned as though a hot poker had ripped through her skin.

She took a steadying breath and focused on her mission. To their credit, the Russians had played their hand brilliantly. Not only did they have a good plan, but they had executed it with a woman who was clearly an elite operative. In addition to her flawless English and acting skills, she was also a good shot.

Her eyes darted around the hall as she rested, but she saw no sign of the imposter. *Maybe she left the building.* It occurred to Amanda that the woman might be calling for backup. Her chest tightened at that thought. If the Russian commandos stormed the station then, it would all be over.

After catching her breath, Amanda started moving down the hall. She planned to make sure the front door was locked before beginning a systematic search of the building for the mole. She also wanted to make sure Sunny was safe.

As she neared the foyer, Amanda heard a distant voice. She stopped to listen. To her surprise, there were actually two voices, both of them female. Her stomach did another flip as she imagined the imposter luring Sunny in as a hostage.

A moment later, footsteps came down the stairs from the second floor, and a flashlight beam cut through the darkness. Two silhouettes crossed the foyer then went out through the front door. Amanda had thought about calling out, but her gut told her to wait. The last thing she needed to do was get into a gunfight in the dark.

Amanda followed as fast as she could. Remembering that she was about to go out in the cold, she pulled out a knitted cap and slid it over her head. Unfortunately, it was all she had on her, and there was no time to grab the rest of her outdoor gear.

She opened the front door and went down the steps. Immediately, a gust of frigid wind hit her bare face. Her body, already weakened by the loss of blood, trembled uncontrollably. In a normal climate, her three shirts, a sweater, a light coat, and the knit cap would have been enough. But not here. If she was lucky, the clothing she had on might keep her alive for a few minutes at most.

Amanda swept her gaze across the snowy landscape. *There.* A flashlight beam was bouncing toward the garage. As the light disappeared around the corner of the building, Amanda caught a glimpse of two people behind it. One of them wore a red coat, and the other wore a bright-white coat with a fur-lined hood. Amanda had seen both coats many times before. One belonged to the person posing as Christine Pageau, and the other belonged to Sunny Lee.

Feelings of shock and betrayal rippled through Amanda, cutting her to the core. *Is Sunny working with the mole?* If so, then Amanda had some soul-searching to do. She had roomed with the woman and hadn't picked up on anything suspicious. She had even bought the nurse's story about being a committed Christian. Looking back, Sunny had probably known everything about Amanda going in.

Pushing those thoughts aside, Amanda considered her next move. She was weak and cold, which meant she needed to act quickly. She had to make the call on whether to go back inside and wait for Zane and the others to return or go after the two women right then and there. Amanda suspected they were about to drive off in one of the Hagglunds. If they knew where the battery was hidden, then it would be easy to get one of them up and running.

The more she thought about it, the more Amanda realized she had to stop the women from leaving. If she didn't, they would probably return with the commandos. She couldn't let that happen. Better to face two than ten or twenty.

After pulling the cap down over her cheeks, she ran out into the storm.

41

Stretched out on the floor, Zane kept his eyes trained on the spot where the men would come out of the corridor that linked the two bays. Positioned just twenty feet away, he was in a vulnerable position. If any of the men looked to the right when they came in, they would see him. But he believed that things would go according to plan, and they would keep their sights fixed straight ahead.

Zane had finally figured out why the Russians were making their move. Up until that point, they had probably seen value in letting the American team of experts lead the way into the alien spaceship. But now that they'd served their purpose, the Russians had decided to take them out. Zane wasn't going to let that happen.

As he waited, footfalls sounded a short distance away. The noise was faint but distinct. A small group of people was moving stealthily through the corridor.

They're here. Zane's pulse quickened.

Moments later, the barrel of a rifle protruded from the corridor's mouth. Soon, another appeared. Then one more. Within seconds, four silhouettes slipped into view, their weapons up and ready.

Although things could still go wrong, everything was playing out just the way Zane had hoped it would. The Russian commandos were all looking straight ahead, their gazes fixed on the flashlights Freja had positioned strategically on the other side of the bay.

One of the commandos gestured for the other men to come closer. He then whispered what Zane assumed was a series of instructions. Once he was done, the four men fanned out like football players breaking a huddle. One man went to the right, walking right past the place where Zane was hidden. Another one went left, with the remaining two—including the man who had given the instructions—continuing on a path that ran straight across the bay and toward the lights.

As he'd predicted, their plan was straightforward. They would infiltrate the bay and position themselves in a semicircle around the unsuspecting Americans. They would then mow their quarry down in a hail of gunfire. Unfortunately for them, Zane had planned for that.

Careful not to make a noise, the operative got up and followed the soldier that had walked past him seconds before. The man was about twenty yards ahead but was moving at a crawl.

If the goal had been to simply kill the man, it would have been an easy task. Zane could just slip behind the target and put a bullet between his shoulder blades. But for the plan to work, he would have to take the man down without making a sound. If the commando managed to get off a shot or shout for help, then everything would fall apart.

After tucking his pistol away, Zane closed to within a few feet of his target. Fortunately, the soldier's sole focus was on the flashlight beams across the bay. It was a mistake born out of overconfidence, and it would cost the man his life.

Zane tensed his arms, increasing blood flow to his muscles. As he always did before initiating an attack, he visualized the attack—the moves he would make, the possible countermoves his opponent might make, and what he should do if things didn't go as planned.

When the moment was right, Zane sprang. He wrapped his right arm around the man's throat. At the same time, he used his knee to kick the rifle out of the man's grasp. It all happened so quickly that the soldier had been unable to respond.

But the man wasn't about to give up without a fight. Arms flailed. Legs kicked. He even threw back his head a few times in an attempt to smash Zane's forehead. But it was all to no avail. Zane's arms were like ribbons of steel, and each time the man moved, Zane tightened his grip further, cutting off the supply of oxygen.

As the struggle went on, the man began to twist his head, trying to free his mouth long enough to shout for help. Zane couldn't let that happen. He drew his knife and finished the job. The man sagged as the blood spilled from his throat.

Although the task had been carried out quickly and efficiently, Zane knew he still had work to do. He had just taken out the man assigned to the right flank. The left flank was next.

He set the corpse aside then sprinted into the darkness.

42

Igor Svechnikov and his partner, Viktor, moved silently across the large bay. A dozen or more floor-to-ceiling towers looked down at them like the massive columns of an ancient Greek temple. Under any other circumstances, it would have been a beautiful sight worthy of closer attention. But Igor had business to do, and he wasn't about to let anything distract him from finishing the job.

As best as he could tell, the American team had gathered on the far side of a large column directly ahead. It must have some importance because the Americans had been there for a long time. Unfortunately for them, it would be the last thing they studied before dying.

As they drew nearer, Igor got a bad feeling. For the last minute or so, he had noticed the lights had remained perfectly still. He guessed it was because the researchers were so focused on whatever it was they had found.

Still, he couldn't shake the unnerved feeling growing inside him. Concerned, he placed a hand on Viktor's shoulder, bringing his partner to a stop.

He leaned closer and whispered, "Those lights haven't moved in a while."

Viktor nodded. "I noticed that too."

"Do you think it's a trap?"

Viktor shook his head. "No. I don't think we're looking at their flashlights anymore."

"Then what are we looking at?"

"That pillar is much larger than the others." He paused for a moment, his gaze running up the structure. "I think it must be some kind of elevator or stairwell."

"An elevator?" Igor asked.

Viktor nodded. "I think they may already be on some upper level of the ship."

Igor swore softly. If the Americans were no longer in the bay, then their job had just gotten much more difficult.

.

43

TREMBLING FROM THE COLD, Amanda opened the side door of the garage just enough to have a look at the interior. A single workbench light glowed across the other side of the space. Seeing and hearing nothing, she slipped in and shut the door behind her.

She remained in place, surprised that she didn't already hear the sound of voices. She had expected to find the two women putting a battery in one of the Hagglunds. Instead, the garage seemed empty. If the women were inside, then they must've been in the very back.

Before taking a look around, Amanda leaned back against the wall. Her shoulder was throbbing, and she was still shaking from the cold, a reaction that was undoubtedly exacerbated by the loss of blood. Fortunately, the bleeding no longer flowed freely from under the fabric of her layers.

After resting for a full minute, she pushed off the wall. She needed to get her blood flowing. The short break had been nice, but she was still cold inside, and movement was the only way to warm herself up.

As she started walking, Amanda found it odd that she hadn't even heard the women talking. *Is there a back door?* If so, then they might have slipped out to retrieve one of the batteries. She would simply have to wait for them to come back if that was the case.

When she was about halfway across the garage, Amanda turned left toward the trucks. She wanted to look inside them, and she also wanted to stay outside the periphery of light from the workbench.

Keeping the pistol at her side, Amanda approached the nearest Hagglund and peered through the front passenger's window. As far as she could tell, there was no one inside. She then went to the next vehicle, but there was no one there either.

Seeing no signs of life, she had to consider the possibility that the women hadn't even entered the garage. After all, she hadn't actually seen them go inside. She had only assumed that was what they had done after they'd gone around the side of the building. If that was the case, she needed to keep watch in case they came in behind her.

After taking into account her weakened state, she decided not to venture outside to search for the two women. Her body couldn't take the frigid temperatures in the clothing she had on. Instead, she would remain inside and check the back of the garage. Although it wasn't likely the women were there, she at least needed to take a look. She might even find a good place to hide.

She turned and began moving toward the rows of shelves containing various parts and tools used to service the station's equipment and vehicles. There was so much junk that Amanda was beginning to wonder if there might even be an old battery hidden in one of the piles. She made a mental note to search for one later.

She had just started down one of the aisles when the garage's overhead light came on. But when she spun around and looked behind her, she didn't see anyone.

Footfalls sounded close by. Amanda dropped to one knee, gripping her pistol tightly. Soon, another noise reached her ears.

Strangely enough, it sounded like someone was whimpering. Confused, she stood and edged back toward the front.

As she neared the end of the aisle, two figures stepped out in front of her. Amanda backed up and lifted her pistol with both hands.

"I wouldn't do that if I were you," a female voice said in heavily accented English.

The two were backlit by the workbench light, making it difficult to see much more than a silhouette. But Amanda didn't have to see their faces to know she was looking at the mole and Sunny Lee.

"Put your gun down," the woman with the accent said.

Amanda stepped forward. As she got closer to the two women, she noticed the mole had a gun to Sunny's head. Was it a ruse, or had she taken the nurse hostage?

"Don't worry about me." Sunny's voice trembled. "Just shoot her."

Momentary relief washed over her. The nurse hadn't betrayed her, although it wasn't much consolation in light of the present circumstances.

"You heard me," the woman said with a Russian accent she was no longer trying to hide. "Put the gun down, or your little friend dies."

"Let's both put our guns down and talk this through," Amanda said.

Using a free hand, the woman grabbed Sunny's hair and yanked her head back, causing the nurse to cry out in pain.

Amanda took another step forward. "Let her go."

The woman pressed the pistol's muzzle into Sunny's cheek. "I'm giving you one last chance."

Amanda knew the woman wasn't bluffing. She wasn't some crazed citizen with a gun. She was an elite Russian operative who had probably killed too many people to count. That meant she certainly wouldn't hesitate to put a bullet in Sunny's head.

Realizing she had no other options, Amanda crouched and set the pistol on the floor.

"That's a good girl," the woman said.

Amanda stood. "Now let her go."

The woman laughed. "Sorry, my dear. But that's not going to happen."

Amanda needed to keep the woman talking until she could come up with some way out of the present predicament. "Who are you?"

"I guess it is time I formally introduced myself," the woman said with a smile. "My name is Natasha."

"I take it you were already here when we arrived."

Natasha nodded. "I must say, it wasn't comfortable sitting in that vent for so long, but it was worth it."

"I have to admit it. I'm impressed." Amanda paused as she tried to think of another question. "If you're the mole, then how did you know when we would get here?"

"That was easy. Someone told us."

Amanda frowned. *Someone? A second mole?*

"Don't worry," Natasha said, seeing the concern on her face. "We don't have anyone working on your team. Not that we didn't try."

"Then who told you?"

"We have someone at Parks Station. He's one of those... I can't remember what you call it. The person who cleans."

"A janitor."

"Yes, the janitor."

"He's Russian?"

"No, he's Chilean. He used to work at one of our stations before though. I must say, the man gets around."

"So you paid him to pass along information?"

Natasha smiled. "It's amazing what someone will do for five hundred US dollars."

"Where is your team now?"

"The last I heard, they were about to follow your people into the ship."

"What are they planning to do?" Amanda asked.

"Now that we have access to the technology, well… I think you can fill in the blanks."

If true, and Amanda had no reason to believe it wasn't, then the situation looked grim. Zane and the others would be outnumbered and outgunned. Still, she had seen Zane get out of situations that looked bleak many times.

"I know it can't be easy hearing that, but this is what our two countries do," Natasha said. "Unfortunately, your team just wasn't good enough this time."

"You don't know Zane like I do. I guarantee you, he'll walk out of that ship alive. And if he does, it's going to be in your best interest to let us go. If you don't, then I promise you he'll hunt you down."

Natasha laughed. "Lots of empty bluster."

"I'm not bluffing. Zane is the best at what he does."

"If he's so good, then why did he just lead my people to the very thing they were looking for?"

"And if your people are so good, why did they need us to do it? I guess it's the same reason you hack into the servers of our companies—to steal what you couldn't develop yourself."

Natasha's expression soured.

Concerned she might have gone too far, Amanda quickly posed another question. "So, what are you planning to do with us?"

"Unfortunately, you won't be needed." Still holding a clump of Sunny's hair, she shook the nurse's head. "But I'm going to keep this one alive for a while in case any of my people need medical attention. If they don't, then…"

As Natasha spoke, a *thud* sounded in the distance. The mole didn't seem to notice, but Amanda searched the dark for the source of the noise, her ears burning. Maybe she hadn't shut the door all the way and the wind had blown it open. She also considered the possibility that someone had come in. The only ally she and Sunny had left on the surface was Brady Arnott, and he was dead. They were totally alone. *Or are we?*

"One more question," Amanda said.

"Make it good because it's your last."

"What happened to Patrick Rider?"

Natasha frowned. "Who is that?"

"He was one of our helicopter pilots. He tried to fly back out on the night we arrived."

Amanda didn't expect the Russian would know, but it might keep her talking for a couple more minutes.

A smile flickered on the Russian agent's face. "I'm sorry to report that he's dead. We shot the helicopter down a few miles from here."

Amanda flinched. There was no way of knowing if that was true, although there had been a look of confidence on the woman's face when she'd said it.

"In case you're wondering if I'm telling the truth," Natasha continued, "I was told it was one of those large helicopters. An Agusta, I think? I may not have the name right."

Amanda felt like she had been hit in the chest by an anvil. She had hoped the British pilot had made it safely back to Parks. It was one more tragic death to add to all the others. There was no way to spin it. Barring some miraculous turn of events, Operation Whiteout had been a complete disaster.

She could still be lying. Amanda did her best to hold onto hope. After all, Natasha could have gotten information about the kind of helicopter from their source at Parks Station. If he knew when they were flying out, then he likely knew the model of helicopter that they were in.

"And now it's time to say goodbye," Natasha said. The Russian agent's arm extended, training the muzzle of her pistol on Amanda's chest.

"Let's talk about this," Amanda said.

"We've done enough talking," the Russian said. "I've got work to do."

Amanda closed her eyes, but it wasn't because she was afraid. She needed to concentrate on her next move. Natasha was about ten feet away, so Amanda felt certain she could close the distance in a second or two. If she dove for the woman's legs, she might be able to knock her to the ground.

She hesitated. *What about Sunny?* An abrupt attack could get them both killed. As Amanda wrestled with the plan, a shot rang out.

Sunny screamed, but strangely, Amanda felt nothing.

Acting on instinct, she dove behind some boxes to her right. As she tumbled across the floor, she heard a thud that was followed by the sound of approaching footsteps.

A few seconds later, a male voice with a British accent spoke into the silence. "You may have shot my bird down, but you didn't shoot *me* down."

4 4

THE CLOSER THEY came to the large column, the more suspicious Igor Svechnikov became. He didn't believe it was the sort of elevator shaft Viktor had proposed. To him, the whole thing smelled like a trap.

One minute, there'd been flashlight beams waving in every direction, then the next, there was only one steady source of light. He supposed the American team could have exited the bay through another corridor, but he knew they would want to spend more time studying the room.

He grabbed Viktor's shoulder. "Wait."

Viktor gave him a surprised look. "What?"

"Something's not right." He nodded at the massive column. "This doesn't look like an elevator. And what's the light we're looking at?"

Now that he thought about it, the light could have been there all along. Perhaps they'd only mistaken it for one of the flashlights, and the Americans truly were no longer in the bay.

"Why don't you try Sergei or Anatoly?" Viktor asked. "Maybe they're in a place where they can see the other side."

When setting out, Igor had told his men to go radio silent, and he wasn't going to break that rule now. "It's too risky. The Americans might hear them talking."

"So we're just going to wait?"

After mulling it over, he decided it wouldn't hurt to get a little closer. As long as they didn't move into the light, then they wouldn't tip off their quarry. "We'll take a quick look. But if I see one thing that seems out of place, then we're pulling back."

Viktor nodded.

The two crept forward, their rifles up and ready. When they were about twenty yards from the column, Igor tapped Viktor on the shoulder and signaled for them to head left so as not to enter the circle of light. Soon, the other side of the column came into view. Although he couldn't see its source, Igor noted that the light seemed to emanate from the intricate machinery at the column's base.

"What did I tell you?" Viktor whispered. "The Americans aren't here."

"No elevator though."

"I think it's there. We just can't see it yet."

Seeing no signs of the enemy, they moved toward the light. Igor scanned the area, looking for any clues that they might be walking into a trap. He didn't see or hear anything, but he still couldn't shake the feeling that they were being watched.

As they neared the outer edge of the light, he held up his hand.

Viktor looked over at him. "What?"

"They're here. I can feel it."

"If you're so sure this is a trap, then answer this—how did they know we were coming?"

Igor didn't have an answer. He was operating solely on the gut feeling that had developed over the last several minutes.

"I'm going in," Viktor said. "If you don't want to, you can wait here. I'll let you know what I find."

As he walked off, a sense of frustration and anger welled up inside Igor. Viktor had always been a bit of a rebel, but his current act of disobedience was going to put them all in danger.

Even so, Igor knew he couldn't stay back. If this wasn't a trap, then he would look like a coward. Cursing under his breath, he hurried forward. As he came alongside Viktor, he could see there was no door at the base of the column. That meant there was no elevator, nor was there a stairwell. Viktor had been wrong.

"What did I tell you?" Igor hissed.

"If this was a trap, then we'd already be dead," Viktor assured him.

There was only one question left. With the Americans nowhere in sight, all they could do was examine the light's source. It seemed to come from behind a row of pipes. Igor moved in for a closer look. When he did, he saw something that made his blood run cold—several flashlights had been lined up on a metal shelf, their beams pointed at the column's base.

They had been placed there on purpose.

Suddenly, Igor remembered something that had happened back in the corridor. Sergei's foot had hit a piece of metal, causing it to clank against the wall. At the time, he hadn't thought much of it. He recognized it for what it was too late. *A trip wire.*

"Go!" he shouted.

But the warning did no good. Two shots rang out from somewhere above. Based on the height, he guessed it had come from another catwalk in a part of the bay that they couldn't see.

As Igor turned to flee, he noticed Viktor wasn't moving. A blank stare was frozen on his face, and a gurgling noise came out of his mouth. Seconds later, he folded and crumpled to the floor.

Knowing what would happen next, Igor tried to duck for cover. As he did, another shot rang out.

45

AMANDA, Sunny, and Patrick Rider stood around the body of the mole. A red splash on the back of Natasha's coat marked the place where the single round had entered between her shoulder blades. In all likelihood, she had died instantly.

Still in shock, Amanda tried to piece together the last few minutes. She remembered deciding to charge the Russian agent, but before she could act, someone had fired a shot. Everything after that had been a blur. Then, when Amanda got to her feet, Patrick Rider was there. Somehow, the British pilot had made it back, and he had done so just in time to save their lives.

To Amanda, the whole thing was providential. She had been seconds away from dying, and Sunny wouldn't have been far behind. She lifted a silent prayer of thanks up to God.

Rider nodded at the corpse. "Who is she?"

"A very crafty Russian agent," Sunny answered.

Amanda spent the next few minutes telling him how they had found the woman in an air duct and how she'd impersonated an astronomer as Christine Pageau. Without going into much detail, she then briefly went through the events of the last hour leading up to the garage.

"So she was planted here before we arrived?"

Amanda nodded. "It was a brilliant plan, and it almost worked."

Sunny looked at Rider. "Speaking of dead people, I must say, I'm a little surprised you aren't."

"At one point, I did have a foot in the grave."

"So you made it back to Parks Station?" Sunny asked.

He shook his head. "No, they shot me down about ten or fifteen miles from here."

"She told us they had shot the helicopter down, but I thought she was bluffing," Sunny said.

"She was telling me the truth. They used a shoulder-fired SAM."

"SAM?" Sunny asked.

"A surface-to-air missile, probably a Russian SA-7 or SA-14."

Amanda frowned. "And you survived that?"

Rider described what had happened after flying out on that first night. He told them about seeing the distant flash at the base of a mountain, which he'd recognized as a shoulder-fired missile. In a snap decision, he'd directed the chopper toward the wall of the ravine.

After Rider told them about the death-defying jump he had made right before impact, Sunny interjected, "I can't believe you survived the fall."

"That was the miraculous part. I landed in a snowdrift in the middle of the ravine."

"So the missile never actually hit the helicopter?" Amanda asked.

"I'm not exactly sure," Rider answered. "It all happened so fast. I was out the door in seconds, and it took me a while to get my bearings after digging out of the snow. By that time, the chopper was a ball of fire. Either the missile hit it, or it exploded in the crash."

"So that's when you hiked back?" Sunny asked.

He shook his head. "I knew the people who shot me down would come to make sure I hadn't somehow survived, so I dug in and watched. As I suspected, they showed up a few minutes later. At first, I thought seeing the wreckage would be enough for them, but they eventually spread out to search the area for survivors."

Rider then described his close call with the commando who had come within a few feet of finding him.

"What would you have done if he had seen you?" Sunny asked.

"I probably could've killed him, but the gunfire would've drawn the others over. I was outnumbered and outgunned."

"You were very fortunate," Amanda said.

He nodded.

Sunny frowned. "Just one more thing. How did you survive out there?"

"It wasn't easy, I can tell you that. Once the commandos left, I started the slow journey south. I'd walk for several hours then find a place to get out of the wind and rest. That's the good thing about these mountains. They're riddled with caves, overhangs, and tunnels."

"What about food and water?" Amanda said.

"I grabbed my backpack before jumping out of the chopper. Everyone who works down here, particularly those who are in transportation like me, keeps the essentials with them. Basically, I was able to make it on seven bottles of water and a pack of protein bars."

"Well, we're just happy you made it back," Amanda said.

"You're not the only one," Rider said. "That said, if you don't mind, I'd like to go in and warm up a bit. I'd also like to see my best mate. That bloke has probably written me off as dead."

Niles Hawke. Sunny and Amanda exchanged a glance but remained silent. Neither was anxious to tell the pilot that his friend had been killed.

"What?" Rider asked when they didn't respond.

Amanda knew they had to give him the news. He deserved to know, but she was afraid of how he would take it. "Patrick, I don't know to tell you this, but…"

Her pause was enough for Rider to fill in the blanks. His eyes filled with a wet gleam. "No."

"I'm so very sorry," Amanda said.

He dropped to one knee and rubbed his face with both hands. "It wasn't supposed to happen like this. I was the one who was supposed to die."

Amanda went over and placed a hand on his shoulder. She was about to say something else then thought better of it. Words weren't going to help him deal with the grief.

He visibly shook as though trying to cast off the pain. Looking up, he asked, "How did it happen?"

"You're still in shock," Sunny said. "Maybe we should go back inside—"

"I need to know how he died." His voice trembled.

Sunny nodded at the corpse.

Rider followed her gaze. "She did it?"

Sunny nodded again.

"That bloody woman killed my best mate?"

"She killed at least two people. Maybe more," Sunny replied.

Rider slowly rose to his feet, his gaze still fixed on the corpse. "Then I'm glad it was me who did this."

Amanda was about to suggest they return to the main building when a soft *click* came from the other side of the garage. *The door.* It could've been the wind, or someone might have come in. *Natasha's allies?* The door's hinges groaned, confirming her fears. In the seconds that followed, Amanda heard the distinct sound of slow and stealthy footsteps moving across the floor. As best she could tell, there were at least two people, maybe more.

"Get down," Rider whispered.

The three backed farther into the aisle and crouched low. The garage went silent. Amanda strained to see from her hiding spot, but she couldn't make out the number of hostiles since the row of vehicles blocked their view.

Hit with an idea, she got down on her stomach and looked underneath the vehicles. From what she could see, there were two sets of boots near the door, although there could have been more still hidden from view.

"See anything?" Rider whispered.

She rose to one knee then held up two fingers.

Rider nodded.

"Who is it?" Sunny asked.

"Probably some of Natasha's friends."

A muffled voice came from the direction of the door. If these were commandos, Amanda guessed they were using headsets.

The footsteps started again. Amanda dropped down to her stomach again for another look. Now she could see three sets of boots, and they were fanning out. She looked at Rider and held up three fingers.

"Let's move to the back," he whispered.

It was the right thing to do. The workbench light didn't reach the rear of the space, which meant it would be the best place to set up.

Before leaving, Amanda grabbed Natasha's pistol and handed it to Sunny. Staying low, the three then crept to the rear of the garage. They moved carefully, making sure their feet didn't hit any of the stray containers and tools strewn across the floor.

Once they reached the end of the aisle, Amanda got Rider's attention. "If there are only three, then we have a chance," she whispered. "We need to spread out and take down two at the same time."

He nodded. "Roger that."

Amanda gestured for Sunny to follow her then scooted a couple of rows down, finally crouching at the end of one of the shelves. After Sunny settled in next to her, Amanda leaned left and looked toward the front of the garage. There was no movement in the aisle.

Sunny held out the pistol. "I don't know how to use this thing, remember?"

Amanda put her lips close to Sunny's ear. "You won't have to unless someone threatens you. Leave the rest to Patrick and me."

"At least tell me how to—"

"I don't have time to give you a lesson. The safety is off. Just aim at their chest and pull the trigger."

Sunny looked like she wanted to say something else, but Amanda put a finger to her lips.

Hearing a faint noise, Amanda leaned out again and took a quick peek toward the front. A commando was coming down the aisle. He wore winter camo with a matching helmet. The butt of a semiautomatic rifle was pressed against his shoulder.

Amanda considered her next move. The best option would be if she and Rider took down two of the hostiles at the same time. Unfortunately, it would be difficult to coordinate such a move without radios. For the moment, she would simply put the commando in her crosshairs and wait. If she heard Rider shoot, then she would fire right after.

As the commando came toward her, Amanda recognized something vaguely familiar about the way he moved and his thin but athletic frame.

As seconds passed, she realized she couldn't wait for Rider to fire first. The man could turn at any second, and they would lose their advantage of surprise. Gripping her pistol in both hands, she aimed at the man's chest.

The commando stopped, lifted his wrist, and spoke into a microphone. "All clear so far."

Amanda stiffened at the sound of the familiar voice. The he was actually a she.

Amanda stood, revealing herself. "Carmen?"

The woman whipped the rifle in her direction.

"Don't shoot," Amanda said. "It's me!"

After taking a few seconds to digest what she had just heard, Carmen Petrosino finally lowered her rifle and spoke into her microphone again. "Stand down. We have friendly forces in the building. I repeat, stand down."

Having alerted the others, the woman clicked on a flashlight then came toward Amanda. A smile played on her face as she drew near. "You're lucky I didn't shoot you."

"No, you're the lucky one. You didn't even see me until I said something."

"Touché."

Sunny stood just as Patrick Rider and the other men arrived. Carmen introduced her associates as Special Forces operators. According to her, the group was part of a twelve-person strike team that had been sent to Ellsworth Station on a hovercraft. Carmen told them there were more reinforcements on the way.

"What on earth were the three of you doing out here?" Carmen asked.

"It would take several hours to bring you up to date," Amanda said. "Unfortunately, we don't have that much time."

Carmen nodded. "Okay, just tell us what needs to be done. We're here to help."

"We need to take a little trip," Amanda said.

"A little trip where?" Carmen asked.

"Down to see an alien spaceship."

46

ZANE and the other members of the team stood near the base of the giant column, a dead Russian commando at their feet. The trap had worked, although not perfectly. As best they could tell, one of their targets had managed to slip away.

"We need to be careful. There could also be more than the four we saw," Zane said. "Who knows? The place may be crawling with Russian commandos."

Freja's eyes narrowed as she walked toward the column.

"See something?" Zane asked.

She nodded. "I think so."

Zane watched as she approached a display screen like the one they had seen before. The glass pane glowed red, with one line of script flashing over and over.

"It's some kind of warning," Martini said.

As if on cue, both Reimer and Stone began coughing. Zane could feel a tickling in the back of his throat as well. Strangely, he hadn't felt anything just a few seconds earlier.

"We fired several shots." Cignetti ran his flashlight around the column's base. "Unfortunately, I think one of them may have punctured a pipe."

Freja pointed. "Over there."

Zane followed her gaze. A dark liquid oozed out from the column's base.

"We should probably leave," Freja said.

"It's just fuel," Reimer said. "Our lungs will adjust in a few minutes. We need to stay and collect a sample. We also need to find the engine room, which can't be far away."

Martini looked at him. "Lucas, she's right. We need to—"

"Don't you understand how important this is?" Reimer said, his voice rising. "We're on the verge of unlocking the key to interstellar travel. Can you imagine the treasure trove of information our scientists could glean from examining the ship's fuel and its engines?"

Zane's gaze went back to the glass screen, which was now glowing a deeper red than before. *Definitely a warning.*

"We're leaving," Zane said. "For all we know, the fumes from this substance could be toxic."

After coughing a few times himself, Reimer stood his ground. "I'm not going anywhere. I was sent here to do a job, and I'm going to stay until it's finished."

Cignetti aimed his rifle at him. "It wasn't a request."

Reimer glared at the SEAL. "I'll make sure the authorities know who decided to tuck tail and run."

"You do that," Cignetti said.

While he was no psychiatrist, Zane was beginning to wonder if Reimer had multiple personality disorder. At times, he could be calm and reasonable. He had even managed to get into a relationship with Morgan Martini, who seemed to be a stable person. But if he didn't get his way, or if he was placed in a stressful situation, then his dark side quickly came to the surface.

Sensing the urgency of the situation, Martini put a hand on Reimer's arm. "Lucas, they're right. We need to go." She coughed several times before continuing. "Once this is all settled, we'll come back with a team that's properly masked."

Zane wasn't about to sit around and debate the issue. He was in charge, and the others would have to follow his orders. "Let's go." He stared at Reimer. "And you're coming with us."

Cignetti pressed a hand on Reimer's back, urging him forward. Surprisingly, the DARPA scientist complied without protest. Perhaps the soothing words of his lover had helped him snap out of his rebellious state.

With the others in tow, Zane walked back across the bay and into the corridor. Several minutes later, they emerged in the first bay and found themselves walking through a fog that was much worse than it had been before. *Did something happen while we were gone?*

Forced to slow their pace, they silently made their way past the rows of specimen tubes. Zane hoped they weren't walking into a trap. If there was a commando on one of the catwalks, then they would all be sitting ducks. Unfortunately, they didn't have any choice but to keep going. If there was a massive leak, then the whole ship might soon be filled with toxic fumes.

Freja tapped Zane's arm and pointed to yet another flashing red screen. "Apparently, this leak is a serious thing. If the fumes are dangerous, I'm starting to worry that this section of the ship may get sealed off."

"Like an auto-response to the leak?"

She nodded.

He hadn't considered that possibility. "Hopefully, we still have time to get out. If we can just reach the upper corridor, then we should be fine."

After making it past the tubes, Zane started up the stairs.

"Wait a minute," Martini said.

Zane stopped and looked back at her. He didn't like the tone of her voice.

"Where is Lucas?" she asked.

Everyone turned their flashlight beams on each other. Lucas Reimer was nowhere to be found.

As frustration seared through him, Zane turned to Cignetti. "I thought you were watching him."

"I was. But with the fog, I couldn't see anything for a while."

Zane swore softly. Not only was he frustrated with Reimer and Cignetti, but he was also angry at himself. He should have realized Reimer had calmed down too quickly. It had all been a ruse so that the SEAL would let his guard down. He had planned on slipping off the entire time.

Stone shook his head. "I hate to say it, but I warned you something like this would happen. Now that little SOB has run off to join his friends."

"He hasn't done any such thing," Martini said.

"Then what's he doing?" Stone asked. "Trying to find a restroom?"

"He probably got lost."

"Oh, he got lost but didn't know to call out for help?" Stone asked, his voice dripping with sarcasm. "The really strange thing is that you actually dated this dude."

Martini glared at him but said nothing.

Still not through, Stone turned to Zane. "I just wish you had listened to me when I found that gun. I delivered Judas into your hands, but you wouldn't have it."

Zane paused before answering. "In the end, you may be right. But caution was warranted in that situation."

"I found the man's *gun*," Stone said through clenched teeth.

"I understand that. But it still doesn't mean it was his. Say what you will about Reimer, and there is a lot we could all say, but the man isn't dumb. With all of us searching for a mole, it would have been the height of stupidity to keep the gun under his mattress."

"Then how did it get there?" Stone asked.

"I think it was planted," Zane said. "Although, I have to admit that theory isn't looking good right now." Sensing it was time to get moving, he looked at Freja. "Take the others back. I'm going to find him and will catch up later."

Her eyes widened. "You can't be serious."

"It won't take long. I think he went back to take a sample of the fuel, so he shouldn't be hard to find."

"You saw the warning on those screens," she replied. "This place may get locked down soon."

"At least let me go with you," Stone said.

Zane shook his head. "I need to do this."

While it was tempting to let the mechanic come along, Zane didn't trust him to bring Reimer back unharmed. The two men had almost come to blows earlier, and there was a fair chance Stone would look for an excuse to take him down.

"He's probably going to die in here," Cignetti said. "I say let him go."

"I'm in charge of the team's security," Zane said. "And that even includes people who make irrational decisions."

"He's a traitor," Stone said.

"If so, then we need to bring him back to face justice," Zane said. "If he dies in here, in my opinion, that's letting him off the hook."

Stone shook his head and mumbled something under his breath.

"Maybe Lucas just got a little behind," Martini suggested. "If so, then maybe we should just wait a few minutes then—"

"No, Vince was right. He could have called out if he fell behind or got lost." Zane looked at Freja. "I won't spend much time looking for him. I'll go back to the fuel spill, and if he's not there, then I'll come straight back."

Freja hesitated then nodded.

Without waiting for anyone else to protest, Zane turned and walked off. Finding Reimer was his responsibility, but he also wasn't about to spend the next several hours searching every nook and cranny of the ship. If Reimer wasn't in either of the two bays, then Zane would leave him behind.

As he continued past the specimen containers, Zane began coughing again. The fumes from the fuel lines were now spreading throughout the ship. But that wasn't the only problem. He was also getting short of breath. If things got much worse, he might have to cut the mission short.

A minute later, Zane entered the corridor linking the two bays. Almost immediately, he heard something he hadn't expected—a man's voice. If it was Reimer, then who was he talking to? Was he the mole? If so, then maybe this whole thing wasn't about collecting a fuel sample. Maybe Reimer had slipped off to meet with his handlers.

The voice went quiet, and silence fell over the corridor. Concerned he might be seen, Zane turned off his flashlight then stepped quickly to his right. Using the wall to orient himself, he crept forward. About thirty or forty yards ahead, the thin beam of a flashlight appeared in the foggy haze.

"You're so beautiful," a man said.

Reimer. There was no mistaking his voice. *Who is he talking to?* Zane thought about the low oxygen levels and the harmful fumes present inside the ship. He wondered if the man had fallen into a confused state. Maybe he was having hallucinations.

Zane slowed his pace. He could now see Reimer's silhouette about thirty or forty feet away, backlit by the beam of his flashlight.

"I won't hurt you," Reimer said. "I promise."

Zane stopped. *He's gone mad.*

If so, he would probably have to remove Reimer by force. Though he was a small man, it wouldn't be an easy job to drag him across the foggy bay and up six flights of stairs. Looking back, he should have brought Cignetti along to help.

Zane was about to make his approach when a large shadow moved in front of Reimer's flashlight beam.

Zane stiffened. "What the—?"

As the shadow moved closer, several sets of long legs stretched into the light.

In that moment, everything clicked in Zane's mind. The specimen containers. The scaly limbs. The suddenly thick fog in the other bay. Another one of the containers must've broken. Zane shuddered.

Reimer began to slowly back away, perhaps realizing the danger staring him in the face.

Turn and run, you idiot.

The creature continued toward Reimer, its long legs alternating in pairs like a spider slinking toward its prey.

Zane considered his options. Grabbing Reimer might be the only way to shake the man out of his fearful state. Then again, simply shooting the creature might be the better option. Either way, he had to get closer.

Gripping his pistol with both hands, Zane started forward. He had just come up behind Reimer when his boot kicked something hard. He flinched as his water bottle skittered across the floor then clanked against the wall. Horror washed over him. *The water bottle.* He had triggered the very trap he had placed there earlier.

Startled, the enraged creature shrieked and charged in their direction.

Left with no other options, Zane lifted his pistol and fired.

47

AFTER REACHING THE CAVERN FLOOR, Zane dropped to his knees and took in huge gulps of air. Deprived of oxygen and suffering from the effect of the fumes, his lungs burned like never before. He hoped they hadn't been permanently damaged.

At this point, he was just happy to be alive. Getting out of the ship had been nothing short of a miracle. He remembered firing his pistol several times in defense of Lucas Reimer. As far as he knew, none of the rounds had hit the mark. The creature's thin body made a difficult target, and Reimer's flashlight had been knocked away, plunging the corridor into darkness.

Unscathed by the bullets, the creature had pounced on its victim. Zane could still remember Reimer's horrific screams. The sickening sound of ripping flesh and snapping bones would haunt him for the rest of his life.

Even though he had wanted to help, sticking around would have only resulted in two deaths instead of one. In any battle, he had learned there were times to fight and times to retreat.

After resting for a few minutes, Zane's lungs began to recover. Anxious to get back to the station, he got to his feet. He doubted the creature would be able to find its way out of the ship—at least not for a while—but he didn't want to take the chance that it had followed him out. He needed to seal up the entrance to the tunnels as quickly as possible.

As he set out for the ice bridge, Zane's thoughts turned back to the alien ship. He wondered what the US government would do once all the dust had settled. He doubted the knowledge of a dangerous life-form lurking inside would stop them from sending in another team. If there was only one creature on the loose, then they would likely be able to handle it. Even a predator like the one Zane had just encountered wouldn't survive an attack by a well-armed platoon of Special Forces.

Once the storm was over and they made contact with the government, he would suggest they wait a few weeks before going in. In that scenario, the creature would likely die of starvation. Or, if it had managed to reach the surface, it would freeze to death.

Several minutes later, Zane reached the bridge. *Almost home. The others must've already made it back.* He decided to take his time crossing it. He was still weak from the fumes, and he would have to be careful when passing through the slippery section that had almost taken Freja's life. The irony of escaping the horrors of the alien ship only to be killed by a slippery patch of ice would be too much.

Zane had just started making the journey across when a faint *thump* reached his ears. He paused to listen. It seemed to come from the field of stalagmites, but the cavern's acoustics made it almost impossible to know for sure.

He waited for a full minute, but the sound didn't repeat. Had he imagined it? The oxygen levels were low underground, which meant hallucinations weren't out of the question. Still, he was almost certain the noise had been real.

Warier than ever, Zane turned and started walking again. When he did, he heard the sound of something moving across the ice. Was he being followed? He wondered if it might be the

Russian commandos. He was convinced there were more onboard the ship than the four they encountered.

Zane picked up his pace. As he did, the noise behind him grew louder. Something was skittering across the ice, and the sound didn't suggest boot-wearing commandos.

It would be foolish to break into a run on the slippery bridge, so Zane prepared to defend himself. Reaching down, he removed the pistol from his coat and put in a fresh magazine. He then whipped around, bringing the gun and his flashlight up at the same time. At first, the bridge behind him seemed clear. Then, seconds later, a large shadow came into the light. Long, spindly limbs moved across the ice, the same limbs he had seen going toward Reimer.

The hairs on the back of Zane's neck stood on end. Somehow, the creature had tracked him. He stood in place, mesmerized by the sight. In the ship, he had thought it was some kind of arachnid that had been plucked off the surface of a distant planet. But now that he could see the invertebrate more clearly, its features were more like an arthropod's. It had a heart-shaped head that was protected by a hard chitinous shell. Its front legs were covered with the same hard material, and they were tipped with crab-like pincers. Its shape was something akin to a praying mantis, only in this case, it was the victims who needed to pray.

Zane's gut told him to get moving. He'd been standing in place for too long, so he aimed at the arthropod's abdomen and fired a single shot. A blood-curdling shriek echoed across the space. The creature had been hit, but Zane wasn't sure how much damage had been done.

Turning, he sprinted down the bridge. As he neared the midway point, a plan formed in his thoughts. It would be risky, but it might be the only way to make it back to the station alive. Trying to kill an armored arthropod with his nine millimeter would be suicidal.

Having settled on a course of action, Zane slowed his pace as he entered the slick portion of the bridge. The skittering of legs behind him slowed as well. The creature seemed to sense the path was more precarious there. It was much more intelligent than its appearance suggested.

Moving carefully, Zane veered to the left. As expected, his feet began to slide underneath him. Once he was about five feet from the edge, he unhooked the ice ax from his belt. He lifted it high above his head then brought it down as hard as he could, driving the sharp point deep into the ice.

Once he stopped sliding, Zane turned and directed the beam of his flashlight back down the bridge. He didn't have to wait long. Seconds later, the first pair of legs came into view, its pincers opening and closing in anticipation.

As it got closer, the creature's legs struggled to find firm footing. It was losing its ability to move forward, which was exactly what Zane had been hoping for. Now it was just a matter of letting the slick surface and gravity do their work.

But Zane's celebration was short-lived. The creature did something he hadn't expected. Sensing its predicament, the arthropod let out another excited shriek and charged in Zane's direction. Either it saw him as something to grab onto, or it had decided to grab its meal on the way down.

Gripping the ice ax with both hands to anchor himself, Zane prepared to absorb the hit.

The creature sped toward him, its forward momentum momentarily overriding gravity's pull toward the edge. Then, just as the pincers reached out, the physics changed. The creature hit an area that was even more sloped, sending it over the edge.

Just as Zane thought the danger had passed, he felt a sharp stabbing pain at the bottom of his leg. *The pincer.* He looked down to see the creature dangling by his ankle.

His muscles burning, the operative held on with everything he had. The arthropod was heavier than he had imagined, so heavy that his anchor was slowly being pulled out of the ice. If he didn't do something soon, they would both fall to certain death.

As the creature shook frantically, Zane considered his options. He needed to get the pistol out of his coat pocket, but if he let go of the anchor with either hand—even for a moment—then it would all be over. It was a problem that had no solution.

Eventually, the anchor would give under their combined weight. As the pick continued slipping out of the ice, Zane kicked his legs furiously in a vain attempt to dislodge the pincer. If he could get free of it, he might still be able to make it up the slope. But the creature wasn't letting him go.

Then, just as all appeared lost, a shot rang out.

A second shot followed the first, and this time, Zane felt the weight that was pulling him down release. Realizing what had happened, the arthropod gave a horrifying shriek as it plummeted from the bridge. The cries of fury continued for several seconds before finally ending as the beast fell into the depths of the chasm.

His life literally hanging in the balance, Zane held on with every ounce of strength he had left. Even though nothing was pulling him down, the damage had already been done. The ax was sliding out of the ice, and there was nothing he could do to stop it.

It's over. The haunting words echoed in his thoughts. *So this is how it ends.* He wondered how long it would take to fall to the bottom. Whether minutes or seconds, at least he would die instantly.

Whack whack.

Zane frowned. Although he couldn't see what was happening, it sounded like sharp objects were being driven into the ice behind him.

The shots. He had almost forgotten that someone had fired two shots. As he pondered who, he felt the ax begin to come loose. A feeling of doom swept over him. Whoever had come to save him had arrived seconds too late. He was going down.

"Grab my hand!" a male voice shouted.

Obeying the command, Zane released the ax and extended both of his arms as far as he could. Strong hands grabbed his wrists, halting his descent. A moment later, another set of hands grabbed one of his forearms. All four hands then pulled him slowly but surely away from the edge.

"Move him over here," a woman said from somewhere farther up, her calm and confident tone familiar. She had a distinct European accent, but it didn't sound like Freja.

A half minute later, the strong hands deposited Zane at the center of the bridge. His lungs burning, the operative rolled over on his back and took in deep breaths.

As his strength returned, he finally opened his eyes. Three faces hovered over him, backlit by the beams of several flashlights. A woman's face came closer, likely the one who had spoken with the accent. She had an olive complexion, and her raven-colored hair was tucked tightly under a knit cap. She looked like someone Zane had seen before, but for some reason, he still couldn't place her.

"*Ciao, amico,*" the woman finally said.

Zane's eyes widened as it all came together. The hair. The face. The voice. He pushed himself up on one elbow. "Carmen?"

48

Three Days Later
Hotel José Nogueira
Punta Arenas, Chile

ZANE TOOK the elevator down to the first floor then made his way to the hotel's famous watering hole, the Shackleton Bar. With its dark wood molding, antique furniture, and ornate chandelier, the space had a distinctly Old World feel to it. Even the staff's starched white shirts and formal black vests looked like the kind of attire one might see at any upscale lounge in Madrid or Barcelona.

Upon entering the bar, Zane found his group seated around a long table near the window. Carmen, Amanda, Cignetti, Freja, Sunny, Martini, and Rider were all there, which meant he was the last one to arrive. Although he hated being late to anything—especially the celebration of their last night together—he didn't regret taking the three-hour nap and long shower. His body still hadn't completely recovered from all it had been put through and probably wouldn't for quite some time.

Three days had passed since the operative's near-death experience on the bridge. Once he'd been brought back to the station, Carmen filled him in on what he'd missed, including Arnott's tragic death and how his disappearance had led Amanda to uncover the mole's identity.

As it turned out, Arnott's body had been hidden in the warehouse at the back of the main building. Even though Zane knew he shouldn't dwell on things that could no longer be changed, he still felt a small twinge of guilt over the cook's death. Having trusted Arnott with the task of getting into the laptop, he probably should have given him a weapon to protect himself with. That or he should have asked Amanda to watch over him.

At least the outcome had been better for others on the team. According to Carmen, her group had arrived only minutes after Patrick Rider had finished Natasha off. Amanda had then led Carmen's team to the tunnel entrance just as Zane's remaining team emerged from below.

After hearing that Zane had been left behind to look for Reimer, Carmen insisted on going down to help him. Led by Freja, Carmen's team had traveled through the tunnels and just started to cross the bridge when they saw Zane in a death struggle with the creature.

Although he wasn't one to use the word lightly, Zane knew that his rescue had been nothing short of a miracle. Had Carmen's team arrived a second too late, then both he and his attacker would be dead.

As more details began to emerge, Zane learned his rescue was even more miraculous than that. Carmen told him that she and Ross had debated over what to do in response to the silence coming out of Antarctica. After reviewing weather reports, Ross wanted to wait one more day to see if communication could be established. But Carmen wasn't having it. Like Zane, she often operated on her instincts, and her gut told her that something had gone horribly wrong.

After a heated discussion in Delphi's executive offices, Ross eventually agreed to authorize a rescue operation. Looking back, it had been a decision of monumental importance. Waiting another day would have resulted in disastrous consequences.

Amanda had a unique take on all the events. As a woman of faith, she had assured Zane that all the various pieces had come together as part of a divine plan. She told him she had been praying fervently throughout the entire ordeal and that he had continually come to mind.

A skeptic of religion in general, Zane wasn't so sure. Things often happened that defied statistical odds. He was old enough to remember the Miracle on Ice in the 1980 Winter Olympics when the experts had said a US victory was impossible. He also remembered Jaycee Dugard being saved from her kidnapper after being missing for almost twenty years. While beautiful and gratifying, her discovery had been nothing more than a statistical anomaly.

Still, he had to admit his rescue had taken place in a way that seemed providential. Miraculous, even. If someone were to make a movie about the events that had taken place over the last week, audiences would say the ending was too unrealistic to be true. Truth be told, he wouldn't blame them for thinking that.

As he walked toward the table, Zane made a mental note to discuss the matter more with Amanda on the way back to the States. Whenever she prayed, she seemed to get results. He wanted to know more.

A server approached Zane before he had a chance to sit down. "Can I get you something, *señor?*" she asked.

"I feel like a bourbon tonight," he said. "Do you have Woodford Reserve?"

"I think we do," she replied.

"Over ice, *por favor.*"

As she walked off, Zane slid into the only open seat, which happened to be between Carmen and Amanda at the head of the table.

"We reserved the place of honor just for you," Cignetti said.

"I don't feel too honorable," Zane said as he scooted his chair in.

Carmen nodded at all the appetizers spread across the table. "Sorry, but we didn't know when or if old Rip Van Watson was going to come down."

"I guess an old guy like me needs my beauty sleep."

Carmen raised a brow. "Old guy? Last I checked, you were in your forties."

"I feel like I'm in my sixties," he countered.

"Your beauty sleep must have worked," Freja said. "You're looking much better than before."

"Thank you, I think," Zane said with a smile.

"We all looked a little ragged before," she added.

Zane held her gaze. "So, you finished your debriefing?"

"I did," she replied. "I'm not sure they believe everything I shared, but they took it all down."

As it turned out, the Danes had sent their own people down to Antarctica. From the beginning, Ross had been in constant communication with Argus Frieberg, the director of the DSIS. Frieberg was also concerned about the situation at Ellsworth Station, and he insisted they be included in the rescue operation. Since the Americans were already providing enough muscle, the Danes didn't send any military personnel. Instead, they sent down three of their best intelligence officers, all of whom remained at Parks Station. Once Freja had been brought there, those agents had begun what turned out to be a long debriefing.

"I'm sure my recollection of events will raise some eyebrows as well." Zane suddenly remembered something he had wanted to ask her about. "By the way, have your people learned anything about our Russian mole?"

Since the Danes were already conducting an investigation into Russian operations in Denmark, the US had asked them to look into Natasha's background. They hoped to find out how she had been communicating with the commandos and about how she'd infiltrated the operation.

"We found a radio in her room but little else," Freja replied. "We're guessing she hid some things around the station that haven't been found yet."

"So it was a dead end?" Zane asked.

Freja shook her head. "We *were* able to unlock a treasure trove of information from her fingerprints."

His curiosity piqued, Zane leaned forward and put his elbows on the table.

"We believe her real name was Natasha Kafelnikov," Freja continued. "As it turns out, she'd lived in several European countries using fake passports. Our research shows she was an accountant in London for two years, and she worked at the Russian embassy in Paris on several occasions. Oddly enough, she was even married to a Danish man for six months."

Zane frowned. "I assume he was working for the other side."

"We're not sure. We currently have him under surveillance while we look into his past. Either he's a spy, or he's an honest man who got duped by a spy."

Zane was thankful they had discovered the mole even though it had come too late to save Natasha's victims. Now that the Danes knew something about her background, there was no telling what they might uncover once the investigation expanded. The woman had likely been in touch with dozens of Russian agents operating in Europe.

Seemingly anxious to move on to lighter things, Rider looked at Zane and held up a mug. "Where is your pint?"

Zane managed a smile. It was good to see the Brit in good spirits again. For the last couple of days, Rider had fallen into a state of depression over the loss of Niles Hawke, his colleague and friend. Sunny had been counseling Rider, and whatever she was doing seemed to be working.

"My bourbon is on the way," Zane replied. "It's the first drink I've had in a long time, so you may need to carry me up to my room."

"Shall we tuck you in and read you a bedtime story as well?" Cignetti asked.

Zane saw through the SEAL's smile. Unlike Rider, Cignetti seemed to have suppressed his feelings after losing a good friend. Zane didn't think that was wise, and he just hoped the soldier would seek help if he needed it.

Zane looked at Rider. "Are you headed back to the UK?"

He nodded. "I wasn't supposed to be off for another month, but I think a little holiday is warranted."

"After all you've been through, I'd say you deserve a long vacation," Amanda said.

Cignetti took a pull on his beer then set the bottle on the table. "Must be nice. I've been told I'm being deployed again after I get back."

Amanda looked at him. "You have to be kidding."

"Well, my commanding officer did say we could talk about it when I get back," Cignetti said.

"Why don't you come across the pond for a visit, mate?" Rider said. "We'll hang out at the local pub and swap a few war stories."

"That's tempting," Cignetti said with a smile. "If they give me the green light, I'm there."

Silence fell over the table. Each person stared into their drinks, seeming lost in their thoughts.

Finally, Freja looked at Carmen. "So, I heard your people are sending a team down into the tunnel."

"Yes, but they aren't holding out hope of finding anything," Carmen said.

Carmen's remark reminded Zane of the earthquake they'd felt after making it up to the station. The shaking had lasted for a full thirty seconds, but he'd known immediately it wasn't a natural event. The alarms they had previously heard inside the alien ship must've been a harbinger that the craft's self-destruct mechanism had been triggered.

An hour after the tremors stopped, Carmen led a small team down to check things out. As they suspected, the tunnel that led to the bridge had partially collapsed. While they probably could have found a way through the debris, they'd decided not to risk more casualties. Even if the team could somehow have made it past the cave-in, there was little hope that the ice bridge remained intact.

For the moment, most of the ship's secrets were likely buried under tons of rubble. Fortunately, it wasn't a complete loss. Vince Stone had taken dozens of photographs while inside the ship, which would be examined closely by government engineers. Stone had also collected a few samples of metal. Those samples had been placed on a C-130 transport plane and were currently en route to DC. Once there, DARPA scientists would begin analyzing their chemical makeup.

The server brought Zane's bourbon and placed it on a napkin in front of him. He took a long sip and let the warmth run down his throat.

"Is it safe to go down into the tunnel?" Cignetti said.

"Probably not," Zane said after taking another drink. "But I'm guessing they'll take the risk because of the technology that might be down there."

"As fascinating as it might be to examine them, let's hope all the specimens were destroyed," Carmen said. "It's not worth the damage should one of them escape, not to mention any communicable diseases they might be carrying."

"That explosion was powerful," Rider said. "Nothing could have survived that."

Cignetti nodded. "Total incineration of any living organism."

"Let's hope you're right," Carmen said.

Zane was about to say something when his phone buzzed with an incoming text. He found that odd. Only four people had the number, and two of them were sitting next to him. The other two were Alexander Ross and Brett Foster, but Zane had just spoken to Ross before he'd gone to sleep.

While the others continued talking, Zane dug the phone out of his pocket and unlocked the screen. A single text was waiting for him, and it had been sent from a number he didn't recognize. Frowning, he opened it and read the message.

An ominous feeling rose inside him as he realized who had sent it.

How did he get my number?

Zane eased his chair back and stood.

Carmen looked up at him. "Where are you going? You just got here."

"I need to get back to someone."

Her brows pinched together. "Who?"

She could see the look on his face and knew something was wrong.

He decided not to answer the question directly. "I won't be long."

As Zane left the bar, he realized he hadn't been honest. He probably wouldn't be back for quite some time.

* * *

ZANE WALKED QUICKLY through the hotel's maze of ornate corridors. He might have to place a call, which meant he needed to get as far away from the bar as possible. He didn't want anyone to hear the conversation that was about to take place.

After crossing the lobby, he passed through the revolving door then exited onto the sidewalk. A strong gust of cold air snapped the flags hanging over the front entrance. A few flakes of snow spun around like dandelions blown by the wind. It was spring in Chile, but he never would've guessed it by the weather.

Just to be safe, Zane crossed the street and stood underneath the awning of a closed check-cashing company. He then removed his phone and read the message once again.

It's Ryan. I got your number from your boss. I need your help with an urgent matter. Please text me back when you get this.

Zane only knew one Ryan, and that was Ryan Shafer. He and Ryan Shafer had become friends during their sophomore year at NC State University. In an interesting twist, they had met while dating twin sisters. Neither of the romantic relationships had lasted long, but the two men had remained friends.

After graduation, Zane and Ryan had tried to get together from time to time. But like so many friendships, their communication had grown more infrequent over time. Zane had gotten into a serious relationship that took up his time, and Ryan had moved away to pursue a career as a diplomat.

The last time Zane had seen his friend was shortly after taking the job at the Delphi Group. Ryan had taken a job at the US Embassy in London, and he had stopped by Delphi headquarters to see Zane before flying out of Dulles. After a brief tour of the office, they had grabbed dinner at a restaurant in downtown Arlington. Ryan had flown out the next day, and Zane hadn't seen or talked to him since.

What concerned Zane most about the text was the trouble Ryan must have gone through to find him. Delphi had no listed numbers, and there were only a few people in government that had access to the organization's two landlines.

But the other thing that bothered Zane was his friend's use of the word "urgent." Ryan Shafer was perhaps the most grounded person he had ever known. He was the kind of man who took everything in stride, and he wasn't prone to exaggeration. If he said something was urgent, then it meant there was a matter of grave importance that needed to be addressed immediately.

Zane was about to dial Ryan's number when he noticed the last sentence of the message. His friend had specifically asked for a text reply. Maybe he had given that as an option in case Zane was in the middle of an important operation. Or maybe Ryan wasn't at liberty to discuss the matter over a phone conversation.

Erring on the side of caution, Zane quickly typed out a response. **It's been a while my friend. Is everything okay?**

The answer came a minute later. There were no pleasantries or small talk of any kind. **I need to share something with you as soon as possible.**

Zane shot another message back. **Do you want me to call you?**

This time, it took longer for Ryan to respond. **No, I can't talk right now. I need you to come see me if you can.**

A frown tugged at the corners of Zane's mouth. He wondered what was so important that Ryan couldn't discuss the matter over the phone. He needed more information. **What's going on? Where are you?**

A minute later, Zane's phone buzzed with the reply. **I'm in Europe. I was told you were out of the country but would be coming back soon. When you get back I should be in a better position to tell you more.**

Zane found the exchange a bit frustrating. He knew Ryan wouldn't reach out unless it was extremely important. Then again, his friend still hadn't shared the slightest bit of information, and Zane wasn't about to commit to a meeting unless he knew more. Depending on the nature of the problem, he might not even be able to help.

He tried one more time. **You know I'll help if I can but I need to have some sense of what you're talking about.**

While he waited for a response, Zane took a look around. Across the street, a woman led two pugs on a leash. Both of them were dressed in what the woman must have thought were cute red outfits. Neither of the dogs seemed to agree with her.

Several minutes passed without a response. Zane wondered why it was taking his friend so long to respond. It was after midnight in Europe, so he should be alone at home or at least around people he trusted.

Zane was just about to type another text when his phone buzzed again.

I've uncovered something big. And I fear what I've found is just the tip of the iceberg. I apologize for being so evasive but I think you'll understand when we speak.

Zane read the message two more times, furrowing his brow. Ryan was a diplomat—at least he was the last time they had spoken—which meant he could have come across anything. A network of spies. Money laundering by government officials. Sordid affairs. Double agents. The list was endless.

To get some idea of what his friend might be up against, Zane needed to go online and figure out where his friend was working. If he could determine that, then it might give him a hint as to what sort of secret he might have uncovered.

On the positive side, Zane could start that night. He would celebrate a while longer with his colleagues then excuse himself and go upstairs. There was a new mystery to solve, and he wasn't going to wait to start figuring things out.

After putting the phone back in his pocket, Zane checked the traffic and hurried back across the street.

* * *

From John Sneeden:
I hope you enjoyed reading *The Anomaly*.

Rest assured, Zane and the rest of the Delphi team will be back soon for another adventure.

As you wait for the next installment to come out, have you read *Retribution* yet? It's the first novel in my Drenna Steel thriller series, and it's my highest rated work to date. At the time of this writing, it has a whopping 4.8 out of 5 stars on Amazon!

Someone made a big mistake. They put a bounty on the head of the CIA's most lethal assassin, and now she's faked her own death to hunt them down.

Drenna is a kick-butt protagonist who will remind you of a female Jason Bourne. Want to follow her as she hunts down the people who tried to kill her?

Buy Retribution now. (Or keep reading for a sneak

peek.)

RETRIBUTION

PROLOGUE

Harpers Ferry, West Virginia

The man dropped onto his stomach and slithered onto the granite ledge, careful to stay beneath the overhanging limb of a thick fir tree. Even though he was several hundred yards from the cabin, he didn't want to expose himself too much. His target was the kind of person who was always aware of her surroundings, even while on vacation.

Once in position, he took out a monocular and placed it against his eye. He aimed it down the slope and turned the focus wheel. The valley was a blanket of emerald broken only by a few clearings. Even from his spot on the mountain, the man could see the wildflowers sprinkled across the fields. Spring had arrived in the Appalachian Mountains.

The man hated America with a passion, but he had to admire its great natural beauty.

He moved the monocular to the left and found the narrow dirt road that snaked through the forest. At its end, a roof peeked out through the trees.

The cabin.

He turned the focus wheel again, sharpening the image. The property looked just like the satellite image he had reviewed earlier that morning. The cabin was small, no more than twelve hundred square feet. He guessed there were three or four rooms maximum: a living room, full bathroom, and a bedroom.

As he surveyed the rest of the property, he saw the top of a white pickup truck parked in front.

Chill bumps spread across his arm.

They were there. More importantly, she was there.

The man had heard whispers about the woman's existence for

years. She was the most sought-after spy in the world, a cold-blooded killer wanted by governments, terrorist organizations, and criminal enterprises around the globe. She was said to have eliminated at least two dozen high-value targets in the last five years alone. But it wasn't just the number of kills that gave the woman such a frightening reputation—it was her ability to find and take out people who thought they were well protected. No one was beyond her reach, it seemed.

Over the years, many were convinced that the female assassin worked for the CIA, since her kills and information theft always seemed to benefit the United States or her allies. But others held different opinions. Some, for example, believed she worked for Mossad. In a way, that made sense because Israel's geopolitical goals often aligned with those of the US. Others claimed she was an independent contractor, an assassin who took work from any government or organization as long as the price was right.

There were even a few intelligence analysts who believed she didn't exist at all. According to them, the killings were unrelated, and tales of a shadowy female assassin were unsubstantiated myth.

But the woman *did* exist, and her identity was no longer a mystery to the man watching the cabin. She was a real person, she worked for the CIA, and she was about to die.

When the man and his squad had been asked to take her out, they had been given a blurry photograph of the woman's face and the details of where she would be for the next several days. They had a short window of time in which to complete the work. They would fly into the US, kill her, then slip out again.

The man had come to the mountain alone to determine how they would carry it all out. He leaned toward making her death look like an accident. They could, of course, take the safe route and shoot her from a distance with a rifle. But that had its own set of problems. If the US intelligence community knew it was an assassination, they would go after the killers with all the resources of the US government. The woman was the CIA's most prized human asset, and they would stop at nothing to track down and punish whoever was behind her death.

Still, trying to make the whole thing look like an accident had its own set of challenges. Unlike the movies, a staged event was extremely difficult to pull off. So many pieces had to fit together perfectly to be believable. One mistake and the entire operation would be exposed. Worse yet, the target might even escape alive.

Escape alive.

Those two words triggered unpleasant thoughts. Failure wasn't an option. If the assassination attempt wasn't successful, they might as well start typing up their own obituaries. The woman would come after them. And once she found them, she would probably kill them in a way that involved unthinkable pain.

Turning his thoughts to the present, the man studied the property a second time. He thought about what might happen if they stormed the property in the dead of night. There was certainly enough cover around the house for them to make a stealthy approach, but the woman would be heavily armed. And like most spies, she was probably a light sleeper. If they went in, they would have to use overwhelming force, and even that might not be enough.

As the man put the monocular away, he thought about the road he had come in on, and another plan surfaced in his thoughts. The plan would require perfect execution, but if they could pull it off successfully, the authorities would believe the woman had suffered a tragic but accidental death. It would also allow the man and his team of assassins to live the rest of their lives without looking over their shoulders.

That's how it will happen, he thought. *That's the way she'll die.*

CHAPTER ONE

Drenna Steel stepped onto the back porch of the cabin and let the screen door close behind her. She crossed the porch and wrapped her left arm around the support beam. Surrounded by fresh air, she closed her eyes and waited. She was a visual person but was determined to enjoy the bouquet of scents before anything else.

Soon, her nostrils were filled with the fragrance of honeysuckle. After that, the faint scents of fir trees and freshly cut grass pushed their way in.

Heaven.

The honeysuckle brought back childhood memories of playing along the creek behind her house. She remembered pulling off the flowers and placing the drop of sweet nectar on the tip of her tongue. Those were simpler times, wonderful times. And while she could never go back, she would at least try to recreate some of that innocent joy over the next several days.

As she waited to see what else she could smell, Drenna felt a hand come down on her shoulder. Then a body pressed against her.

She was startled but remained in place.

Lips pressed against her long dark hair.

Trevor.

She had been caught up in the moment and hadn't heard him come out.

Keeping her eyes closed, she leaned into him, feeling the warmth of his chest against her back. She smiled. If only they could remain like this forever.

"I thought you might want this," he said, breaking the silence.

Feeling movement, Drenna opened her eyes to find a glass of red wine in front of her. As she took it from his hand, he pressed more firmly against her, his arms encircling her waist from behind.

She reached back and ran her fingers through his hair. "You're not allowed to move for the next ten minutes."

"Unfortunately, I'm not sure my stomach will agree to that."

Smiling, she dug an elbow into his abdomen. "It's always about the food. *Always.*"

"I'm a man, aren't I?"

"Yes." She turned around to face him. "And just my kind of man."

Their heads moved slowly together. When their lips touched, they both stopped, allowing warm breath to pass between them. As the anticipation heightened, Trevor placed a hand under her chin and pulled her into him. They kissed lightly for a time, enjoying the delicate intimacy as a mountain breeze swept across the porch.

A minute later, Trevor's stomach intruded with an extended growl.

Drenna laughed and pushed him away playfully. "Go. It's obvious your stomach has won your affections."

"Since you don't seem to be hungry, I'll just put on one steak for now."

"Do that and you may not touch me again all week."

"Things are getting awfully Victorian around here. You've already insisted I sleep in a separate room."

"I saw a shack at the edge of the property. Push your luck and it may get worse."

Trevor smiled. "Two rib eyes it is."

"Medium rare, please."

Trevor raised a brow. "You're a medium girl."

"I guess this mountain air has brought out the carnivore in me."

Trevor walked over to the grill, lifted the hood, and placed his palm over the cooking grate. "I think she's ready."

Drenna took a sip of wine as she watched him adjust the controls. Trevor Lambert was a classically handsome man, with short dark hair and an athletic build that came from hours spent hiking and kayaking.

But it wasn't his looks that had caused Drenna to end her long absence from the world of dating. After all, she had crossed paths with hundreds of attractive men over the years. Despite their good looks, most of those men were arrogant, prideful, and domineering. Trevor was the antithesis of that. He was stable, fun, and genuine. He was also humble, although his wasn't a weak humility. He was strong when he needed to be.

In short, he was everything she wanted in a partner. Not only had he drawn her out of isolation, but he was the reason she had decided to retire from the CIA.

"How is the wine?" Trevor asked, interrupting her thoughts.

"Lovely," she said. "Is this the Malbec?"

"It is. Jessica suggested it."

Jessica. Trevor's sister. The very mention of her name caused Drenna's stomach to tighten. Although they had been together only twice, Drenna got the distinct impression Jessica didn't like her brother's new girlfriend.

"Please tell her I approve."

"I will. She'll be glad to hear that."

Drenna grunted.

Trevor looked at her as he closed the grill's lid. "What?"

"Maybe it might be better not to mention me."

"Why do you say that?"

"I don't think she's a big fan."

"Don't be silly. Jess likes you."

"It's part of my job to read people, but it doesn't take professional training to see—"

"Drenna." He came over and put a hand on her shoulder. "Trust me on this. I'm her brother. I know her better than anyone."

She held his gaze. "I'm not upset. I know I don't always make a great first impression, but I'm determined to win her over."

"That's just it. You don't have to win her over. Just be yourself, and she'll eventually warm up."

Drenna smiled. "So you admit she doesn't like me."

"No, I didn't say that." He paused as if searching for the right words. "Jessica's just protective of me after all that happened with Maggie. She'd be a little distant no matter who it was."

Maggie was Trevor's ex-wife. The two had been married for five years before Maggie finally realized she wanted the social life she'd never had growing up. She also had a penchant for bad boys, something Trevor certainly was not.

According to him, things had begun to deteriorate in the fourth year of their marriage. Despite being in her late thirties, Maggie began to spend more and more time out on the town with friends. There had also been rumors of affairs with a couple of different men, including one who had spent time in prison.

It all ended when Trevor came home to an empty house. Maggie's belongings were gone, and a note had been conspicuously placed on the kitchen table. In it, Maggie said she was doing what they both wanted—breaking off a relationship between two people who couldn't be more different. She went on to say that even though it might be painful in the short term, she truly believed he would thank her one day.

Two days after she left, Trevor heard from her attorney.

Knowing the story, Drenna couldn't blame Trevor's sister for being wary of any woman her brother became involved with. She probably thought they were all going to be the next Maggie. And truth be told, Drenna knew she could intimidate others. She had a sharp intellect, a tough demeanor, and a gift for analyzing people when she first met them. That scrutiny was a natural outgrowth of her job in intelligence.

But if she truly wanted to adapt to the real world, Drenna knew she needed to let her guard down. She needed to trust people until and unless they gave her reason not to. She had probably come across as cold when she first met Jessica, and the next time they were together, she resolved to turn that around.

"As I said, just give her some more time," Trevor said when she didn't answer.

She smiled at him. "I will."

"I'll schedule something for the three of us to do when we get back." He removed his hand from her shoulder. "Now, if you'll excuse me, I need to go grab our meat."

Once he stepped away, Drenna took another sip of wine and thought about how much her life had changed recently. Just three days before, she had requested a meeting with Nathan Sprague, the man she reported to at the CIA. During that meeting, she had turned in her letter of resignation. Sprague had tried to talk her out of it, but she refused to budge. Her time was over, and she wasn't going to change her mind.

Drenna had worked as an operations officer for most of her thirteen years at the agency, and the job had taken her around the world. At last count, she had conducted missions in over thirty countries and used dozens of false identities. As the agency's most elite operative, Drenna was always given the blackest of the black projects. She had seen and heard things that would never be revealed on the news.

The bulk of her work involved gathering information vital to the strategic interests of the United States. But there was also a darker side to her job, and that was her role as an assassin. No one outside the agency knew that Drenna was a cold-blooded killer. Not her sister Elena. Not even Trevor. And that created a dilemma. Should she tell him, or should it remain a secret until the day she died?

However difficult that decision might be, Drenna was certain about one thing: She would have to leave her past behind. If she couldn't do that, she would never be able to have anything close to a normal life. She didn't like shrinks, but she might have to see one if she couldn't rid herself of the dark memories that haunted her. Seeing that much death changed people forever.

Pushing aside thoughts of her work, Drenna stepped to the edge of the porch. The view behind the cabin was stunning. Emerald mountains rose up on every side, their forested slopes broken only by the occasional outcrop of granite.

Directly overhead, a hawk screamed as it soared on a current of wind. Even from a distance, Drenna could see the raptor turn its head back and forth, looking for prey in the open fields that dotted the valley. West Virginia marketed itself as being wild and wonderful. Drenna couldn't think of a better way to describe it.

As the hawk glided out of sight, Drenna thought about how fortunate she and Trevor were to have such a pristine vacation spot. Located a few miles outside of Harpers Ferry, the log cabin and the acreage that came with it was owned by Preston Kerr, Trevor's uncle. In his late seventies and suffering from painful arthritis, Kerr rarely used the retreat anymore. He probably would have sold it if not for his desire for the family to enjoy it. If her relationship with Trevor continued, Drenna could see them spending a lot of time here. After all, it was only a ninety-minute drive from DC.

The hawk screamed again as it soared back into view. As Drenna turned her head to watch it, she saw a flash of light on the mountain to the east. It was brilliant, like the setting sun being reflected in a mirror.

She frowned. *What was that?*

She tried to find it again, but the flash had been too brief to lock in on.

Trevor had told her most of the property on the east end of the valley was owned by the Nature Conservancy. He said it was a biologically sensitive area that would never be developed. So if that was the case, what was someone doing up there with a mirror?

Maybe it's a surveyor marking off property.

Suddenly, there was another flash of light on the mountainside.

This time, Drenna's eyes moved quickly to the spot. It seemed to come from an area just to the right of an opening in the trees. She located an outcrop of rock, but it was too far away for her to tell if anyone was there.

The screen door groaned open behind her.

"Something wrong?" Trevor asked, a plate of rib eyes in one hand.

Drenna turned toward him. "What do you mean?"

"You're frowning," he said. "I've seen that look before. It's your 'something is wrong' sort of frown."

"It's probably nothing. I saw something flash up on the mountain."

"Flash?"

"It was reflected light, like a mirror or shiny piece of metal."

Trevor opened the grill. "Oh, I think I know what it might have been." After setting the plate aside, he used a steel brush to clean the cooking grate. "There are mountain bike trails up there. I always see at least a few bikers when I'm hiking."

"So how would a bike create a flash of light?"

He shrugged. "Mirrors."

"Mountain bikes have mirrors?"

"Some do. Or it could have been the shiny metal."

Drenna nodded but said nothing.

"We're on vacation, babe. This isn't Bosnia or Morocco."

"You think I'm worried?"

Trevor used tongs to place the first rib eye on the grill. "Yes, I do."

"Well, you're wrong. I just thought it was odd. That's all."

He looked at her. "I just want you to enjoy your time here."

He was right. Her nerves had been on edge since they arrived, and she didn't know why. She guessed it had something to do

SNEAK PEEK AT RETRIBUTION - CHAPTER 1

with her transition to normal life. Her old life—the one with dark secrets, lies, and death—didn't want to let go.

Trevor set the second rib eye on the grill then closed the lid.

"I'm sorry," Drenna said.

"Sorry for what?"

"For snapping."

Trevor picked up the plate and went to her. "And I'm sorry too." He nodded at a nearby rocking chair. "Now sit down and enjoy your wine. That's an order."

She smiled. "I think I will."

As he went inside, Drenna sank into the chair and rocked. It was soothing, one of life's simple pleasures.

Closing her eyes, she enjoyed the moment.

He's right. Not everything is trouble.

Ready for more? **Buy Retribution now.** (And be prepared to stay up late.)

Want a FREE novella by John Sneeden?

Sign up for John's newsletter and get the novella *Betrayal* for free. You'll also be the first to learn about John's future releases and special discounts. You can sign up here:

www.johnsneeden.com/newsletter/

The process is quick and simple, and your email address will not be sold to anyone else.

ABOUT THE AUTHOR

John was born on the coast of North Carolina, and thanks to his mother, a voracious reader, he began discovering books at a very early age. If not outside playing basketball or fishing with friends, he could be found curled up in a living room chair with an Edgar Rice Burroughs novel. In fact, it was Burroughs who first kindled his love for escapist fiction.

After a twenty-five year career in banking, John decided to turn his life-long passion for reading into a career as an author. He still lives in the southern United States, and when not writing he loves to travel and follow NHL hockey.

If you get the chance, email John at johnsneedenauthor@gmail.com. He loves to hear from his readers.

ALSO BY JOHN SNEEDEN

Delphi Group Thriller Series

The Signal

The Portal

The Hades Conspiracy

Betrayal

The Island

The Chamber

The Anomaly

Drenna Steel Thriller Series

Retribution

Silas Beck Crime Thriller Series

Death List

Cold Blood

The Anomaly
Copyright © 2021 by John Sneeden

All rights reserved. No part of this book may be used or reproduced by any means whatsoever without express written permission of the author, except in the case of brief quotations embodied in critical articles and reviews.

This is a work of fiction. Names, characters, businesses, places, events and incidents are either the products of the author's imagination or used in a fictitious manner. Any resemblance to actual persons, living or dead, or actual events is purely coincidental.

Cover design by Damonza

ISBN-13: 978-1-7329458-6-9 (Paperback Edition)
ISBN-13: 978-1-7329458-7-6 (ePub Edition)

Made in United States
North Haven, CT
04 February 2022